DEEP WITHIN THE STONE

BOOK 2 OF THE SUPERSTITION SERIES

TERESA J. REASOR

Copyright © 2017 by Teresa J. Reasor
Print Edition

Contact Information: **teresareasor@msn.com**
Cover Art by Tracy Stewart
Edited by Faith Freewoman

Teresa J. Reasor
PO Box 124
Corbin, KY 40702

Publishing History 1st edition 2017
ISBN-13: 978-1-940047-18-8

TABLE OF CONTENTS

PROLOGUE

Isle of Skye, Scotland
1354

COLD PERMEATED FINLAY MacLeod's body, bone-deep and damp. A small finger of reflective light crept across the floor from above. The sun was going down, and he knew the chill would grow worse. He had been imprisoned in the oubliette for two days, with only a heel of bread dropped down into the narrow cell from above.

It wasn't the hunger gnawing at his belly that preyed on his mind, but the thirst and the cold. He could no longer control his chattering teeth. He winced at the pain as he clenched his teeth in an instinctive effort to still them.

The side of his face hurt where Tearlach struck him. The fool almost broke his jaw. Finn's chin, cheekbone, and temple ached, and his eye was swollen to a slit. His head pounded relentlessly, making him queasy. Had he anything in his stomach, he would have bocked.

He twisted against the ropes binding his arms to his sides, but only managed to further chafe the skin. The insides of his elbows were raw and painful, his ribs bruised. Surely his cousin, Ian Ciar MacLeod, wouldn't leave him here to freeze to death and die a lingering death of starvation and thirst.

A shudder of cold and pain shook him. His cousin was not known for his warmth and generosity. Ian Ciar could be brutal, his moods mercurial. Finn understood why his cousin was upset with him. But all this over a woman?

Granted, she was the Druid's daughter, but no more valuable than any other lass.

And perhaps if he truly believed she was not, he would not feel an icy finger of fear trailing up his spine.

The old *draoidh* seemed to know things others in the clan should, but did not. Ian Ciar depended on the Druid to alert him to troubles long before they struck. While morning prayers were reserved for the castle priest, Finn was not sure what the Druid Cinead MacLeod worshiped, but everyone had a healthy fear of and respect for the *draoidh*.

Finn shook his head and nearly groaned aloud when his jaw and temple throbbed like a punched bruise. He closed his eyes and rested his head back against the hard stone wall.

Why had he gotten it into his mind to seduce Isabel? She was too innocent to be interesting. But so ripe for the picking. And once picked, so desperate to please. He had lost interest about the time she came to him with the news she was bairned, and now 'twas he who was paying for the deed, when she had been just as eager as he.

His resentment died as quickly as it started. He did not wish Isabel to be beaten. Surely her father wouldna go so far as that. He would not see her punished and possibly have the bairn harmed.

She was a sweet lass, and deserved better than he was capable of giving her...or any other woman. It was not in his nature to remain faithful, and even if it were, that alone would not make him a good husband. He had no property of his own, no way to provide for a family, and lived largely off what he could earn with his fists and his sword. Obvious impediments to making the lass happy.

They were both in a sorry state.

At the sound of the bolt above being thrown, Finn cracked open his one good eye. The iron grate screeched as Tearlach swung it aside. Finn gingerly tilted his head back and gazed up at the two men standing at the mouth of the small cell.

Isabelle's father glared down at him with disgust. Though the man wore braes and a rough shirt, just like the rest of them, there was nothing common about him. He stared down his long nose with the arrogance of a king. The cold, hard glow in his dark eyes promised retribution, and the chiseled bones of his face were sharp with hatred. His gray beard hung against his chest, iron gray and coarse.

"Ye have disgraced my daughter and broken trust with yer own people. 'Tis not only m'child ye have preyed upon. There are others who have come forward. Ye will face them now."

He gestured toward Tearlach, and the huge man bent to pick up a short ladder and lowered it into the pit.

Finn eyed the two men warily. They'd probably beat him again once he was out of the oubliette, but at least he would be free of this hellish, small dungeon. He rested his back against the wall, and, bracing his feet, shoved upward until he was standing. The ground seemed to sway beneath him as he approached the ladder and clumsily gripped the rungs with hands he could only lift waist high because his arms were bound. He paused there for a moment, waiting for the dizziness to abate. He had to lean into the ladder and search for each rung with his feet to ascend. Weakness dragged at his legs, and he had to rest between each step.

Tearlach gripped his shirt as soon as he was within reach and dragged him onto stable ground, then dropped him like a sack of oats.

Finn grunted in pain, and his vision went gray as the agony in his head and jaw soared. It hurt to breathe. He lay still a moment, willing the pain to subside a wee bit. Perhaps his ribs were more than just bruised. He rolled to his knees and clumsily staggered to his feet. With his elbows tied at his waist and the room spinning with every move, it was difficult, but he managed to get to his feet. He swayed unsteadily and fell back against one of the close, cold walls. The vision in his right eye blurred, then dimmed, and his stomach rolled.

He had been beaten before, and the pain was bad then, but this fierce agony pointed toward his hurts being far worse. "If ye mean to kill me, ye may only need to wait a wee time. Tearlach has done his job well." His words sounded slurred, and the only thing keeping him on his feet was the wall at his back. He closed his eyes as the room pitched.

Was he facing his death? No fear rushed out to embrace him. Death seemed so foreign, so distant, and he was focusing too fiercely on staying on his feet for the emotion to take hold.

"He will never make it upstairs without help." Tearlach cut Finn's bindings and tossed them aside, then gripped his arm, slung it over his shoulder, and half-carried, half-dragged him to the stairs.

Every step jarred Finn's ribs and jaw. His eyes watered from the pain, and he swallowed back more than a few groans while he put pressure on his ribs, hoping to hold them in place. Once they reached the landing, he gulped in a breath of relief, more like a sob.

The castle's great room smelled of burning wood and roasting meat, overwhelming Finn until he gagged and finally bocked. As soon as Tearlach released him, he fell to his knees and curled into a knot. The painful throbbing inside his head worsened with every heave. He collapsed on the floor and lay on his side.

"He is dying." Tearlach's deep murmur reached him.

"Nay. Not yet. Not until he has paid."

"If he dies, is that not payment enough?"

"Nay, 'twill never be payment enough. He shamed my daughter. She was meant for better than he."

"And better than me as well?" Tearlach asked.

Finn lay still, grateful the two had forgotten him.

Tearlach wanted Isabel? Had he known, he would have never touched her.

Many's the time he stood shoulder-to-shoulder with him, defending the clan. But he had never noticed Tearlach's interest in Isabel. Why had he not seen it?

And what difference did it make now? It was too late. He could not change his actions any more than he could change the consequences of them.

"Ye shall have her after the bairn is born, if that be yer wish. She will be grateful to have ye after the likes of him." Cinead tossed a scornful gesture toward Finn.

Through the slit of his one good eye, Finn now recognized the man's thirst for revenge. It was not his daughter's honor he was defending, but his own.

What punishment had Cinead heaped upon the girl? He

wanted to turn and search the large tables for Isabel and reassure himself she had not been harmed, but to move would once more stir the pain into a maelstrom, and draw the devil bastard's attention. And at the moment he did not feel strong enough to survive even the man's harsh words.

Despite the huge fires burning at each end of the room, the cold penetrated deeper into his bones. The vision in his one eye was growing fuzzy, and he could not discern the faces of those few sitting even a short distance away.

The room was strangely still and quiet, the only sound the popping of the fire as it consumed the huge logs.

Would Tearlach stand between the old Druid and his daughter to protect Isabel? Finn would appeal to him to do so, because he knew he would not live much longer. The pain in his head was growing worse, throbbing relentlessly behind his eyes, against his ears, as though it were a thing alive, trying to push its way free of his skull.

"Raise him so his accusers may look him in the face," Cinead demanded.

Tearlach stepped over his body and bent to grip Finn under the arms, lifting him into a sitting position.

Finn couldn't bite back the groan of pain as an ax seemed to split his forehead above his eye. Had Tearlach not been holding him up, Finn could not have been able to remain erect. He snagged Tearlach's sleeve between his fingers. "Dinna let him hurt Isabel or the bairn."

"Nay, he winna do so." Tearlach said, just above a whisper.

Tearlach would protect them. Finn leaned his head back against the man's knee and his lids dropped.

"Open yer eyes, Finn MacLeod."

It took all his effort to do so. He could see nothing. Everything was black.

"Ye have shamed many women of this clan and deserve a harsh punishment."

One blow and the pain would be gone. Tearlach would strike it, and it would be over.

"What say ye, Finn MacLeod?"

"I didna take m' pleasure without givin' as well as I received, Cinead MacLeod. Can ye say as much?"

He could not see the man, but when the punch landed on his jaw, a sword of pain lanced into his brain. Blackness closed in around him, and awareness fell away.

Seconds later it seemed he was awakened by a cold liquid dashed over his face all at once. He choked as he breathed in some of the water and rolled facedown as he hacked and coughed, the pain in his ribs unbearable. His body was one huge ache as he gasped and finally dragged air into his starving lungs.

His face felt strangely numb.

"Open yer eyes, Finn."

Cinead's commanding voice did not impress him. "Leave me be, Druid."

"Ye will face the women ye have spoiled."

A booted toe hit his ribs, and again he could not breathe. He coughed and tasted blood.

Tearlach once again tried to intercede. "Look about ye, Cinead. What do the people's faces tell ye? What does yer daughter's face tell ye?"

"They are weak-willed and foolish to have sympathy for

the very man who has shamed them."

Finn's head was beginning to thunder again, but the vision in his one eye had cleared enough for him to see Cinead MacLeod's hatred. If he could provoke him, would it end this? He gulped enough air to speak. "'Tis you who have shamed them, Druid. I have never spoken of any lass I have been with. Who has born witness against any of the lasses here? Or have ye frightened them all into saying they have been with me?" Finn coughed again and spat blood. "No matter what ye do to me, 'tis ye they will hate for this. Their kin will hate ye as well."

"Then I will give them more than hatred to think about." He thrust out his palms toward Finn.

"Yer heart has hardened to stone,

"And for that ye shall remain alone,

"Trapped in yer own hardened shell,

"Until ye learn to tell,

"Respect and affection from lust,

"Or until ye crumble into dust.

"No sunlight will ye feel.

"Only at night will the monster in ye steal

"Sustenance for ye to remain

"The monster ye will claim.

"By the power of me and thee,

"So mote it be."

The wind spiraled around Finn, and a force like a large hand picked him up and set him on his feet. He hunched forward against the pain.

A violent rush of panicked movement came from the large tables and benches in the great room, the clansmen and women scrambling to get away from the hot air roaring around the chamber, knocking over tankards and whipping their clothing against their bodies.

Finn's head felt too heavy to hold upright, and his chin dropped to his chest. He cried out in agony as a piercing cold raced from his fingertips and toes inward, consuming his arms and legs, burrowing into his torso. The leaden weight of his limbs dragged at him, threatening to tear them from their sockets.

He screamed as shards of pain like a thousand knives pierced him. His shoulder blades ripped from his back and bowed outward, growing into more. The weight of the projections dragged against his skin, against his bones, until he thought his back might snap in two. He fell to one knee, the sound wrenched from his throat more an animal growl than a scream. Power raged through his body, stiffening his limbs until they solidified in a crouched position.

He caught one last breath and howled a curse upon the Druid, his voice like crushed stone.

"Revenge is a double-edged sword, *draoidh*. Ye will pay as steep a price as I. Ye will know every loss I do and more."

Finn's lungs seized, everything turned gray, and he knew nothing more.

CHAPTER 1

Edinburgh, Scotland
Current Day

THE GRAYISH, BUFF-COLORED stone building façade, so different from the slick glass exterior of their New York office, looked, like many of the other buildings in Edinburgh, as though it had risen from the ground whole and in place. The entire city seemed to have been built of stone quarried from close by.

Genevieve Warren stood in front the auction house, the cobbled street hard and uneven beneath her feet. A light drizzle pattered against the black umbrella she held over her head.

She allowed herself a shiver of excitement and strode forward. Air whipped down the street and tugged a long strand of dark brown hair across her chin. She tucked it back behind her ear and turned to lower the umbrella and give it a shake before pushing open one of the large glass doors.

A well-dressed man strode down the entrance foyer and paused to greet her and introduce himself as Mr. Jonathan Taylor. His face was narrow, and his light brown eyes had a hint of gold. His blond hair, a few inches too long to be considered traditionally immaculate, hung over his shirt collar, and had her studying him with interest.

"I'm Genevieve Warren." She offered her hand. "I'm here to inquire about the gargoyle from the Dunvegan Castle grounds."

"Yes. My secretary notified me you'd be coming. I'll get a bag for your umbrella, and we'll go down the hall. The statue is so heavy, we decided it would be best to keep it on the ground floor. We haven't moved it to a room yet. But I've had it uncrated in the storage room at the back of the building. I hope you won't mind viewing it there."

"No, not at all." She studied the golden glow of the floor and the high ceilings while she waited for him to return. After maneuvering the umbrella into the plastic bag he handed her, she walked alongside him down a wide hallway.

The storage area was well lit, and had handcrafted shelves, some with slots where paintings could rest on their edges until they were hung. Reinforced shelving for pottery, ceramics, and other three-dimensional artworks stretched against all four walls. Her gargoyle—the one she hoped would be hers by the end of the day—was close to the large shipping bay doors. She recognized him from the back. A tail curved around his muscular thigh, while his wings stretched up and back, partially folded.

She first saw the statue in the garden at Dunvegan Castle and asked about it then. Years of exposure to the elements and nature had discolored and streaked the stone, leaving it mottled. The pattern of weathering looked like melted candle wax, but it didn't detract from the sculpture's power and beauty.

Genevieve circled to face the piece and was struck once again by the raw emotion depicted in the creature's face, a combination of torment and rage. He was ugly, yet she saw a dash of humanity in his features. It was the human element that drew her. His expression had remained in her thoughts long after she left the castle and moved on to her bed and breakfast there on the Isle of Skye.

In medieval architecture of the Gothic period, gargoyles were used mostly as downspouts on roofs to project water away from the buildings during rainstorms. To find a full sculpture of this kind was very rare. The owners had to want a fortune for it.

But then again, maybe not. Instead of being a curiosity, and drawing the attention of visitors on the castle grounds, she'd been told it had often frightened them because of the suffering depicted in his expression. He was life-sized, and that in itself made him intimidating. Had he not been down on one knee, he'd be at least six feet tall.

Another oddity was the sculpture had impressive, realistic sexual organs—a strange detail, since gargoyles had always been depicted as sexually neutral, though most gave the impression of being male. To find such nudity in a sculpture of that period was shocking.

During the medieval era, artists and society as a whole were focused on eradicating sin. Nudity of any kind in paintings and sculptures was adamantly discouraged, and was almost nonexistent. In fact, she was surprised the sculpture hadn't been defaced.

"He of course needs to be cleaned, what with the pigeons having roosted on him, and the natural weathering of the stone. The fact that he hasn't been tended will work in your favor, and the price will be adjusted."

"I'm a sculptor. I know how to clean stone," she murmured, taking in the shape of the gargoyle's ears. They lay against his head, and were pointed at the top, which made him look a little like a Vulcan.

"A professional sculptor?" Jonathan Taylor asked.

"Yes. I work in stone and wood."

"Genevieve Warren." His brows rose. "I read an article in a magazine just recently about your work."

"You may have. It's beginning to come along."

He smiled. "And they say the Scottish are masters of the understatement." His accent had grown a little thicker.

"I am part Scot and part French. My father's family came from La Varenne, my mother's family was from the Inverness area. Those two so different cultures wrapped up in one person may be why I am always at odds with myself. May I touch him?"

"Certainly." He gestured toward the statue with a long, expressive hand.

She stepped closer and knelt to cup the gargoyle's snarling face in her hands. From her position, she gazed directly into his eyes. She read suffering in the narrowing of his lids, but also defiance, and more than a glint of rage.

A strange, tumbling sensation attacked the pit of her stomach. His bunched jaw muscles felt almost real. For several moments, she was content to caress the shape of his chin. The artisan who sculpted this was a master.

She braced a hand against the muscular slope of his shoulder to rise while she studied the line of his wing, caught in the moment when it had just started to flex.

"What do you think about him?"

"I think he's so ugly he's beautiful."

Taylor laughed.

The pelt of thick, wavy hair following the contours of the gargoyle's head was strange as well. He was a chimera—part human, and part beast. She rested her hand upon his head, tempted by the detail to smooth the disheveled strands. She stepped away to circle him again and study his wings. Bony fingers fanned out from his shoulder blades, and veins branched from the joint to trail through a thin membrane very similar to a bat's. The detail was exquisite, and would show up much better once he was cleaned.

To his credit, Taylor stood by silently, and didn't pressure her for a sale. "How much are they hoping to get for him?"

"Twenty thousand pounds. But there is a hitch."

She raised her brows. She wasn't surprised.

"Historic Scotland will not allow any sculpture of the period to be sold outright and transported to another country, but it can be put on permanent loan. Which means you would not be able to purchase him outright, but can instead pay for the right to have him relocated indefinitely."

So she would be paying twenty-five thousand US dollars to house and care for him, but could not claim ownership since she lived in another country. Twenty-five thousand dollars she could use for materials to do more sculptures. Stone didn't come cheap. But she could do some smaller things, or work in wood to make up the difference. Her work was moving very well these days.

She studied the gargoyle a few more moments. "The transport to get him home will cost me dearly," she murmured. Possibly as much as five thousand. And then transporting him from the ship to her studio another two or three. She was probably looking at close to thirty-three thousand, maybe more.

She'd gone insane. She was going to spend as much for a sculpture as it would cost to house a family of four for a year in her neck of the woods. And he wouldn't even belong to her.

"They could easily get five times what they're asking at auction and sell him to someone here in Scotland."

This statue was a one of a kind, and would be well worth the money.

Why was she so drawn to him? He couldn't fit in her studio with all her own work. He'd have to go on the porch outside her studio. The insurance would probably be astronomical.

She cupped his cheek and felt the curve against her palm. He had to have been fashioned after a real man. She'd do some research and find out. She bent and whispered in his pointed ear. "Do you want to come to America with me?"

Taylor chuckled.

She looked up and smiled again.

"We can help you with the transport arrangements. We often ship things stateside via plane and ship."

"I'd appreciate it." She reached inside her coat pocket and withdrew a business card with her name and contact information on it. "You sound very sure they'll sell him to me."

"I can't be completely certain, but they remembered your interest in him when you visited the castle a few weeks back. 'Twas from them I got your number. They seemed interested in giving you right of first refusal."

"If they decide my offer is enough, I'll give him a good home, and he'll be in out of the rain and snow."

Taylor grinned, his light brown eyes alight with amusement. "You talk about and to him as though he's alive."

"My own sculptures seem alive to me. I breathe life into them with my hammer and chisel. Whoever sculpted him"— she nodded toward the gargoyle—"thought the same."

Taylor turned his attention to the statue with a thoughtful look. "Too bad they didn't give him a more pleasant expression. But then he wouldn't have scared away evil spirits nearly as effectively."

"He wouldn't be nearly as interesting, either." Genevieve wandered toward the exit, and Taylor caught up to walk with her.

"Would you care for a cup of tea?" he asked.

"I've taken up enough of your time, and I'm sure you have other responsibilities waiting for you."

"Actually, I'm through for the day, and I'd be pleased if you'd join me. There's an Italian restaurant just up the street." He gestured for her to go ahead of him through the door.

Genevieve studied his narrow face with its warm brown eyes and shaggy blond hair. A quick twinge of grief assailed her, and she started to turn him down…but hesitated. She'd only be in Scotland another three days. But it might be pleasant to spend an hour with an attractive man. She'd never see him again.

And Simon, her agent, wasn't here to warn her away from him as he always did.

They came to a stop in the entrance foyer. "Italian sounds good."

Taylor smiled, his eyes alight with pleasure. "I'll just get my coat and umbrella."

CHAPTER 2

F INN SIGHED WITH some regret as the man and woman disappeared through a doorway. When she looked into his eyes, he had read curiosity and wonder in her expression. And she had touched him like his flesh was not stone, but alive beneath her hands. It had been a century since anyone stood eye to eye with him, or really looked at him.

Though he was a monster, he was still human beneath the layer of stone and ugliness. He'd been pure monster after Cinead MacLeod cursed him, and it took him some time to learn to control it. He had slaughtered the clan animals for food and frightened the people, but, as he had predicted, they turned on Cinead and held him responsible.

The man's death had not lessened Finn's pain, because he still suffered each dawn as his body turned to stone. He still craved human touch and human congress.

He fought constantly to hold on to his humanity. If he allowed the monster to take over, he would be mindless, and live by instinct alone. What was to keep the monster from slaughtering humans? He had not in the past, but... After six hundred and sixty-two years, he no longer believed he would ever return to his human form.

Though he could not see the sun go down, his body sensed

it coming, and even now the transition from stone to flesh hit him like a broadax. He caught himself on the tips of his fingers as he pitched forward, his muscles knotted from being in one position for the past fifteen hours. He had nine hours to spend alive and in motion before the sun rose and he again became the cursed stone statue.

But in all but thought, he remained the monster.

He rose from his crouched position and stretched to his full height. He bowed his back and extended his wings, relieving his cramped muscles. He flapped his wings, rose into the air, and flew to one end of the storage area and back.

Being banished to this dark, crowded space was worse than being out in the garden. At least there he had not been missed when he needed to forage at night for food and water. Since arriving here, his one attempt to escape the storage area caused the eruption of an ungodly racket, and two men with weapons had rushed in. He pretended to be frozen into the same pose he was forced into every dawn until they left. He had to find a way out of this place, or at least into the rest of the building, where he might find food to fill his rumbling belly and water to slake his thirst.

He discovered four windows set into the roof. Why would anyone fashion a window in such a place? He paused in wonder to study the clarity of the glass. It looked much thicker than any he had ever seen.

The sky had turned a deep purple. Clouds partially obscured the moon. If he could open the window, he could fly out and find food and drink with no one the wiser. He flew up and ran his hands around the frame and discovered a latch. He tried to open the door the day before and set off a commotion, but perhaps this time he could slip out before the guards arrived. But then how would he get back in?

His stomach rumbled. He would figure out a way back in later. He shoved open the window, flew through the opening, and then hovered above it. No ungodly noise. He started to ease the window shut, then thought better of it. The latch might lock, and he would be forced to break it to get back in.

He searched the top of the building for an object to wedge in the frame, but the area stretched flat and empty but for some pipes. He flew back through the opening, and hovering low, scanned the area.

The panels of the wooden box in which he was transported lay stacked against one wall. He wrenched one of the narrow slats loose from the top and broke it in two. With two flaps of his wings, he was back up at the window, where he wedged a small piece beneath the latch so it could not catch.

He flew away from the auction house, leaving the stifled, trapped feeling behind, and soared high above the flat-roofed buildings. He had heard the man mention sharing a meal. He scanned the streets below for a glimpse of the woman who'd looked into his eyes.

Not in hundreds of years had he felt such a strong stirring from a human glance or the touch of a woman's hand. But then he had seldom experienced either. She wanted to buy him and have him conveyed to her home. He would be her property, just as he had been Ian Ciar's from the moment he was turned into this grotesque creature.

There was something morally wrong in one human owning another. But he was no longer human. And he spent more time as a stone block than the monster.

But there were freedoms that, as a human, he would never experience without his curse. Flying was one of them. He twisted in midair and shot straight up, until the cold took his breath. He folded his wings, jackknifed, and allowed himself to plummet toward the earth headfirst. The glint of the moon on the tile shingles of the buildings warned him he was close, and yet he waited. At the last moment, he snapped his wings open and glided along the rooftops, following their crenellated heights.

He spotted a rain barrel atop a roof and landed on it. Though the water tasted a bit strange, he drank deeply, then flew on.

The scent of seawater reached him long before he arrived, passing high over several ships at berth. He maintained his heading until a glimmer of light caused the water to shimmer as though thousands of candles rode the chop, then turned back inland.

He fancied some fish, and where better to find a few but on one of the fishing vessels coming in? He followed high above one of the larger boats late to reach port. Though it was dark, gulls still followed in its wake, screeching, dipping, and wheeling, alert for an opportunity to snatch a free meal.

The boat docked, and Finn and the gulls hovered, waiting for the fishermen to unload their cargo. Fascinated with how things had progressed since his time, he watched while loud machines sucked the fish out of the boat's hold with huge hoses and dumped them onto a belt that carried the carcasses to holding vats filled with ice. Four men worked in tandem, scooping ice into the large tubs while the fish tumbled into them.

Finn swooped low over the base of the belt, its high sides keeping him out of sight of the men, and hovered there while he grabbed two of the larger fish and a few smaller ones.

He flew low along the deserted quay between the docked ships and then out into open water, with two large gulls following him. He flipped one of the smaller fish up in the air, and one gull snatched it, its beady black eye glowing as it flew away with its prize. The other bird flew alongside him, its high-pitched screech a jealous protest. Finn laughed and tossed him a fish as well.

He turned back inland and followed the coast on the look-out for a private place to enjoy his meal. He settled on a long point of rocks that had tumbled down from a high cliff and into the water.

Using his long talons, he ripped the heads off the fish and tossed them aside. Splitting their soft underbellies proved easy, and he pulled loose the guts and dumped them over the side of the rock onto the sand below. Gulls would find the leavings and clean up the mess. He rinsed the prepared carcasses in the surf, crouched upon the rocks, peeled the soft meat away from the skin and, rolling it into balls between his fingers, popped them into his mouth.

While he ate, he remembered roasting his catch over an open fire, sharing it with his men. Men long dead. Even after all these years alone, he still longed for the sound of another's voice, sharing conversation with him. Instead he had to settle for the murmur of the sea. He ate his meal, then tossed the bones away for the gulls to pick over later.

Finn gazed out over the watery horizon. What was the point of this solitary life? What purpose did he serve, other than the ornamental when his body hardened into stone? He could sleep away the hours while in that form.

But as the monster, he only served himself by staying alive. What if he did not eat? Would he eventually die and become the stone statue for an eternity?

He did not have to return to the storage room.

He could find his own home, away from those who would claim him.

Two hundred years alone in a garden, shat on by birds, climbed on by other creatures, stared at and insulted by thousands of people wandering through, was more than enough. He had even been urinated on several times through-out the years.

Yes, he could be free of it all. But he was vulnerable when unprotected. Turning into the stone creature, even one less monstrous than he was right now, left him at the mercy of people. Should someone find him and decide to take a hammer and chisel to him while he was defenseless... He shuddered. He was haunted by the fear that he would live through the destruction, only to die once he changed to monster.

The laird of the castle through every generation had protected him. Until now. Now they wanted to be rid of him, though he had been careful of his behavior for the past fifty years or so.

Finn raked his fingers through his thick hair. He stared at his hands and grimaced. He needed a bar of soap. Just because he was a monster did not mean he had to stink like one. He flew down to the water and waded in to his knees. He bathed the best he could by rubbing sand against his skin and rinsing it in the frigid salt water. When he took flight, he turned back toward the building where the woman had visited him, spoken to him, touched him.

He landed on an impressive church not far from Edinburgh castle and folded his wings around him. From his perch on one of the spires, he studied the surrounding area. The city had always been a busy port, but the castle above was built of wood in his time. The hulking stone structure that sat atop the great hill in the middle of Edinburg was much more intimidating and regal, as was the church beneath him. The roads were no longer packed dirt, but stone.

The numerous stone buildings surrounding him created a maze of crosses and streets. People scurried up and down, wandering in and out of the pubs and shops. When the people's movements became sluggish and sparse, he tired of watching them.

His thoughts turned morose. He focused on the cobbled street below. He could leap and let himself fall to the pavement below. If he allowed himself to topple from this spire, would he shatter into pieces like the stone statue, or would he die of his wounds? If he could die, it would end this constant waiting.

But if he did not die…if he made himself a cripple, what then would happen?

How many times would he have this debate? His fear of being maimed and helpless for an eternity always prevented him from acting.

With a sigh, Finn left his perch and flew west, toward the building he had escaped.

CHAPTER 3

G ENEVIEVE RAN HER hands over the hard, smooth surface of the six-foot tall block of marble. It was a beautiful piece of stone, perfect for the sculpture she planned. She liked to live with the block a few days, touch it, and visualize the form trapped within, before starting the work. A finished clay sculpture sat close by, ready to be fired as soon as the clay dried.

In the meantime, she wanted to spend time with the gargoyle on the covered concrete patio outside. And the first thing he needed was a bath.

She strode into the mudroom, and after wiggling into well-worn blue coveralls, she tugged on rubber boots and gathered a bucket of soapy water, a soft brush, several rags, and rubber gloves.

As she walked out on the porch, a gentle breeze carried the sweet scent of the white freesia blossoms tucked among clusters of colorful tulips and drooping, bell-shaped daffodils planted in carefully maintained beds along the front of the house.

She breathed in their perfume and tilted her face up to the tender midmorning sun. After weeks of rain, the weather had turned fine, promising several days of clear skies and warmer temperatures. She pushed back the metal doors of her studio to air out the space, and invited in the greener smell of blooming flowers and rain-washed grass.

Carrying the bucket and cleaning tools, she cut across the soggy grass to the covered concrete patio. The slab butted up against her studio on one side, and the porch that stretched across the front of her long ranch-style house on the other. French doors in the breezeway, connecting her studio to the house, opened onto the patio.

Butterbean, her orange tabby, looked out at her, his mouth moving in a plaintive meow she couldn't hear. She set the bucket down next to the gargoyle and ambled up the steps to open the door and let him out. He wove through her legs for some attention, and after a few head-to-tail strokes sauntered off, leapt up on the porch, and settled into one of the rocking chairs.

Genevieve turned her attention back to the statue. The gargoyle's suffering was laid bare in the full sun, and a burst of sympathy swamped her.

"Maybe you'll feel better once you're clean." She tugged on the rubber gloves and started with his hair and his taut, forbidding face. The soapy water and soft brush cleaned the algae and dirt off the stone, leaving it grayish white.

As she splashed and scrubbed, she studied gargoyle's features more closely. Though set in a grimace of pain and rage, his face had the musculature and physiology of a human, except for the heavy brow ridge and the displaced chin and exaggerated teeth. His cap of hair curled around his ears, along his neck, and across his forehead.

Once he was clean, she'd study him more thoroughly. She worked steadily for an hour, changing water when she needed to, and had cleaned a fair collection of pigeon droppings, dirt, and algae off most of his upper body. She was working on his back and shoulders when a car pulled into her driveway. The low-riding charcoal gray Jaguar gleamed like a troop of shoe shiners had worked over its entire surface.

Simon Martin emerged from behind the wheel with the grace of a dancer. His black suit fit his tall, trim frame to perfection, setting off his dark hair and chocolate brown eyes, although his rich gray shirt paired with a black and red silk tie looked too dressy to be anywhere near her studio.

Hyperaware of her appearance, she looked down at her dust-coated coveralls and sighed. The jeans and T-shirt beneath the coveralls weren't much better.

"What are you doing?" Simon asked.

Simon wasn't usually so obtuse. "Cleaning this statue."

"I can see that, but what is that thing?"

"It's a gargoyle, sculpted in the fourteenth century."

His brows rose, and he started toward her, but stopped a safe distance away from the garden hose and water-slick concrete. "And it's sitting on your patio because…?"

Genevieve gave the area just above the statue's wings a swipe or two with the brush. When had Simon's prissiness begun to test her patience? Was it before or after her trip to Scotland? The two weeks she spent in Scotland had given her a breather from the pressure he often put on her to produce, produce, produce. He didn't seem to realize that art couldn't be forced. And if she kept working when she was too tired, she made mistakes. The materials she sculpted were expensive, and she couldn't afford to make many.

He was a good agent. And he was so good to her after

Andy's death…. "I like him, and I want him here." Did her tone sound as intractable to him as it did her?

His brows rose, and he sidled closer to the gargoyle. "He's ugly as hell."

She smiled. "Yes, he is. But he's one of a kind, and very valuable. I'm getting ready to rinse him, so you'd better step back if you don't want that beautiful suit ruined."

He danced away *tout de suite*, and she smiled as she sprayed the gargoyle down to remove the soapy residue. When he was properly rinsed, she turned off the water and said, "You arrived just in time. I'm ready for a break. Would you like some iced tea, Simon?"

"Yes. I could do with a drink."

"Come into the kitchen with me."

Genevieve led the way up the steps of the breezeway, where she took off her boots and padded in her sock feet into the kitchen.

"Have a seat if you like." She flipped her ponytail over her shoulder and went to the sink to wash her hands.

Simon hiked a hip on one of the metal stools at the breakfast bar off the back of the island. "The kitchen looks great."

"Thanks. I'm very pleased with it. And the house is much more comfortable now this and the bathrooms have been remodeled."

She scanned the space and its ceiling-high green cabinets. Their glass doors gleamed, and her grandmother's antique dishes added style and color. With travertine tile as a backsplash and marble countertops, the kitchen also brought a bit of her studio into the space. She had an office in the studio, but found herself spending more and more time at the kitchen table in front of the bank of windows looking out onto her front yard.

She filled two glasses with ice, poured fresh-brewed, sweetened tea into them, put a slice of lemon on the rim of the glass, and set one down in front of Simon. "Is this just a visit, or is it about business?"

"A little of both. I've only seen you twice since you returned from Scotland."

"I've been doing some sketches for a new sculpture and finishing the clay sculpture of the one I'm working on now. And doing a little gardening."

"I'm glad to see you're staying busy. I've been busy, too. I sold *Reclining Woman* to a collector yesterday for thirty thousand dollars. He was very impressed with the sculpture. It's going to have a front and center place in the window of his office building in New York."

A small twinge hit her. She always grieved a little over every sculpture when it sold. A piece of her went with them each time. "What kind of business is it?"

"A fashion magazine. He said they were all about the beauty of women, and the sculpture is big enough to make a statement. He also asked about the model."

"She wants to remain anonymous, Simon." If anyone approached her, Juliet would never agree to sit for her again. "You could make me lose one of my best models, plus she has an extremely protective boyfriend."

Chase wouldn't physically harm anyone… Or would he? But since he was a police officer, he could definitely make things difficult for anyone who tried to harm Juliet. And then there were Juliet's abilities. Genevieve got a glimpse of them last time she visited, and she had a newfound—and pro-found—respect for witches.

"Okay, but if ever she changes her mind, she could hop a plane and have a job on a fashion runway in half a second."

For a moment Genevieve wondered if Juliet would be tempted by such an offer, considering the work she did at the bar. "I'll be sure to tell her."

"What have you been working on?" he asked.

The table was littered with sketches of both the gargoyle on the patio and ideas she had for a series of nude male sculptures inspired by him. She didn't want Simon poking into them. Not yet.

"I've finished the clay sculpture for the latest work. We can wander out there, and you can check it out. It's too wet to be fired yet, but it's drying."

"You always hold your cards close to the vest, Genevieve. I wish you would talk to me about your ideas."

But she didn't feel she could. He tried to guide her to safer subjects, more mainstream art forms, and it wasn't where she wanted to go. She made money because she pushed the envelope instead of staying inside it. "I want to do more nudes. Male and female."

He raised a brow. "They're harder to sell."

"But they do sell eventually. And I want to look at applying for commissions for public art."

"Most of the time those are created from metal."

"Which won't be a problem. I do the sculpture and create a mold from it. Then the mold is poured in bronze and constructed."

"You make it sound very easy."

"Not easy. But with public works, you build a far-reaching reputation because of the number of viewers, depending on the venue."

"Don't you think you may be reaching a little far?"

Why was he representing her if he didn't believe in her? She glanced toward the drawings on the table. She'd never doubted her ability. Other things, certainly, but never her sculpting. It was a gift, and came to her as naturally as breathing. "No. I don't think I am."

She reached for her iced tea, taking a sip to cover a tangle of feelings. "Why don't you bring your drink, and I'll show you the clay sculpture."

She started toward the breezeway again, but Simon caught her arm. "I didn't mean to insult you, Genevieve. You are an extraordinary talent. It's just that I don't want to see disappointment interfere with your creativity."

She studied his patrician features. "Simon, you have a fantastic eye for what will sell and what won't, but by its nature, art is a series of experiments that sometimes work and sometimes don't. I didn't learn without some disappointments. And if I stay with what's safe, I might as well sell my art to a corporation that mass-produces it in miniature, so everyone can have a copy instead of the few who want a piece that's been a creative struggle to produce.

"The mass production would probably make more money, but it wouldn't make me happy, because it wouldn't really be mine." She appealed to the business side of him. "But to produce a work everyone can view, discuss, and enjoy will make the pieces I sell more valuable."

He flashed her a self-deprecating smile. "Okay. I understand. I'm a greedy bastard, always wanting to steer you toward projects that sell quickly."

She allowed him to charm her and laughed. "Sometimes. But not always." There were times she could almost be attracted to Simon, but his controlling nature put her off.

Besides, she wasn't ready to let any man into her heart again. Not yet. Andy's loss had left her reeling emotionally. Going to dinner with Jonathan Taylor while she was in Scotland was as close to a connection as she wanted right now.

"Do you want to see the next sculpture?"

Simon inclined his head. "Of course I do."

They crossed the breezeway and went into the studio. The gentle breeze drifting through the open door had freshened the air, and sunlight glinted off the five-foot square block of marble.

She paused beside her clay model. The clay still retained a few darker damp spots, and it would need to be bone dry before she could fire it. Otherwise it would explode. She ran her fingers over the woman's arm, enjoying the silky-smooth feel of the dry clay.

"That block won't be big enough for her, will it?" Simon asked.

"No. It isn't for her. I'll be firing this one and using her as the sculpture with a wooden base. I'm going to use a polymer to create the impression of water trickling down her body and pooling around her, a sort of modern Venus rising from the sea. The wooden base will be part of the piece."

"Have you used the polymer before?"

"I used it in a series in college This one will be very different from the first." She rested her hand on the sculpture's knee. "She'll be the first of three, based on classical themes. I want to experiment with some different materials before I do another stone carving, and I'm saving the marble block for something special. I have a large wooden block coming for another wood sculpture, too. It will be here next week."

"Your diversity is remarkable, Genevieve."

"So many ideas... Sometimes my mind won't let me sleep because I have so many of them."

"Be careful not to burn yourself out."

"I won't. This is what I was meant to do."

Her worktable was empty of tools until she needed them, but was covered with scattered drawings of the sculptures she planned. "Come see what I mean."

He followed her to the worktable. "You've drawn her from every perspective." After a moment's study, he looked up. "Have you thought about framing and selling your drawings?"

"They're just working sketches."

"They're beautiful. And they'd sell."

He was always looking for ways to turn a profit from everything she produced. Which was what she paid him for. She thought about it for a moment. "If they're still in good shape after I've finished with the project... Sometimes I have to make notations and adjustments."

His attention still rested on the back view. "Your grasp of human anatomy is amazing."

"I studied anatomy in college, and took several other classes on human physiology before I went to Florence to study. When I sculpt, I see the structure beneath the stone, or build it from within the clay."

"Like Michelangelo, who said he saw the angel in the

marble and carved until he set him free."

She smiled at the quote. "Something like that."

Had the sculptor of the gargoyle seen him hiding beneath the surface and freed him? Was the agony she saw in his face from the struggle and pain of birth? Or was it some other agonizing experience? Who was the inspiration for the sculpture, and who was the artist? She should have done research and learned more about them both before leaving Scotland.

"This isn't the same model as *Reclining Woman*?"

"No. Someone younger. She's twenty, going to school, and doesn't want anyone knowing she's sitting for me. I've changed her features so she's anonymous."

Simon studied the sculpture a moment longer. "She's lovely. And you'll make her famous, yet no one will know who she is."

"In today's world, it'll keep her from being hounded on social media, and possibly harassed by the people around her."

"I see what you mean." He studied the other drawings closely.

"Who will you get for the male sculptures?"

"I haven't chosen anyone yet. I've been doing some free-hand sketches, but I'd prefer a model."

"You need to be careful about the type of man you approach for this, Genevieve. By the very nature of what you're asking them to do, it may leave you open to... unwanted advances. Why don't you call me, and I'll hang out and act as a buffer?"

Touched by his concern, she smiled. "I may do that. Thank you for offering."

"I want you to be safe."

She read sincerity in his brown eyes and nodded. "I know you do." He had been very attentive after Andy's death. Offering to stay until she found her feet again, although she'd preferred to mourn in private. "I promise I'll be careful. There are professional models I can hire."

"I'm sure whoever he is will find it gratifying."

His wry tone triggered a laugh. "It isn't any different for me than drawing a female body, Simon. They're called models for a reason. You don't date your models. And it can screw up a good working relationship...when you find a good one. I've even been known to invite their girlfriends so they can see nothing is going on. I just want to do my work."

He fell silent for a moment while he carefully set the drawings aside on the table. "That will change one day, Genevieve."

Her eyes stung, and she looked away. "I'm not in any hurry. Andy and I had a past together. We went through school together from the first grade. Parted ways when I went to college and he went into the Marines, but we always stayed in touch. It seemed natural for us to be together when we found each other again here in Superstition. There was a history there. I loved him before I fell in love with him. I didn't just lose my lover, Simon. I lost a dear friend. He's not replaceable."

As she turned, she glimpsed impatience—or was it anger?—in his expression before his features returned to their usual careful charm.

"He wouldn't want you to lock yourself away, Genevieve." Simon rested a hand on her shoulder. "I'd better go. I'll transfer the money for *Reclining Woman* to your account this week, as soon as the check clears."

She dropped her gaze to hide her uncertainty. "Thanks, Simon."

Ice rattled in the glass as he set it on the worktable. "Call if you need me."

She wasn't certain about that, either. There was a tension between them that hadn't been there before Andy was killed. Simon seemed to resent her grief. Was it because he thought it might interfere with making money? Or something else?

She hoped not. Their relationship had always been about business more than friendship. She couldn't imagine there being anything more than that between them.

Simon sauntered out the open door, and when she heard his car start, she breathed a sigh of relief.

CHAPTER 4

SIMON PULLED OUT of Genevieve's driveway, the pressure building inside him until he pounded the steering wheel in fury.

He made sure she got top dollar for her work. Worked to get her exposure with magazine interviews and television coverage. Helped her line up workmen to get her house remodeled in record time. But no matter what he did for her, she wouldn't let Andy's death go.

Two years. It had been two years. How much longer did he have to wait? They needed to be together. She needed him there to keep her focused. Otherwise she wasted time with her friends. And unplanned trips to Scotland. She'd waited until he was out of touch in New York before arranging for the trip. Who arranges a major transatlantic vacation in a matter of days?

Who had she gone to see?

And why had she returned with that hideous monstrosity? Why would she waste money on it? And why did she have to set it on her patio? To scare the wildlife away?

The gargoyle was a distraction. Just as Andy had been. As were her friends Juliet and Miranda.

A squirrel scampered into the road ahead of him. Simon

stomped on the gas and aimed the Jaguar at it, felt the tiny bump, and glanced in his rearview mirror to see it dead behind him.

Genevieve was going to be as famous as Michelangelo and Bernini, but she needed to focus. He, Simon, was all she needed. He'd keep her working. Keep her sculptures selling. Keep her name out in front of the public.

When she mentioned wanting to do public works, he played it just right. Reverse psychology worked so easily. Whenever she thought he might want to talk her out of an idea, she'd dig in deeper and go after it even harder. She was so easy to manipulate.

About everything but Andy. She hadn't listened to him about Andy. She brought him into her house and into her bed. And now she was holding onto her grief. He'd become larger to her, more important in death than he was in life.

Simon hadn't expected that. It was a huge miscalculation.

He punched the steering wheel again. It had taken everything in him to maintain his pretense of sympathy and not grab her and give her a hard shake.

Andy had taken up her time, and kept her away from Simon. He couldn't tolerate that. He was building her into a star. She'd appreciate all his hard work one day. Appreciate him even more once her eyes were open to what she really needed to be. What they needed to be to each other.

Reaching Superstition's city limits, he slowed while he passed some of the newer homes. The town was growing, with new industry moving into the mountains. Some of the coal mines, closed years before, had been repurposed, their damp, dark corridors manipulated to create the perfect conditions for growing mushrooms. The factories were running strong, and pumping jobs and money into the community.

Simon wove his way through town, past the college campus, then turned into Moon Bow Acres, a gated community. He shot down the main road to Wicket Street and to his large, two-story brick house. Using the remote he opened and entered the two-car garage. The garage door was closing behind him when he let himself into the house.

He walked through the mudroom, into the immaculate kitchen, and paused long enough to pour a glass of wine before wandering upstairs to his office. Settling behind his desk, he flipped open his laptop and keyed in his password. One tap of an icon on the screen, and the monitor came alive with a grid of images from inside Genevieve's house.

In her bedroom she opened dresser drawers, removed clothing, and went into the bathroom.

Simon cursed. Why hadn't he wired the bathroom with a camera? If she left for a weekend, he'd be sure to do it.

He settled in to watch her for the evening.

CHAPTER 5

ROM HIS POSITION behind one of the large oaks that shaded the house during the day and offered him cover and a perch at night, Finn watched Genevieve. Her feet were propped in a chair close to the window. Their strong arches curved while she pointed her toes. The bottoms, unmarred by calluses or dirt, looked baby-soft and pink. Finn rarely thought feet beautiful, but he decided this woman's feet might change his mind.

She wore thigh-length shorts, and her long, slender legs seemed to stretch on forever, pale and smooth.

Women's fashion had changed much over the years—for the better, in his opinion. Thank God for the books the families in residence at the castle left lying about, along with newspapers, shiny-page magazines, even letters. The written word had helped pass the time, and kept Finn tethered to the human world. Plus it had helped him evolve along with the humans.

So very much had changed since the year of his birth as the monster. Had a woman displayed herself in garments baring her legs for anyone other than her husband, as Genevieve was doing, the entire village would have been outraged and moved to punish her. And now it was accepted, had been for decades.

But for him such a display was a double-edged sword. She represented everything he had lost, could never have, and yet craved. He could not wrench his gaze from her. He was fascinated, even when she did nothing more than turn the page in the book she focused on so intently, and reached for the small, long-stemmed glass of golden liquid sitting on the table next to her to take a sip.

Her long, twisted tail of brown hair curved against her cheek and lay draped across her shoulder. A long T-shirt, almost as long as the shorts, covered her upper body, but outlined the sweet shape of her breasts. Those same breasts had been close to his face earlier today, covered by layers of bulky cloth, and he had ached with the need to rest his head just there and feel the soft, womanly flesh against his cheek, beneath his lips, and cupped in his hand.

But no human woman would allow him so close. And there were no other beings like him with whom he could share comfort, conversation, or the fulfillment of any other need. Would he even be attracted to one if there were? Probably not.

Seeing her sitting at the table, so completely feminine, brought once again to agonizing light every long, barren, empty year he had spent alone. A sense of loss, piercing and painful, stormed through him. A howl of pain and rage rose from the very depths of his being. With difficulty, he choked it back.

Unable to bear watching her any longer, he took two long leaps and sprang into the sky. His wings snapped open like freshly washed sheets caught in a gale. The sound was satisfying in its intensity. He needed to fill his empty belly, then bathe the monster so he would at least be as clean as the stone he became.

The area was surrounded by woods and isolated, with a creek snaking along one border. He dove down in search of fish, startling a doe getting a drink with her twin fawns. They leapt into the brush, their white tails a flicker of movement. He started to follow them, then decided against it. He would not do them harm, and there was no need to terrify the wee ones.

Instead, he watched for movement beneath the water. How sick of fish he was. Birds were always easy to catch, but he was not in the mood for the hour of work required to pluck feathers for only a bite or two of meat.

He glided over the water, observing the effect his shadow had on the smaller animals and birds. Then, coming to a field, he swooped down low and scared a rabbit from its hiding place in the tall grass. He was after it in a second, caught it by the scruff and, with a jerk, snapped its neck. He circled back around to the water and landed on the bank, where he ripped the skin loose from the carcass and gutted it, leaving the mess for other animals to eat.

He missed being able to cook his meal over a fire and dampen the wild flavor of the meat. He missed sitting at table like a civilized human and sharing drink with his clansmen. His memories of them were as sharp today as they were six hundred years ago. Was that, too, part of his punishment? To be reminded every day of what he had lost?

A wolf came slinking out from the deepest part of the brush, possibly drawn by the smell of fresh blood. His hunger killed by his thoughts, Finn stayed motionless until she crept close. On a whim, he tossed the skinned rabbit to her. Her teeth gleamed white as she caught it in her strong jaws and bounded back into the brush.

Finn slogged to the creek and washed his face and hands in the chilly water. He crouched there for several moments, drinking deeply, and then, looking up, noticed several pairs of eyes glowing from the underbrush. Wolves, possibly a pack. He eyed them with wary concern, then with interest.

Could they end this for him? Could he remain unresisting while they attacked and devoured him? He folded his wings back and bent to rest his forehead against his knee and waited.

The musky smell of their fur was familiar, and took him back hundreds of years. When he felt a muzzle brush against his arm, he froze, though every human instinct screamed at him to leap to his feet and run, and every monster instinct told him to fight and fly.

Sounds came from behind him, wet and nauseating, while they gobbled up the innards of the rabbit. He raised his head a wee bit, and met the golden gaze of a huge wolf. For several seconds they froze, taking each other's measure.

The feral gleam he glimpsed in other animals' eyes was absent. Instead, Finn saw a patient watchfulness. Testing the waters, he raised a hand and, curling his fingers so his sharp, lethal nails were tucked into his palm, extended the back of his hand to the beast.

The wolf sniffed it and sat down.

Stunned, the words "What are you?" burst from Finn. "Have ye been cursed like me?"

The wolf shook himself as though to say no. He gave a short, sharp bark, calling his pack together. Finn watched in despair as they followed their alpha back into the woods.

After that one brief contact, they had no interest in further congress with him. He rose and did the only thing left to him.

He flew back to Genevieve's house.

Careful to avoid large patches of interior lights cast onto the lawn, Finn reached for one of the dingy cloths Genevieve used earlier to scrub his stony exterior. He poured some soap onto the cloth, then studied the knob connected to the garden hose. His overlarge hands, with their deadly claws, gripped the circular metal clumsily, but he managed to turn it.

The sound of running water was evident, but none came out the end of the hose. He gripped the metallic thing preventing the water from pouring. He gave the lever a cautious squeeze, and cold water sprayed out, hitting him in the chest. With a grin, he sprayed himself down and wet the rag, delighting in the process of soaping his hair and body until he was covered with lather. He even soaped the parts of his wings he could reach, then sprayed himself down with the hose before giving a violent shake, scattering drops across the patio. There were so few pleasures left to him, but being clean and not smelling like an unwashed beast was one of them.

After taking a long drink, he returned everything to its place and turned off the water. He had just moved to his spot on the patio when the door behind him opened. In a blink, Finn took his normal position. Only if she came close enough to touch him would she recognize the difference.

Out of the corner of his eye, he saw her check the valve that controlled the water. She paused for a moment to scan the yard. His footprints stood out on the concrete and led right to him. His stomach tightened with part dread, part excitement. What would happen if she discover his secret? She would be terrified, horrified. But after that passed… He didn't want to think about what she might do. All he knew was the truth of his existence had remained secret for too long.

He tensed to stand, but hesitated when she followed the footprints and came to stand directly in front of him. She was too close. He did not want to frighten her.

He breathed in the sweet scent lingering on her skin and gazed at the long, smooth length of her legs. Without the barrier of the window and the distance, they appeared softer, more well-muscled. The shorts hugged her buttocks and hips, outlining the womanly roundness. His body responded to the sight with a fierce joy and need, and he quickly closed his eyes to block out the sight.

Should he approach her in such a state, she would be doubly terrified. He swallowed against a knot of despair. It took all his control to stay in position.

"Just someone passing by, I suppose. They must have gotten a drink and then left," she murmured to herself.

Nearby, to the west, a wolf howled, and Genevieve caught her breath and swung around to look.

She rubbed her arms, as though warming herself against a chill, then went back inside.

Finn slumped in disappointment. Had he been on the verge of alerting her to his presence before the wolf howled and she fled into the house? The wolves he had concluded were not wolves at all?

He stretched his wings and folded them around his body, not for warmth, for he was seldom cold, but because it provided him with a wee bit of comfort.

✧　✧　✧

GENEVIEVE MOVED FROM window to window, trying to catch a glimpse of whoever had been outside her house. Why had she positioned the gargoyle on the corner of the patio, where she couldn't see him except through the breezeway windows? Whoever it was had sprayed him with water and been barefoot.

There was no rational reason to be afraid. She was secure inside her house. But the hairs on the back of her neck were still raised, and every nerve continued to prickle with alarm.

She'd felt someone watching her. She was certain of it, and she'd learned over the years to trust her instincts and her impressions. Traveling abroad by herself, she'd saved herself from many a mishap by paying attention to those feelings.

She retrieved a sweater from the mudroom off the kitchen and dragged it on.

Because she'd cleaned the gargoyle, and the light reflected off his features, he now looked more lifelike. She could swear she'd seen the light glint in his eyes, as though he were looking right at her. Maybe it was just his startlingly lifelike gaze which made her feel watched.

She crept into the breezeway and peeked out the window. Butterbean looped through the statue's legs and rubbed his chin against his calf, marking him. Surely if someone was around, the cat would be a little more wary.

Whoever it was had to be gone now.

She returned to the kitchen, poured a glass of wine, but pulled the curtains across the window before taking a seat. Through the glass she heard the wolves howl once again, the sound sorrowful. Goose bumps cascaded over her neck and arms, and she swore.

She'd never known them to come so close to the house.

But they'd surely scare off anyone who lurked.

But Butterbean was outside. She'd read about coyotes hunting family pets because they were easy prey. Wolves would do the same, probably. She rose to call the cat in and found him perched on the gargoyle's muscular shoulder.

"Butterbean, come in, baby."

His plaintive meow was her only response. He butted his head against the gargoyle's pointed ear.

"Crazy cat." She stepped out on the top step. "Here, kitty-kitty-kitty."

In typical cat fashion, he ignored her and continued to heap affection on the statue.

"Come on, Butterbean. You don't want to be eaten by wolves." Another mournful howl, closer this time, intensified her anxiety. She descended the steps. Fear, like a cold wind, sent a frisson of apprehension through her. As she approached the gargoyle, she told herself there was nothing out here to be afraid of, until a yap sounded from the front yard.

Her voice was swallowed to a whisper. "Butterbean—come on, baby." She reached for the cat, and he leaped out of her reach onto the patio.

"Damnit, Butterbean," she breathed, and moved around the gargoyle to scoop the cat up before he could run.

Not daring to look into the statue's face, she rushed inside, shut the door, and threw the bolt. Her heart pounded against her ribs, and she couldn't seem to catch her breath.

Whatever spooked her earlier in the evening now made her hypersensitive to every creak and pop inside the house. She went from room to room, checking the windows and peeking out. Nothing moved. And the wolves had ceased calling to one another.

It was time to get her mind on something else. She was allowing a feeling and some wet footprints to frighten her. She sipped her wine with more determination than normal, and after a time the alcohol seemed to ease her tension.

Finally she settled into bed with a book and Butterbean. He kneaded his blanket at the foot of the bed, and wandered up to be stroked now and then while she read. When she set aside the book and turned out the light, Butterbean cuddled into the crook of her legs, and she reached back to rub his head, the only part of him she could reach. The warm feel of his fur and the sound and vibration of his purring relaxed her.

While her tension lessened, she was able to mull over her reaction to a random set of wet footprints and the wolves howling.

She wasn't easily frightened. Otherwise, she wouldn't be living out in the woods by herself.

It wasn't just the wolves that had frightened her, or the fact that someone had taken a drink from her garden hose.

She'd allowed her imagination to run away with her, too. It was the sculpture. He was a monster. If he was real, his claws and teeth would be lethal. He would probably be ferocious, brutal, and violent.

He was only a statue, but for reasons she didn't understand, tonight she'd been unable to look him directly in the face.

She rose up on an elbow and gave the cat one final head-to-tail swipe. "But you weren't at all afraid of him, were you, Butterbean? You were all over him." She needed to take a cue from her cat and relax. The gargoyle was a sculpture, for Pete's sake. A harmless, stationary piece of stone. There was nothing to be afraid of.

She closed her eyes, and after a short time the tension began to leach away, and her breathing leveled out. She was on the cusp of sleep when her eyes flew back open.

Why had the footprints led to the statue, but never trailed away?

CHAPTER 6

G ENEVIEVE COVERED HER mouth and nose with the painter's mask, shoved safety glasses on, turned the exhaust fan up to high, and covered her ears with safety headphones. She braced the weight of the saw and cut into the stone block several times, scoring it. Dust flew despite the powerful fan drawing it out. She stepped away, set the saw down, and took up a large hammer. When she hit the marble, the area broke away cleanly and fell to the floor.

She moved back to the model she'd completed in the past few days, and, using the calipers, measured the area she wanted to transfer, and marked the stone. It was meticulous work. Once the stone was cut away, it couldn't be put back, so she did everything in her power to minimize mistakes. So far the project was going well. If only she could get a full night's sleep, she might be moving along at a steadier pace.

She set aside the calipers and pencil after marking the stone, stepping back from the block. Her shoulders ached from the weight of the saw, but more so from the concentrated burst of creativity during the past forty-eight hours.

The non-drying clay cut out the need to fire the model and made work on the stone more immediate. The down side was there would not be a fired sculpture to sell, because she'd reuse the clay for another one. Simon would not like it. He was used to being able to sell the model as well as the finished piece. Well, he was going to have to get over it.

Her snippy mood gave her pause. She needed to stop for the day, take a shower, and perhaps grill some chicken or fish for an early dinner.

She could call Juliet and Amanda. If they weren't too busy with their boyfriends, they might come over and hang with her for a few hours and enjoy eating dinner.

And perhaps she'd get up the nerve to share some of the things keeping her awake at night. Butterbean's obsession with the gargoyle being one of them. And maybe once they laid her fears to rest, she might get some sleep.

Two hours later, Genevieve poured three red wines to go with the grilled steaks and baked potatoes. Holding her glass by the bowl, she said, "I also have apple pie from The Dish and ice cream for dessert." She took a seat across from Juliet.

Juliet sprawled in her chair. One arm hung over the back while she rested most of her weight on one hip, one leg looped around the other. Miranda, her identical twin, sat back in her seat, knees together, and feet squarely on the ground.

The twins were a study in opposites. For all their similarity in looks, their different attitudes, different personalities, different styles of dress, and different body language assured they'd never be mistaken for anything other than individuals.

While they ate, the three of them talked about the new library expansion and the fund-raiser to build the new wing. "I'd love to have the sculpture you just finished to display in the entrance foyer, but she's nude, and I don't think the library council would go for her." Miranda looked regretful. "Is there any hope you might do a sculpture for us? It would be fantastic to have one of your pieces, since you're a local artist."

"I'd love to. What exactly are you thinking about?"

"Nothing libraryish, since the nude in your studio is really what I'd have my heart set on." She gave a sigh. "I suppose we'll have to go with something introspective that will represent the college and the community."

"I'll give it some thought and do some sketches."

"I'll present the idea to the library board and see what they think. It would be a feather in our cap. And we might even be able to put in some display cabinets for the art department, so they can show off their work in the library, too."

"They might want to choose an artist from the college to do the piece, Miranda," Genevieve suggested, then took a bite of her steak.

"If any of them did the caliber of work you do, I'd say they would, but there isn't anyone who does sculpture the way you do, Gen."

Pleasure flushed her cheeks. "Thanks for saying so. I sometimes feel as though I was born to do this one thing, so I pour everything into it."

Juliet leaned forward in her seat. "You can have something else in your life, Gen. You've done nothing but work these past few years."

Genevieve looked away. "I'm content with things as they are right now. My trip to Scotland was a breather from work, and I got to study some interesting architecture, see several castles, meet some of the local folk, and found him." She nodded toward the gargoyle crouched under the awning with them.

Genevieve went inside to get dessert. She tucked a bottle of dessert wine beneath her arm and returned with a tray with their pie and fresh wineglasses. After pouring the wine and serving the pie, she sat and propped her feet on one of the table's metal supports.

Juliet held the wineglass under her nose. Her brows rose, and she turned the glass to sniff the bouquet, and rolled the golden liquid around the bowl. She took a sip, her movements graceful and unhurried.

Miranda took a sip, held it in her mouth, then swallowed. "This is excellent, Gen." She leaned forward to rest her elbows on the table.

"It's really fine," Juliet agreed.

"Thanks. I'm not at all a wine connoisseur, but a buyer of one of my commissioned pieces had six bottles of this shipped to Simon for me as a thank-you. I've been waiting to share it."

"So what's the occasion?" Juliet asked.

Genevieve took a sip and had to pause a moment to savor the flavor and bouquet. "I need to ask you both about something."

Their expectant looks were so similar, she had to smile. "It's about my friend from Scotland." She pointed to the gargoyle crouched close by.

They both rose to look him over, though she'd noticed them doing so earlier.

"Why would you lease something like this?" Miranda asked.

"He called to me. His suffering is so...human."

"How did you hope to change that?" Juliet asked.

"I know I can't change it but..." She paused, just realizing what Juliet had said. "He was sitting in a garden, neglected and perched on by birds, squirrels and whatever else found him. And he was so unique... I just wanted to clean him up and offer him a more protected environment."

Miranda placed a hand over the sculpture's head but didn't touch him. She and Juliet exchanged a glance. Juliet did the same, but went further when she walked all the way around him, her palm hovering over his form without making contact. Coming full circle, she stepped close to lay her hand atop his head.

Miranda grabbed her wrist. "Don't take any chances, Juliet." With her brows knit in a troubled frown and her mouth taut with worry, Miranda looked every bit as tough as her twin.

It had taken Genevieve a long time to understand and accept what these two sisters could do. After all, this was the twenty-first century, and most people believed magic was only an illusion. "What do you sense about him, Miranda?"

She moistened her lips. "There's a very old, very dark magic around him. It's as if he's encased in it, and it's very powerful."

Genevieve's mouth parted in surprise. Her gaze went to Juliet.

Juliet's expression said it all, but she added, "She's right. It's scary strong."

If she was saying it was scary... It was serious. Juliet didn't frighten easily.

"The other night I got the feeling I was being watched. And there were wolves close by. They seem to be coming closer each night, and I'm getting a little spooked. I've been keeping

Butterbean in with me."

"How does he react to your friend here?"

"He adores him. He'll rub against him, perch on his shoulder, and meow for attention. At night he wants me to let him out to visit with the gargoyle. It's almost as if he thinks the sculpture's human."

Miranda knelt to gaze into the gargoyle's face. The two witches exchanged a look. "He may have been at one time, Gen."

"You mean someone used him as their inspiration for the statue? If they did, he either had a genetic anomaly at birth, or the artist had a hell of an imagination."

"I've seen some powerful magic since we came out of the box," Juliet said, speaking of her and her sister's embrace of their gifts, gifts they had suppressed and hidden for years. "But nothing like this." She offered her sister a hand up. "There wouldn't be any reason to infuse a statue with magic unless he has a purpose."

"What purpose do you think he might have?"

"How old did you say this thing was?"

"It was created in the fourteenth century, so more than six hundred years old."

"Possibly to protect the community from evil spirits or real attacks," Miranda suggested.

"How could a statue protect the community?"

She couldn't really read Miranda's expression as she said, "I'm not sure he was always a statue, Gen."

Genevieve's hand went to her throat. "You mean someone turned a real person into a stone statue?" Her stomach cramped, and an ache settled beneath her breastbone. She read the truth of her guess on the other two women's faces. "Is there anything we can do?"

Miranda shook her head, setting her brown ponytail to swinging. "We don't know what kind of magic this is, Gen. We might do more harm than good. And we don't know why he might have been put in there. What if he was a serial killer or rapist?"

"Which would be a good reason to leave things alone," Juliet said. "This is dangerous magic, Gen."

But if he was still alive inside the stone… How horrible it would be to be trapped like that for over six hundred years. Too horrible to contemplate.

Juliet frowned. "You're very empathic, Gen. Maybe the echo of his suffering is what called to you. But you need to be careful."

"I understand why you don't want to get involved. But I'm going to contact Jonathan, the man who sold me the sculpture, and see if he knows its history. Or if there's any way to trace the history of the piece."

"I think it's a good idea," Miranda said. "You need to understand what you've brought into you home. The magic alone could be dangerous."

A shiver worked its way up her spine. "Dangerous in what way?"

"I don't know, Gen. But dark magic is by nature dangerous. It's created by someone whose magic comes from evil, and their soul pays the price."

Genevieve rubbed her forearms. "Just knowing there's something like that in the world—much less in my backyard—is creepy as hell."

"It is for us as well."

She'd never seen Juliet so serious.

The need to put some distance between them and the statue drove her to return to her seat. The sisters joined her. "What about him would cause the wolves to hang around?"

The women exchanged a look again. Juliet spoke, "If they're more than wolves, they could be drawn to his magic."

"What do you mean 'more than wolves?'"

"We're not the only gifted beings who live here, Gen."

She stared at Juliet. Werewolves? *Really?* When she realized her mouth was hanging open, she closed it. "Wow. I thought they were just made-up stories or myths bred by scary movies or books," she managed after a moment's pause to catch her breath. "They wouldn't hurt anyone, would they?"

"No. It would call too much attention to their presence here in Superstition. But it's likely they're either drawn to something here, or are keeping watch over it."

Genevieve raked her fingers through her ponytail as she scanned the open area around her house for any sign of the wolves. "So our friend has made them nervous, too."

"Or they're curious about him," Miranda offered.

"Do you know any of them?"

"I have several as students, but I'm not at liberty to identify them. It would be a serious breach of trust. It would be dangerous for people to know about them. Humans have a tendency to kill what they don't understand."

Genevieve glanced in the direction of the statue and nodded. "I understand. I was just wondering…if you could ask around, perhaps find out why they're drawn to him. And…"

"And?" Miranda encouraged.

"If any of them would be willing to sit for me."

Juliet laughed. "Only you would bounce from being shocked to learn of their existence one moment and ready to ask one of them to pose for you the next."

"I'm always on the lookout for models. Simon sold *Reclining Woman* to a fashion design company in New York, and they said any time you want a job, you can fly up and they'll put you to work."

Juliet went from teasing to wary in a heartbeat. "They don't know who I am, do they?"

"No! I wouldn't do that to you, Juliet. But both of you could be models. They'd probably go crazy over twins."

Miranda spoke up. "No, thank you. I'm content in my job and with my Caleb." She glowed every time she mentioned him.

"I'm content with Chase, but still looking for a different job," Juliet admitted. "Since we both work at night, the bar is still the most convenient source of employment. But I'd like a job where I don't have to dress like a stripper. I'm taking business classes online during the day to get my degree, since I've served too many of the students at the college to feel comfortable in a classroom with them."

Despite all her strengths, talents, and beauty, Juliet still had moments of uncertainty because of tragic events from her past. "You may end up managing the bar instead of serving at it," Genevieve rushed to say.

"It would be great to be on the floor in charge instead of behind the bar being hit on."

The conversation continued as they carried the dishes into the house. As the twins got ready to leave, Juliet to go to work and Miranda to go home to Caleb, Genevieve began to wonder what else she might have missed in their community, and if there were precautions she needed to take with the statue.

"Any last-minute suggestions about you-know-who?"

The two shook their heads.

Juliet added, "I've been thinking about it...you've scrubbed him down, and nothing has rubbed off on you. So I think it's okay. I also think if he was a danger, Butterbean wouldn't be so enamored with him. Animals are usually more sensitive to metaphysical things than we are. Besides, he's stone. What harm can he do?"

She watched the sisters drive down her winding gravel driveway to the main road, and then turned to follow Butterbean as he jumped off the porch onto the patio. He leapt upon the statue's base and meowed plaintively. She blinked to clear her vision, then rushed to the patio. The base of the statue was intact, but the gargoyle was gone.

A six-hundred-year-old sculpture didn't just get up and walk away.

Her insurance company was going to have a fit.

CHAPTER 7

F INN WATCHED THE men in uniforms circle the property. The lights they carried flitted from one place to the other, back and forth, while others searched the outskirts of the woods.

He had been too hungry to wait for her guests to leave and for her to retire. He stumbled upon the wolves once again and followed them through the valley, where they shared a deer they brought down, saving him the trouble of hunting.

And now the men were searching for him, possibly thinking he was stolen. It had happened a few times in the past.

What would she think when she awoke the next morning to see him in his normal place? Would she put all the things the two sorceresses said together with his absence and realize he was alive part of the time?

If she did, would she send him back to Scotland, to be sold to some other unsuspecting buyer?

What difference would it make if she did? He'd still be trapped inside a lump of stone, no matter who owned him.

But he'd rather stay here with her and her two beautiful friends. They, at least, sensed magic afoot. If he could prove to them he represented no danger to Genevieve or others, they might be persuaded to help him escape this damnable curse.

It was the closest he'd ever been to a chance of being human again. He had to show himself without frightening her too terribly, and plead for her help.

He would do anything for a chance to be normal again.

The men got into their vehicles and drove away. Genevieve stood on the porch and gazed out over the yard as though deep in thought, then turned and went into the house. Finn leaped from the high limb where he perched, opened his wings, and glided across the yard to within walking distance of the stone block he sat on sixteen hours out of every twenty-four.

Butterbean greeted him with a high-pitched mew. He picked up the cat and sat on the cold concrete block to pet him. The cat balanced on his arm and butted his head against his chest. Having the small animal's trust and acceptance was a new experience. Most animals were terrified of him. But then he was hunting them for food. It had never occurred to him to win one's affection, but he truly enjoyed the tabby's attention.

A howl pierced the quiet, and Finn looked toward the west. The wolves were another surprise. They, too, had gone out of their way to befriend him, unlike the wolves and other animals near the castle grounds. If only they could speak. The hunger for a human conversation tormented him.

He moved to the breezeway door, even though it was surely locked. He was surprised to find it wasn't, and opened it a crack to gently place the cat inside, then twisted the lock button and closed it.

He took two long strides from beneath the roof, opened his wings, and leapt into the sky. He circled the house, making certain no one lurked close by. Curious, he turned toward the lights of a car shining from beneath the canopy of trees along the main road. The car was the same one the man drove to Genevieve's house this afternoon. How had he known the police were here?

Finn hovered high above and followed the vehicle's progress toward town. The car turned into an outlying residential area and cut across the business district to another area of larger houses. The houses were more ornate with pillars and gables, their yards well-tended.

High above the car, Finn caught the air currents and glided through the sky hundreds of feet up. The car turned into a driveway, and the house seemed to swallow it as he drove into the garage. A few minutes later, lights came on in two of the windows upstairs. Finn spiraled down to look inside, landing on the chimney that rose from the bottom floor up the side of the house and thrust skyward. He stretched to the side and gripped the windowsill with his fingertips.

Inside the room, the man sat in front of a computer, his shoulders blocking Finn's view of the screen. If he changed position, the sound of his wings flapping would alert the man to his presence, so he clung to the side of the house and waited. His fingertips grew numb and the muscles in his back and shoulders burned with strain.

Finally the man moved, and Finn caught a glimpse of what he was studying. There were a set of pictures on the screen. There was movement in one, but he was too far away to see what it was. There was no way he could identify what the man was doing.

He released the windowsill and allowed himself to fall, landing on his feet before rushing toward the back of the house. Spreading his wings, he launched himself and settled in a tall pine on the border between the yard and the one next door.

What was that man doing? Finn knew so little about computers. He read about them, but had no experience with them. What was on the screen? Not photographs. Something moved in one of them. His hands fisted in frustration. It was difficult to understand what he'd seen when he had no way of learning about it.

If only he could approach Genevieve, but she wasn't ready to face the monster. He had sensed her nervousness and fear out on the patio...but what of the two witches who shared a meal with her? And how could he find them?

He would have to wait for them to return, and hope it happened during a time when he could approach them. He went over everything he overheard during their conversation with Genevieve.

One had spoken of the library. He could find it, and perhaps find a way to approach her another night.

He balanced on the thick branch and let himself fall. His wings caught him, feet above the ground, and he soared higher and flew back toward town.

He passed over residential areas and the business district, then came upon a cluster of large buildings sprawled across the valley. Well-lit signs across the lintels of each structure identified the department. In the center of the cluster was the Harlan J. Collins library. Dim lights shone from inside, and the parking lot was empty, save for two vehicles at the back.

He landed on the structure and clung to the large cupola perched atop its roof, looking in all directions to get his bearings. He'd return and see if he could follow the witch home and speak to her.

A man sauntered out into the parking lot. He stood within the circle of light at the back door and lit a cigarette. He inhaled, and then blew the cloud of pale gray smoke into the air.

Finn swung around the cupola so he could use it for cover when he took flight. Though people rarely looked up, there was no need to take the chance that this man might.

He spread his wings, and was lifted on an air current when loud crack sounded from below. Finn looked down to see a man standing on the sidewalk in front of the library, pointing an object at him. Once again a loud crack came from below, and blood and pain bloomed on Finn's arm, and he clapped a hand over the injury and increased his speed.

The man was shooting at him. He heard the report from two more shots, but they whizzed past harmlessly. He dipped down behind the trees, out of sight. Blood trickled between his fingers, and he swore. The injury would heal once he turned to stone, but it hurt like the slice of a blade, and he needed to stop the bleeding. He turned back toward Genevieve's house.

The sound of an alarm came from behind him. What did the man think he was? One of those bloody giant lizards from thousands of years ago?

Finn swooped down into a yard surrounded by a tall wooden fence. Large towels were draped over the railing of a wooden platform around a body of water. He tore two strips from the closest towel, wrapping one strip tightly around his arm, then tying the other around it to hold it in place.

A car raced by, its engine revving. He waited for the sound to recede before taking off toward home.

From now on he'd have to have to be more careful when flying over the town.

CHAPTER 8

G ENEVIEVE CIRCLED THE statue twice before reaching out and gripping one of the gargoyle's wings. It was hard and unyielding. She shoved against it, and it didn't budge as she had expected.

How the hell did they move him? And how many guys did it take? Small, red-brown splatters of blood stained her patio, and a pinkish stain lay close to the garden hose.

As amazed as she'd been to see the gargoyle gone, she was even more amazed that he'd been returned. She scanned every inch of him to make certain he sustained no damage, and breathed a sigh of relief when she found none.

She called the sheriff's office to let them know, and then, on impulse, dialed Jonathan Taylor in Scotland.

She'd read the brief history provided by the owners, but she needed details. The more she thought about what Miranda and Juliet said about the magical force field that encompassed the sculpture, the more she was convinced it was important to know more.

"I can email you all the information I have. Based on the castle records, Ian Cair MacLeod had the statue carved for his castle garden. No one knows why. He was rumored to have a cruel streak and a bad temper, as did his wife. So perhaps his perverse humor played into it. The gargoyle stayed in the gardens in one spot or another until we moved it here to be sold at auction." He paused. "Is there a problem with the statue?"

Genevieve "No. Not at all. I just wanted more background on him. I've been doing some research about the history behind grotesques. Some of it has inspired changes in one of my own projects."

"I hope you haven't decided to carve garden gnomes," he teased.

Genevieve chuckled. "No. I think gnomes might be too much of a niche market for me."

"So he's settling in?"

She laughed. "He's been cleaned, and has his own spot under the eave of my patio, where he can greet all my visitors and stay out of the weather. I can send you photos."

Jonathan chuckled. "It sounds like we're sharing a pet long distance."

"It does. Is there any mention of who might have carved him?"

"No. But then sculptors of that era didn't sign their work as artists do now. And unless the work was commissioned by a castle owner and contracted, there would be no record of it.

"Although you might want to look in the National Archives online. They have managed to copy many historic records into their system so historians can study them without handling the originals, though you can do that as well on-site. And you might even try calling. They are very helpful with pinpointing information if they know what you're asking about."

"I'll think I'll do that and see what I can discover. This is becoming a treasure hunt. Your history is so rich and diverse."

"And so long," he said, the dryness in his tone inspiring her chuckle.

"Mine is just as long, just not confined to one country. I appreciate your help, Jonathan."

"You're quite welcome. If ever you get back to Scotland, don't hesitate to call me. We'll go out for Greek or Chinese next time."

She'd found him good company, and he hadn't tried to pressure her into more, so she came away with the feeling she'd made a friend. "What, no haggis or blood pudding?"

"I could take you out for that as well, but trust me, neither will live up to their hype."

"We have a few dishes here in Kentucky I could introduce you to if you decide to visit the US. Nothing as colorful as haggis, unless I did traditional burgoo, which used to mean whatever roadkill you found, or whatever animal you could hunt, like opossum, raccoon, or squirrel."

The sound of Jonathan's laughter made her smile. When she hung up a few minutes later, she opened her computer and went on the Scottish National Archives site to see how many answers she could find there.

There were a few documents involving Ian Cair, but nothing about her gargoyle. She scrubbed her scalp, finger-combed her hair, and rubbed her eyes. Perhaps a student with research experience could do this for her. She certainly wasn't very good at it, and she needed to get some work done.

She reached for her cell phone and called Miranda, who said, "I'm already researching. I haven't found anything yet, but I'll keep looking."

"Thank you. I'll forward everything Jonathan sent. You might find it helpful."

She paced to the breezeway and checked on the statue again. "He disappeared last night, and I called the police. This morning he was back. How many people do you think it would take to move him?"

Miranda's silence stretched on. "I don't know. I wouldn't have thought anything but a forklift could do it."

"The base was still on my patio. Only the statue was moved."

"He wasn't damaged in any way?"

"No. But there was blood on the patio. Whoever stole him may have been injured."

"You need to be careful and lock your doors, Gen. Promise me you'll do that. And it wouldn't hurt if you had a security system installed."

Miranda was the cautious twin, while Juliet was bolder. But after finding the blood, Genevieve did feel a little concerned. Simon had been after her for two years to have a system installed. This might just be time to do it. "I'll think about it. And I always lock my doors. I promise."

She opened her studio door to let in the summer breeze while she worked. She absolutely could not lock up while she worked, even though she turned on the vacuum to suck away the dust.

She worked steadily until her shoulders ached from either holding the saw or hammering away at the stone. She unplugged the saw, brushed it free of stone dust, and placed it in the cabinet. Next she used a soft brush to clear away the fine particles clinging to the sculpture, and did the final cleanup around the project with a broom and dustpan.

She ran her hands over the rough image, which, with its angular edges, looked more like a robot than a person. She would fine-tune with a power chisel tomorrow, and more with a hammer and chisel then sandpaper, but she was pleased with the progress.

She removed her work jumper and, careful to keep the mask over her face, gave it a quick shake outside. After pulling the kerchief covering her hair free, she washed her hands and face with cool water and gentle soap. Handling marble seemed to suck the moisture from her skin, but she couldn't touch the stone with any kind of lotion or oil on her hands. It would stain it. She rubbed moisturizer into her face and hands now to combat the dryness.

She hadn't slept very well after all the excitement the night before, and decided to sit on the patio with the gargoyle in the late afternoon sun to relax before cooking dinner. She closed up the studio and locked it, then went into the kitchen to fix a glass of iced tea.

Butterbean followed her when she went out on the patio. She pulled a lounge chair close to the sculpture and watched the cat rub and loop around his legs. She stared at the gargoyle, once again taking in his pain-filled snarl.

"Who took you? And how did they get you off my patio?"

When silence bounced back at her, she took a sip of tea and shrugged her tired shoulders. "It had to be a prank. Probably a group of football players, or the wrestling team."

She eyed the foot-thick, roughly chiseled base the gargoyle crouched on. It was much less refined than the sculpture itself.

Perhaps the two pieces were the work of two different sculptors. She'd have to mention it to Miranda. She tilted her head back against the mesh and closed her eyes. The idea of getting up and going inside flitted through her thoughts, but she was comfortable here.

Her eyelids drooped, heavy with exhaustion. She drifted off.

CHAPTER 9

F INN STUDIED THE sleeping woman while he waited for the sun to slip behind the mountains, and for night to fall. Her features, relaxed in slumber, were refined and delicate. Just a hint of pink tinged her cheekbones, and her brows formed a graceful arch. He studied the roundness of her chin, the fullness of her parted lips, and a sharp, poignant hunger to taste her lips rose in him.

If she wakened to see his ugly face, alive and as monstrous in the flesh as he was in stone, it would surely frighten her to death.

When her eyes opened, thick brown lashes fluttered as she blinked, then her attention focused on him. Would she recognize the change coming over him? He felt the magic awaken and begin dragging at him, trying to tear him out of the stone.

She swung her legs over the side of the lounge chair, turned away, and stood, stretching. She climbed the steps and went inside just as the sun sank deep behind the mountains.

Butterbean rubbed against Finn's legs, arched his back, and meowed, begging to be picked up. Finn scooped him into his arms, and the cat bumped its head against his jaw. If nothing else had improved in his life, at least he had earned the cat's affection.

Four large wolves loped around the side of the house, their tongues lolling out. They came as far as the edge of the woods last night and waited for him, and tonight they were growing bolder.

Butterbean began to growl deep in his throat, the hair rising on his back, his tail puffing out. The youngest of the wolves whined, intent on the cat.

Using his arm as a springboard, Butterbean leaped free of Finn's grasp, landed on the nearby table, jumped to the ground, and, running for all he was worth, sprinted across the yard. One of the wolves broke from the pack in pursuit, his haunches bunching as he took great leaps toward the cat.

Finn roared, "Nay." He ran forward and took to the sky. The easy flap of his wings seemed slow and laborious, but pushed him forward. He bore down on the pair. The wolf edged closer, his jaws open.

Finn grasped the feline by the back of the neck and swung him up into his arms. The wolf leapt to snatch Butterbean from his grasp, missing the cat's tail by a thumb's width. The cat's claws dug deep into Finn's shoulder, and his hisses and growling cries of panic pierced the air.

The porch light came on, and Genevieve rushed out onto the patio, facing off with the other three wolves with a wooden club of some kind. Finn's roar of warning startled Butterbean, and his claws dug deeper, slashing down his shoulder and stomach. If he dropped the cat now, it might be injured, so he hung onto the animal as gently as possible and soared back toward the house.

When Finn landed a short distance from her, Genevieve

staggered back toward the door, dropping the club, which thudded against the concrete and bounced on the hard surface, setting up a hollow clatter.

His deep-chested roar displaced the air and left it shimmering with sound as he landed between her and the wolves.

"Begone! You are frightening my mistress."

The wolves turned and fled toward the woods, the fourth wolf racing to join them.

Butterbean's back claws dug as deep into his stomach as the foreclaws had his shoulder. The scent of his own blood, coppery and rich, wafted to him. Until the night before, it had been a long time since he suffered any kind of injury, and these scratches nipped and stung with equal vigor, just as the bullet nick had the night before.

He soothed the cat with gentle strokes while he unhooked its claws from his skin.

"You aren't going to hurt my cat, are you?" Genevieve's voice sounded breathy and weak, her breathing ragged, as she retreated toward what she called the studio.

Strong emotion clamped a hand around Finn's throat, and his eyes glazed with tears. He blinked to clear his vision. "Nay. I wouldna repay his affection by harming him." He moved gingerly to turn so his nakedness would not further distress her. In the dim light, her face glowed, pale and featureless. Try as he might, he could not read her expression. "I mean you no harm either, mistress."

Silence reigned between them for several seconds.

"Oh, God. This can't be happening. I'm either hallucinating or dreaming." Her voice climbed to a higher pitch.

He kept his tone even, though he couldn't control the

rough, gravelly timbre of his voice. "I have oft thought the same, living the life of this creature."

She half fell, half sank onto the edge of the patio, as though the strength had left her limbs.

"Ye dinna have t'fear me. I will leave if it is what ye wish."

Her voice was stronger when she asked, "Can you go?"

His hope fell as quickly as it had risen, hollowing his belly.

"I mean…can you permanently leave the base you perch on?"

"No. I have tried, but I am always called back to it."

"Why?"

"'Tis part of the magic that created me." He fell silent for a moment. Surely, being a sculptor, she would understand and wish to protect the stone gargoyle, even if she wished to be free of the live one? "Without a guardian's protection, while I am stone I am most vulnerable. I could be hammered into pieces. My greatest fear is t'come alive once the damage is done and be unable to die."

She leaned forward to brace her elbows on her knees and covered her face with both hands. When she finally dropped them, and used the hem of her shirt to wipe her face, he realized she was crying.

"You–you're bleeding."

"Aye. Butterbean was a wee bit frightened and dug his claws in." He continued to stroke him. "He's calming now."

He started toward her, but thought better of it, and bent to set the cat on its feet. Butterbean meandered over to Genevieve and rubbed against her in a bid to be picked up. She cuddled him close.

"Thank you for saving him."

"You're welcome. 'Tis instinct for wolves to chase anythin' that runs from them. Butterbean has been generous with his affection, and I would have been distressed had he been harmed." He would have a talk with the pack and encourage them to keep their distance in the future.

"Are you friends with them?"

"They have shared their food with me."

Genevieve pushed awkwardly to her feet, still clutching the cat. "I'll get you some disinfectant to clean those scratches."

She was not screaming or beside herself with terror. But once she was locked inside the house, would she call the men who were here last night? Would they come back to kill or imprison him?

Could their modern weapons do what swords, knives, and arrows were unable to do in years past? The bullet nick on his arm had healed as soon as he turned to stone, but had bled badly beforehand.

He looked to the west where the wolves had disappeared into the forest. He wasn't a member of their pack. They would not offer him protection, because it would put them at risk.

He had no pack, or flock, or clan to call on. He had out-lived his family, his son, everyone in his clan. What great loss would it be if they killed him? Who would mourn his passing?

CHAPTER 10

G ENEVIEVE CLOSED THE breezeway door and locked it, for all the good it would do if he decided to attack it. She stood for a moment watching the creature. His head was bent, and he stared at the ground as though pondering some terrible problem. A thin rivulet of blood trailed down his shoulder and chest, and stood out against his skin. Skin that looked all too human.

His hair was a thick, burnished blond, curling about his nape and his pointed ears. Darker hair formed a patch on his chest and a thick crop lower. She averted her gaze from his nudity, because it made her uncomfortable. She felt embarrassed for him.

She dragged air into her lungs as she carried Butterbean through the kitchen and down the hall to her bedroom and shut him inside. She doubted she'd ever let him out of the house again.

In the hall bathroom, she gathered peroxide, gauze pads, and a tube of antibacterial ointment. Her hands shook while she fought the urge to scream, not only from fear, but to release some of the spiraling tension building inside her. How could this happen?

He had thus far been polite, well-mannered, and well

spoken. She'd seen his hesitancy in approaching her. She didn't pose a threat to him. He was large, muscular, and, with his claws and teeth, could easily kill her. If he wanted to hurt her, he could do so easily.

The gentle care with which he'd treated Butterbean soothed some of her fears. He had saved her baby from a wolf.

Her breathing became uneven as soon as she stepped out onto the patio. The gargoyle didn't move, but he looked up to train his disturbing yellow eyes on her. "You dinna have to come near. You can leave the things on the table, and I will see to meself."

She moved to the table and laid the bottle, pads and tube there. She told herself to stand still while he approached, but courage failed her, and she wandered away and pretended to look out at the forest while every nerve was aware of him and what he was doing. "How long have you lived like this?"

"'Twas the year 1354 when I was turned from human to this beast."

She did the math in her head. Dear God. Six hundred and sixty-three years. "I'm—I'm so sorry."

He cocked his head in a way that made him seem more beast than human for a moment, and her heart thundered.

"'Twas not of your doing, lass."

"Use the peroxide first. You'll have to twist the cap…"

She broke off what she was saying when he twisted the top free, reached for a gauze pad, and tilted the bottle to wet it. He wiped the blood away with a dry pad, then blotted the injuries with the wet. Though she knew the medication had to sting, he didn't react to it. How did he know how to use it?

He picked up the tube of ointment, and it looked tiny in

his enormous hand.

"Would you like me to open it for you?"

He laid it on the table, keeping it between them.

She opened the tube and extended it.

The gargoyle stuck out the pad of a finger with a lethal-looking claw. She smeared the salve on it, and he rubbed it over the scratches.

Standing this close to him, he seemed huge—more muscular...and more intimidating. "What is your name?"

"Finlay MacLeod. You may call me Finn if ye like." He wiped his fingers with the piece of gauze. "The two witches who joined ye for food...do ye think they will try t' lift the curse from me?"

"You heard our conversation?"

"Aye."

"You know they have some reservations."

"I am no murderer, and I dinna attack women. But I have no way to prove it."

His features, such a mixture of human and beast, were intimidating, and the gravelly sound of the creature's voice sent a shiver through her.

"If they winna free me from this, I would ask them t' help me die."

He took two long strides across the lawn, his wings unfurled. They had the weathered look of old leather, their surface segmented by veins and the bony sections that made them unfold. His tail whipped back and forth, the dark hair on its end flicking like a lion getting ready to pounce.

With a leap, he took to the sky.

CHAPTER 11

GENEVIEVE PACED THE kitchen floor.

She hadn't been able to sleep for two nights. The first night she watched Finn from the breezeway while he cuddled Butterbean and allowed the cat to climb all over him. When he set the cat down and flew away, she called Butterbean and locked him in with her.

Last night she worked up her nerve to talk with Finn again, but he disappeared as soon as he changed, and then suddenly appeared on the stone platform as soon as the sun rose.

If not for that, she would have thought she'd dreamed the entire thing. But she wasn't asleep in her bed or on the couch when she watched him appear on the stone block as though his molecules were drawn there against his will.

The gargoyle's desperation, the resolve in his expression as he said "I would ask them t' help me die" had almost broken her heart. He was suffering. Had suffered for more than six hundred years. No matter what he'd done, his punishment needed to end. She already read the brief history provided by the owners, but she needed details.

She needed to call Juliet and Miranda and see what their thoughts were. How they would feel about meeting him.

She needed to run some errands and buy groceries. Maybe she could go by the library or Juliet's house so they could discuss it.

SIMON OPENED THE app on his phone to see Genevieve hurrying through the kitchen to retrieve her purse from the pantry. Why on earth did she put it there? Perhaps she felt it would be the last place a burglar would look. When she walked out of the frame, he switched the screen to the garage, where he watched her get into her vehicle and open the garage door to back out.

She always ran errands and shopped on Saturdays, so she'd be gone long enough for him to slip in and install the camera. He rose from behind his desk and strode out to the showroom. Keith Cramer, his assistant, was circling an instillation he just set up. His unceasing, nervous energy kept the man string-bean thin. Black, pencil-thin pants hugged his long legs like a layer of skin. He looked a little like Prince, with his fine bones, close-trimmed beard, and shoulder-length, curly hair, and Simon wasn't certain Superstition was ready for him, but Keith suited the gallery, and he knew art.

"I need to pick something up at my house, Keith. I won't be long."

"Okay. I'll hold down the fort."

Fifteen minutes later, Simon parked in Genevieve's drive-way. The house lay quiet before him. The hideous gargoyle squatted on the patio, his rage-filled grimace uglier than ever. Why did she buy that monstrosity? It just didn't make sense to him.

Camera in hand, he exited the car and got out his keys. Would Genevieve be angry if she found out he had a key to her house? Probably, since she hadn't offered him one.

He let himself in through the front door, meandering through the quiet foyer and living room, and entering the kitchen. Pausing beside a basket of unfolded laundry on the kitchen table, he hooked a finger through a pair of lacy panties, an electric thrill surging through him as he hardened. He couldn't have Genevieve yet, but these panties had been in intimate contact with her body, so he'd use them later to take care of his growing need. He tucked the trophy into his pocket and moved on to the bedroom.

He paused by the bed. Genevieve slept on the right side. The comforter had been neatly spread over the pillows, with others covered by shams propped over them. He flipped the pillows with shams out of the way and reached beneath the covers to get the pillow she slept on. He raised it to his face and breathed in the scent of her shampoo and her while his arousal went rampant, and he groaned. He rubbed his cheek against the fabric, mingling his own scent with hers. Would she notice? He hoped so.

The bedside clock caught his attention. Time to install the camera and get out. He replaced the pillow and smoothed the comforter into place, propping the pillow with a sham next to one like it.

He strode to the bathroom and flipped on the light. The new subway tile gleamed. The claw-footed tub and the shower next to it were where he wanted to aim the camera.

He looked up at the light overhead. She wouldn't notice the bulb camera at all. No one really paid attention to overhead fixtures, and she probably used the lights over the sink most often. It took him only a moment to screw in the device and test it with his phone. The tiny camera gave him a view of the bathtub and part of the shower. It would have to do. There was nowhere else to conceal a camera in this room.

He made one more stop in the studio, and slipped into the office where Genevieve kept her business checkbook, receipts, and bills. He put on a pair of the rubber gloves from a handy box on a shelf above the desk. He'd seen Genevieve wear them when she used corrosive chemicals.

He thumbed through the last few pages of checks until he found the name he was looking for. He wrote the information on a Post-it note, then went through Genevieve's address book for a number and street address, wrote that down, too, and stashed the Post-it in a pocket. Even though he had gloves on, he rubbed the address book down with the rag hanging on the back of the chair and carefully replaced it in its original spot. He looked around the room to make certain nothing was out of place.

He sauntered back down the hall to the front door. Butterbean jumped down from his perch on the hall table. The cat darted out the door as soon as he opened it. He rushed to catch him, but the feline was too quick, and leapt from the porch and sauntered away.

Would she remember whether the cat was in or out? Surely not. He came and went as he pleased.

Simon shrugged, locked the door, and strode down the steps to his car. His gaze snagged on Butterbean as he backed out of the concrete driveway. The cat was perched on the gargoyle's shoulder, and blinked at him as he drove away.

CHAPTER 12

ENEVIEVE STUDIED THE soft, pale sky as she pulled into the driveway. It was getting late, but sundown wouldn't be for another couple of hours. She'd have time to plan for her meeting with Finn this time.

She sat for a moment in the car to study the statue. Both Miranda and Juliet had been unavailable, and the longer she debated about calling them, the more she believed she needed more information before she did. If she could get Finn to talk to her again…

She'd bought a large steak to tempt him. If he was sharing food with the wolves, then it meant he liked his meat rare. But she couldn't sit and chat with him while watching him eat raw meat. He'd have to sacrifice just this once and eat his food cooked. Would he eat a baked potato and some salad as well? She'd fix him some and see.

A nervous cramp settled in her stomach. This was probably a bad idea, but she couldn't do anything until she was certain Finn didn't pose a danger to her or her neighbors.

If she contacted the police, they'd ship her off to the psych ward. And when Finn transitioned…they'd kill him. Or attempt to, and then one of them might end up hurt or killed, because Finn's claws and teeth looked lethal. And since he'd been hunting animals to eat, they obviously did the job.

She called to Butterbean as she entered the house, plastic bags full of groceries hanging off her arms. A new catnip mouse toy might make up a little for his temporary ban from going outside. It and the bag of treats.

When he didn't come running, she stashed the raw meat and other perishables in the refrigerator and then wandered down the hall, mouse in hand. "Hey, boy, I got you a mousie," she called as she entered her bedroom.

He wasn't in his spot on the bed. Or in her walk-in closet, where he liked to hide. She checked the bathroom, though he rarely went in there unless she was in the tub.

"Kitty-kitty-kitty-kitty," she called while she wandered back toward the kitchen. He was asleep somewhere, she was sure, and mad because she wouldn't let him go out. She put the mouse on the kitchen counter and finished unpacking her groceries and cleaning supplies.

She made a salad, put the potatoes in the oven to bake, put the steaks in a marinade, and then exited the house through the breezeway door to clean the grill. She scrubbed a wire brush over the cooking rack, removing any residue of grease and food, sprayed it down with the garden hose, then put it back into the grill.

When she turned off the water, she turned to face the statue. "I hope you're awake, because I want to invite you to dinner. I'll be grilling some meat, and I have other things cooking in the kitchen. I hope you'll join me. We need to talk."

She strode to the breezeway door and gave a startled squeak when something rubbed against her leg. Butterbean greeted her with a high-pitched meow. "How did you get outside?" she asked. Yeah, like he was going to answer her.

She opened the door, and he shot inside. She followed him to the kitchen, where he went to his automatic water dispenser for a drink, then meandered to his food dish.

After Genevieve fed him, she leaned against the counter and traced each step she'd taken before leaving. Butterbean was lying on her bed before she collected her purse from the pantry and left. She was certain he was inside. Then how had he gotten out? Unless he squeezed out when she left. But in that case, why hadn't she spotted him?

Because she was distracted and thinking about talking to Juliet and Miranda. At least Butterbean was safe inside the house now. But she needed to be more careful. He was all she had left. Him and her career. She needed to take very good care of them both.

She poured a glass of wine and carried it into her studio to take a look at the clay figure she completed a few days before. It was drying nicely, would be ready to fire in another week, and the wooden base was prepared.

She moved on to the stone project. She wiggled into her work coveralls, put on her mask and did a bit of sanding on the arm she revealed earlier in the day. The tiny veins rising from the skin looked as though they might pulse with blood. She was very pleased with them.

She tried to lose herself in her work until, nearly an hour later, she stopped and stood back from the piece. It was going to be very emotional, and very powerful. The figure was breaking free of the stone. Much as Finn hoped to break free of his curse. Was it painful for him when he transitioned from stone to flesh?

After cleaning up the studio and herself, she checked the potatoes in the oven. Finding them done, she glanced out onto the patio. In the gathering dark, Finn sat on the concrete seat, his wings wrapped around him like a bat. She opened the door. "Are you cold? I can get you a blanket."

"Nay, mistress. I am well."

She turned on the patio light and descended the three steps. He remained motionless until she came close. His yellow eyes gave her a shiver as he tracked her movements.

"It has been some time since I have eaten a cooked meal. Thank ye for yer invitation."

"You must be as hungry as I am. I'll get the steaks." She turned on the grill to heat and went back inside. When she returned with the meat, she set the plate on the flat platform on the side of the grill. "It needs to heat up a little more. Would you like a drink?"

"Aye. Being hardened into stone all day makes for a fierce thirst."

She retrieved a pitcher of water from the small refrigerator and a glass from the cabinet next to it, pouring him a drink and handing it to him. "You are welcome to help yourself to what's in this refrigerator any time. I try to keep it stocked with bottled tea and other drinks."

He inclined his head again. "I am most grateful."

When she raised the top of the grill, Finn came to stand beside her and study it. Her heart beat like something wild at his close proximity, and her legs turned to jelly. But it wasn't entirely fear that caused the reaction. It was excitement, too.

"How does the fire start?"

She swallowed. "There is gas in this bottle here. I turn it on with this knob. Then I push this button here, and it causes a spark. The spark ignites the gas, and starts the fire."

"Gas?"

"There's a liquid inside the bottle that changes to a vapor-like fog at a certain temperature. It's invisible, but you can hear it escaping the bottle when I turn it on. It hisses."

He nodded.

Using tongs, she lifted the meat out of the marinade, put it on the grill, and closed the lid. "It will be done in just a few minutes. The grill is extremely hot, so you don't want to touch it. I'll get the plates and other things."

She rushed inside with the empty dish, took the potatoes out of the oven, and put in the bread, then went outside with everything to set the table and flipped the steaks.

Fifteen minutes later, when they sat at the table to eat, she was struck by how surreal it was to share a meal with him.

He was interested in everything, the dressing on the salad, the sour cream and butter on the potatoes. She went in and got some shredded cheese to add to the toppings. His hands looked so big with the fork and knife in them. She demonstrated how to cut the meat, and he sawed away at the rib eye. He watched her eat first before taking up a piece of meat on his fork.

When he growled, she started and nearly dropped her fork until she realized it was a groan. He chewed slowly, savoring it.

She took a quick sip of wine to cover her reaction. "What kind of food did you have before?"

"Before the beast, porridge. Stews. Roasted meats, turnips. Ale. I have sorely missed ale. Since becoming the beast, I have hunted for small game and fish, and sometimes dug through rubbish for food. This is a potato?" He held the bite aloft on his fork.

His quick change of topic threw her a moment.

"Yes."

He put the bite in his mouth and closed his eyes while he enjoyed it. "One of the cooks at the castle put food out for the animals. I believe she cooked these, but not in this way. This way is much better."

One minute his monstrous exterior fascinated her, the next frightened her. Listening to him talk, she found herself moved by sympathy for how he'd been forced to live. But it was more important for her to learn who turned him into the monster, and why, before she went to Miranda and Juliet.

They lapsed into silence while they ate. When she could only eat half her steak, she offered the other half to him. He gladly took it.

When the last bite was consumed, she offered him a little more wine, then set the bottle down between them. How wise was it to give a cursed human/monster wine? Probably not very, but he seemed so grateful for the meal...

"I need to know who turned you into the statue, Finn."

"'Twas a Druid priest, name of Cinead MacLeod. He advised our laird Ian Ciar about many things going on within the clan. But Ian was away from the castle, and Cinead was angry with me." He looked away into the forest, his features rigid with emotion. "I took his daughter to me, and she was bairned." He swept his hand from his head to his feet with a wry smile. "This was part of my punishment."

"What do you mean part of your punishment?"

"Isabelle died in childbirth."

Despite his gravelly voice, she heard the regret.

"There were those who said she paid with her life for sinning with me. But she was an innocent lass. She was simply hungry for love and a wee bit of attention." He paused. "'Twas my sin that caused her death."

"And you loved her?"

He shook his head. "I wish I had. I regret that I did not. They buried her in the garden in front of me so I would see where she lay every eve when I awoke. They buried m' son beside her when he died, a score and four years old." He fell silent for a long moment. "I never knew him. Never spoke w' him." His throat worked as he swallowed.

He turned to focus on her. "I watched m' clansmen die away until I was left there alone."

Genevieve beat back the twinges of pity. "How did you learn to speak English?"

"I wasna an ignorant man before I became the beast. I knew how to read and write. And I had been to London and France. Later, back before the Great War, there was one young lad who discovered my secret. He was drawn to the monster even though he was afraid of me. He spent time conversing with me and sharing books. When he was twenty, he wed, and he feared his wife would be afraid of me, so he met with me in the woods or left books on m' slab. I have witnessed wars, and read of them. We watched as the planes flew overhead carrying their bombs to London. I stopped some of them from reaching their destination, but 'twas never enough."

"How did you take them down, Finn?"

"I tore the tails off with my hands."

Dear God, he'd taken down planes. "There have been other wars since then."

"Aye. I have read of them as well. But they havena' been so close to home. Now few people have a newspaper delivered to their door in the early morning, so it has been some time since I was able to borrow one and read it, though I oft find magazines in the rubbish and read them."

It seemed unbelievable that he'd witnessed hundreds of years of history. "We read the paper on the computer now."

"I ken a bit about computers, but I have only seen pictures of them."

"I'll bring mine out and show it to you another time." It seemed time was rushing by. "What was the name of the boy who shared the books with you?"

"James MacFadden. He lived a wee distance from the castle. He died in a lorry accident. It overturned with him inside." She looked away at the grief in his expression. How many people had he lost over the years? Outlived.

"Have there been many who knew about you?"

"Nay. In the beginning, they hunted me with lance and arrow because I killed their animals and frightened their children. I was an abomination, because the turn had stolen my humanity from me. When I came back to myself...I hid away. I didna wish harm on anyone but Cinead, and he was already dead."

"What happened to him?"

"The clan burned him at the stake for being a witch. I told him before the turn that what he wished upon me would return to him, and it did. But by killing him, they left me stranded as a monster. There were no others who could help me.

"Ian Ciar was my cousin, and he protected me for as long as he lived. Then his son banished me to the edges of their property and told me he didna want me anywhere near the castle. Over the years, my statue was moved about the grounds, until now. 'Twas perhaps my trespassing that caused the laird to wish me gone. An unguarded letterbox or an unlocked door was too much temptation for me when there were books within reach. The current laird wanted no part of me."

So that was why the price was so amazingly low. They'd wanted to be rid of him as quickly as possible. And what would she do if she awakened to find Finn prowling the house, looking for a book?

Somehow she didn't think he'd trespass without being invited.

"The magic used to turn you into this creature is very dark, Finn. And very dangerous. I need to do some research about you and it before I ask Juliet and Miranda what can be done."

He studied her face for a long moment. "Aye. I understand." His throat worked as he swallowed.

She stood to clear the table and stacked the dishes. When he started to rise, she waved him back down. "I can do this." She really had to find him some clothes.

She gathered the dishes, but paused just before going into the house. "I might be able to find you clothing to wear if you'd like. At least some pants."

He flashed a quick, toothy grin. "Aye. I would appreciate it."

She nodded. "I'll be right back."

She had to be careful. For all the courtesy he showed her, and all the sympathy she felt for him, he might have moments where the beast was more in control than the human. She put the dishes in the sink and went into her bedroom. Inside the walk-in closet she found the box of Andy's clothes she'd packed and been unable to part with. How would he feel about her giving his sweatpants away to Finn?

If Andy were here, he'd probably be searching for something for Finn to put on himself. He wouldn't like the idea of another guy parading around naked in front of his girlfriend. And she still felt like Andy's girlfriend after almost two years, their connection had been so close. When she pulled a pair of gray sweats out of the box, tears stung her eyelids.

There were times being such a visual person made things more difficult. She could still see him dressed in the sweats, and the way they hung off his slim waist with equal parts threat and promise. His warm brown hair would be dark and damp from his shower, his chin still shadowed with his beard.

She forced the images out of her head and turned away from the box.

Finn hadn't moved from where she left him. She extended the pants and he took them. "They may be a little snug. I'll pick some more up in a larger size tomorrow. I don't know what to do about a shirt. Obviously, your wings make it difficult, so I'll have to come up with a creative solution. Is there anything else you may need?"

"If you will leave me soap and a towel somewhere out here, I would be grateful. Just because I look like a monster, doesna mean I want to smell like one."

"You won't be cold?"

"Nay. I dinna seem to have an issue with cold or hot."

"Juliet said you are encased in magic. That may be the reason."

"Aye."

She gathered up the rest of the dishes and the empty wine bottle.

"I appreciate the meal and these, mistress." He raised the sweatpants.

"You're welcome."

When she came back to get the rest of the dishes, Finn was gone. She scanned the sky, but though the horizon was purple against the black shadow of the nearby forest, she could see no sign of him.

Was he standing somewhere close by, watching her? What if he was? He had been nothing but courteous. But chills bumps ran rampant over her skin.

She gathered the dishes, went into the house, and locked the door behind her.

CHAPTER 13

SIMON PACED THE gallery office, his jaw working. Who the hell was she having over for dinner every night? And why didn't they eat inside the house? It was obvious she'd cooked for someone. Two plates, two wineglasses, two pieces of pie. The meals implied *man*, but that wasn't certain. Since he didn't have cameras outside the house, he couldn't see who was sitting on the patio and sharing the meal. *Damn* it.

He'd looked for areas to place cameras on the exterior of the house, but there were no locations she wouldn't notice. And unless she installed them herself, he was stuck with just watching who came and went inside the house.

He needed to make his move soon. Otherwise she was going to hook up with someone else, and he would have to get rid of him the way he'd gotten rid of Andy.

If the damn wolves in the area hadn't chased him back to his car while the police were there, he might have been able to find out what the hell was going on at her house without reading about it in the paper. Next time he'd take his gun and kill the damn animals.

He opened the app on his phone and watched Genevieve working in the studio. It was time to make his first move and get her attention. He'd take her to lunch and invite her to attend the library fund-raiser with him on Thursday night. Or better yet, he'd bring her lunch so she wouldn't have to change.

He could go to The Dish and get dessert. They had pie, which he knew she liked. But what to get for the main meal?

He settled on food from small deli down the street from the gallery. He ordered croissants, chicken salad with grapes and nuts, and a tray of sliced cheese with sesame crackers. He chose a wine from his own wine collection, and collected two glasses. The pie was still warm when he swung by The Dish and picked it up.

When he pulled into Genevieve's driveway a few minutes later, he could hear the saw going from the open window of his car. He waited until she lowered the tool before shouting her name and waving his hands. She looked up, her eyes narrowed behind the safety glasses, the look of determination he often saw while she worked making him smile.

She put the saw on the table, shoved the safety glasses atop her head, and pulled off the headphones. "Hey. Did I miss a message on the answering machine?"

"No. I thought I'd treat you to lunch today. Just a spur of the moment thing."

Her brows rose, and she continued to look at him for a moment. "Let me knock this area off with the hammer and I'll be right with you."

"Okay." He walked out onto the patio, listening to her pounding away at the stone for several moments, then running water.

Her clothes were covered with stone dust, but she'd pulled the kerchief off her hair and washed her face and hands. She walked around the side of the studio with a brush, and moments later he saw particles drifting through the air.

When she joined him at the table, the imprints from the safety glasses still marked her skin. He stood and waited for her to take the seat opposite him.

"This is really nice of you, Simon. Thank you."

He poured her a shallow glass of wine. "You're welcome." He served her a croissant sandwich in its Styrofoam container and laid out the cheese and crackers. "I have a special dessert as well. I don't mean to interrupt, but I thought you wouldn't mind taking a break to eat."

"Yes. But usually it's just a quick sandwich, nothing as fancy as this." She smiled, and even though she didn't have anything on her face, he leaned forward and pretended to brush away a little dust with his napkin. Her expression shifted, but he couldn't read her emotions.

For a few minutes they talked about the piece she just sold, and when *Water Baby*, which was what she was calling the girl bathed in blue polymer, would be ready to sell. "I've had to move it into the house so the dust from the stone carving won't get into the medium before it dries. I'll show her to you once we've eaten."

"I'm eager to see her." He was. The clay sculpture was beautiful, the girl high-breasted and slender. He hadn't seen the model in person as he had Juliet Templeton. Clothed or not, Juliet was beautiful, but she had a reputation, and he didn't really approve of the friendship between her and Genevieve.

"Did you tell your model for *Reclining Woman* about the modeling offer?"

"Yes, I did. She wasn't interested. She has family here, and a boyfriend. And she's in college and close to getting her degree."

"Really. Everyone seems to be in school these days. What kind of degree is she working toward?"

"Business. She's very sharp. She's given me a few tips that have paid off lately."

"Like what for instance?"

"Just some stock tips. I'd have never pegged her for following the stock market, but she seems to have a knack for it."

He'd never have guessed. He thought her all body and sex appeal. "So beauty *and* brains."

"Yes."

"So you're friends as well as artist and model?"

"Yes. But don't ask me to tell you who she is."

"I think I recognize her, but I'll stay mum about her identity in return for something."

He read the wariness that instantly sprang into her eyes and resented it.

"What?"

"Accompany me to the library fund-raiser on Thursday night."

"Sure. I'm going anyway. I can meet you there."

"I want you to go with me as my date, Genevieve."

She bit her lip. "As friends," she stated, her expression carefully controlled.

"Friends with the possibility of more," he pushed.

She sat back in her seat and reached for her wine, taking a small sip. She kept her eyes on the glass instead of looking at him. "I'm not sure it's a good idea to mix business and dating,

Simon. Besides, I'm not ready for anything romantic yet."

"It's been two years, Genevieve."

"I know how long it's been. Believe me."

"You can have more than one romance in a lifetime."

"Maybe." She looked away. "We work very well together, and it's a relationship that's financially beneficial to us both. I don't want to risk messing that up, Simon."

"I have feelings for you, Genevieve." It took all his control not to scream at her, *You're mine.*

"I've never thought of you in that way. Certainly as my agent, and my friend, but..."

"Because I was giving you time to get through your grief. It's time you tried to get past it, Genevieve. Just think about it, and come with me to the fund-raiser."

She hesitated longer than he liked. "I'll come with you, but I can't promise anything more than friendship, Simon."

"I'm not asking for a promise. I'm just asking for a chance."

He read the resistance in her features and forced his emotions back in their box. "Enough serious talk. Now for dessert. I brought a strawberry-rhubarb pie. Someone told me it's one of your favorites." He got the pie out of the bag and reached for the plastic knife they'd given him to slice it.

"Who told you?"

"The woman at The Dish who bakes the pies. I called and asked if she knew." Although he already knew, since he'd been watching her for months, he made the call in case Genevieve decided to check. He dug the paper plates out of the sack. With the knife and a fork, he managed to transfer the pie to the plate without dropping it. He looked up to find her studying him and smiled. Was that a measured glance? He'd given her something to think about.

It was hard not to push, but he sensed the resistance in her, and didn't want to risk an outright rejection. He wouldn't be able to control himself if she rejected him.

He'd never tasted strawberry-rhubarb pie, and after the shock of the first sweet-tart bite, he decided he probably wouldn't again. He forced himself to eat it despite his revulsion. When he owned up to having made that sacrifice later, she'd better appreciate it.

EMOTIONS BOUNCED BACK and forth inside Genevieve like a ping-pong ball. It never occurred to her that Simon was interested in any kind of personal relationship. He'd blind-sided her with this sudden announcement out of the blue. He was her agent. And if she rejected him…it would ruin their working relationship, and their friendship. She swallowed the last bite of her pie and wondered if she'd associate this moment with strawberry-rhubarb pie from now on.

"I'm leaving the pie with you. Enjoy it at your leisure." He leaned back in his chair to enjoy the wine.

"You didn't like it. Why did you eat it?" And why did it bother her that he pretended to like it?

He raised a brow. "I've never had it before, and was curious. It's a little too bold for me. Isn't pie supposed to be restful? That was a little bit challenging."

She laughed. "I hadn't thought about it in quite that way." She took a sip of her wine. "My grandmother used to make it from the rhubarb she grew along the fence out back. It's still there, and I do cut it now and then and fix rhubarb dumplings and cobbler."

He grimaced. "No."

"Yes." She smiled.

He tilted his head toward Finn. "Your friend over there is looking a little better now he's clean."

"Yes, he is." He was looking better. Something had changed. The color of the stone was lighter, and the surface looked freshly polished. Maybe it was because she'd been treating Finn to regular meals. She couldn't bear the thought of him eating raw meat with the wolves. And the wolves hadn't returned since he sent them off. She didn't understand why they obeyed him. Maybe it was a magic thing.

In any case, Butterbean was happy he could roam free as he'd always done.

And Finn roamed, too. Where did he disappear to every night?

They had spent several evenings together, sharing meals and talking for hours. She was interested in his life before the transformation and after, interested in him. He could speak Latin and a little French. And there was nothing bestial in the way he ate. His table manners were fine, despite his lethal-looking teeth and claws. And she'd discovered how protective he was of her and Butterbean when she saw him patrolling the area around her house at night.

But she'd never been able to catch him at the moment of transformation. His block would be bare one moment, and he would be there the next, frozen in position.

"Why did you buy him? Really?" Simon asked.

Why had she? Had Finn cast a spell on her? He never

mentioned any kind of magical ability, but Juliet and Miranda had both warned her about the magic surrounding him. Or had it been her own empathic ability? Had his suffering reached out to her from behind the magic?

She looked up after a moment. "He was sitting in a garden covered in pigeon droppings. A statue created in thirteen-fifty! And the owners wanted to get rid of him because the tourists didn't really care for him. So I offered to buy him. They turned me down at first, but then decided he'd have a better home with me."

"Your cat seems to like him as much as you do."

She glanced over to see Butterbean perched on Finn's shoulder and shook her head. "He thinks I bought the statue just for him. He's constantly climbing on him." *Even when he's the live gargoyle.*

"Have you made a decision about the drawings yet?"

"I haven't finished the stone carving yet. But I have finished the clay sculpture if you'd like to see it."

"Certainly."

She carried her wine with her to the living room. The figure was on display in the light of two windows.

She'd fastened the clay sculpture onto a wooden block, and from the distance across the living room, the woman appeared to be rising from a pool, with her chin tilted up and her hair streaming down her back. Her shoulders and arms were back in a ballerina pose, as though she was offering herself up to the sun. Her hands, expressive and slender, fanned out at her sides.

The polymer, both clear and with different tints of blue and green, coated her in streams and swirls as it rolled down her shoulders, then over her torso and legs. Color spread like water across the block of wood to the edge where it spilled over the side here and there in heavy drips. The figure glowed in the light of the sun.

"She's...breathtaking, Genevieve." His tone was hushed, his attention focused intently on the sculpture.

If nothing else, he was a fan of her work. She could always trust that. The thought gave her pause. "Thank you."

"I didn't understand what you meant by a polymer. This is extraordinary." Simon circled the figure, studying her intently.

"I'm pleased with her. I had to put a support through the bottom of one foot and run it up through the leg to her internal armature and anchor it to the block. I would have preferred to have her support-free but the figure is too heavy, and the ceramic not strong enough to carry the weight of the polymer by itself."

"You've hidden it well. I couldn't tell you where it is."

"The polymer coats her body and covers the hole I had to drill between her shoulder blades to attach it.

"This one will fly off to a new home as soon as we list it."

She knew it would, as soon as she'd finished it. But with it being part of a series... "I have two more sculptures planned in the series. I think we should wait until they're all finished and offer them as a set."

He continued to study the sculpture. "If that's what you want to do. You won't get attached to it and refuse to part with it?" He was smiling as he said it, but there was a crease between his brows.

"I don't think I will. I can give you the drawings I did while I planned her now, though," she offered to appease him.

But she couldn't promise to give up the next ones, or the stone sculpture in her studio. She'd been working on the drawings for days. She might have to do four sculptures and keep the next one.

She had convinced Finn to allow her to take some photos while he was the stone gargoyle. She'd felt compelled to ask his permission now she knew he was alive. "Ye've paid for that with all the food ye've cooked for me," he'd commented, seeming unconcerned.

Simon started to take his leave. He moved in close, slipped an arm around her waist and held her lightly against him. "I'd like for you to give the idea of us dating some serious thought, Genevieve."

His lean form felt more muscular than she expected. She studied the width of his shoulders for a long moment before looking up into his face, taking in his features with new eyes. She felt no physical response to his nearness, no spark of passion or recognition between her body and his.

Simon pressed a soft kiss to her cheek. "I won't rush you." He breathed against her skin.

She shivered. There was possessiveness in the way he held her.

"Just think about it." He stepped back. "If you'll get those drawings, I'll take them to be framed, and we'll see how they do."

She retrieved them from the studio, went to the kitchen table and took some time to run a kneaded eraser over the edges of the paper where her fingerprints had marred them. The sketches were nice. She'd never thought of herself as an artist, only a sculptor, but she used both skills to complete her process.

Simon appeared from the living room while she finished cleaning up the drawings. She returned to the studio for two pieces of mat board and a cardboard portfolio. With the drawings secure inside, she handed off the portfolio to Simon.

"I believe these will sell as easily as all your other work. I'll let you know when they're framed and hanging in the gallery."

"Thank you, I'd like to see them when they're done. And thank you for lunch."

"We'll do it again soon."

She stood on the porch, watching while he backed out of the driveway and turned his car toward town. When her shoulders fell, she realized how tense she'd become while he was with her. It would be like walking a tightrope, trying balance their business relationship with an emotional one.

CHAPTER 14

FINN STUDIED THE darker shadow of Genevieve's shape where she sat on the steps. He was overwhelmed by her kindness, and did not trust his emotions. She was, after all, the first woman to approach him, speak to him, touch him, in nearly seven hundred years.

But his emotions hadn't kept him from eagerly gulping down the food she cooked every night. He definitely preferred her cooking to the raw meat he or the wolves brought down.

And now she was waiting for him to return from his romp with the wolves.

His blood rushed through his veins, and his heartbeat quickened at the sight of her. Her smile and greeting had other areas of his body quickening.

"I've been doing some research on the internet, trying to find out more about your circumstances," she said. "There was a sculptor Ian Ciar paid to create the base for your statue from the stone floor in the castle great room, but there is no record of Cinead MacLeod."

Finn struggled to tame his willful cock and carry on a rational conversation with her, though the urge to move in close enough to breathe in her scent tormented him. "Cinead wasn't a workman, lass. He was a Druid. He cast spells on Ian

Ciar's enemies, and divined the future. Do ye ken what a fine line Ian Ciar treaded to use him and not be condemned by the clan for it? When Ian Ciar was away and the man made me the monster, they saw his fearsome power and wanted no part of it. Even his daughter wanted nothin' more to do with him."

"So what do you think happened to his historic record?"

"If his name was ever on anythin', it might have been removed. If he could turn me into this monster, what more was he capable of? And just speaking his name would have been a fearsome thin' for the clan, at that time or any other. He had a power none of us understood."

"I see."

She fell silent for so long he shifted on the concrete bench.

"Do ye not believe me?" he asked, his temper rising. He had suffered enough for his mistakes. He would not be labeled a liar.

"If I hadn't witnessed Juliet and Miranda's gifts before you and I met, I would find it hard to believe. But yes, I believe you."

Finn shifted his shoulders and bent his head, releasing the anger. Drawing in a deep breath, he raked his fingers through his hair. It had taken him years to conquer the rage that came with the beast, and he couldn't afford to allow one slight to destroy this opportunity to rid himself of this curse.

When he heard the soft padding of Genevieve's feet upon the concrete as she approached him, he looked up. When she sat down beside him on the stone block, his heart leapt and hammered inside him. She smelled like honeysuckle, and when her arm brushed his, his body quickened again with need. The pants she had given him were truly a godsend.

"I contacted someone on Skye and asked them to look up the information about James MacFadden. Would you like to know what happened after his death?"

Her changed of subject was sufficient to quell his desire. Finn swallowed against the thickness in his throat. "Yes."

"Seven months after his accident, his young wife had a child, a boy. She named him Finlay, because it was what his father wanted. You must have had as big an effect on James as he did on you."

The breeze carried a strand of her dark hair against his bare chest, tickling him. She seemed determined to crack through his determination to keep his distance.

He was torn between his hunger for interaction with her and his wariness of the feelings it inspired. If he should lose control... With slow care, he tucked the long strand of hair behind her shoulder where it belonged.

He dragged his attention back to their conversation. "I did very little. James and I talked of history. How things were during my time and others. He helped me keep my sanity. To be so solitary..." He could not even begin to think of that with her smell, her presence so close. He shook his head as though it would clear the feelings and thoughts from his mind.

Genevieve had too tender a heart, much like Isabel. He had learned well how one thoughtless act could have repercussions that resonated for centuries. He would never again be the cause of someone else's grief. Genevieve protected him, provided for him, and showed him numerous kindnesses. He owed her more.

"I'm going to contact Juliet and Miranda and ask them to come back out to the house to talk with you. Will you be comfortable with that?"

How would the two women react to him? "They may be frightened of me. I know I am a fearsome sight."

"I'll prepare them for their meeting with you. Out of all the other people I know, the two of them are probably better prepared to meet you, and less likely to be frightened, than any others I know."

Probably so, since they were witches. Their weapons could be lethal to him. He'd have to be cautious. "I will bow to yer judgment, mistress."

"And that's another thing, Finn. I'm no one's mistress. A mistress today is someone who is a companion to and sleeps with a married man for money. Which I've never done, nor will I ever."

Finn chuckled at her fierce attitude. "I didna realize I was insultin' ye."

She waved a dismissive hand. "Gen or Genevieve will be fine."

He tipped his head. "Genevieve."

She started to her feet, and he stood to offer her a hand. When she took it, he smiled again. "I am in yer debt, Genevieve."

"Six hundred and sixty years is an unfathomable punishment no matter how terrible the crime."

"Aye. It has proven a cruel penance. What I did affected four people most, but my whole clan for years. I took a woman to me without love and gave her a bairn, and I didna offer to wed her when I learned she carried my child. I had nothing to give her or the bairn. Ian Cair paid me for m' skill with a sword. I was a warrior, not..." he raised a brow, "husband material, as the magazines I've read say. I didna have a house of m' own. I slept in the barracks with the other men. I had only the coin I was paid to protect the Laird's property and people. Tearlach would have been a better husband to her than I, had he been given the chance."

"Who was Tearlach?"

"Another soldier. He was good with a bow. He loved Isabel, but I didna know until 'twas too late. Had I known, I would never have touched her."

"Why did you, Finn?" The dull light highlighted her earnest features. "You knew who her father was. You probably knew what he was. Why would you take that risk?"

He paused to give it some thought. "I was full of m'self. Arrogant and prideful. I was cousin to Ian Ciar, so why couldn't I?" He grimaced, shaking his head.

"What happened to your son?"

"Cinead ordered my friend, Tearlach, to beat me. And because of Tearlach's love for Isabel, he was aggrieved with me as well. So he did. Afterward, I was dying and knew it. Tearlach knew it too. But Cinead didna think that a just enough punishment. So he made me the monster.

"Tearlach took m' son to raise because he had a hand in my punishment. But he loved the lad. I never got to look into m' son's face, one man to another. Never got to speak to him as a father or a friend. Never got to ask my friend's forgiveness or thank him for what he did for m' lad.

"All because of my actions."

He looked up to find her face wet with tears and longed to brush them away. Would she be horrified if he reached out to touch her? His attention snagged on his rough hands with their inch-long claws. Aye, she would, and rightly so. "Dinna cry for me, Genevieve."

"When you speak of your friend and your son, you speak with love and grief, Finn. It moves me to tears." She wiped away her tears flashing a smooth stretch of flesh across her belly in the process.

Her skin appeared so smooth and creamy, he would dream of that small glimpse for days. Her smell, her voice, her long, slender legs, her eyes as green as the glens back home, and the way she approached him, as if it was he who was wary of her instead of the other way around. Everything about her combined to draw him in and make him crave more. If being the monster hadn't destroyed him, caring for her, needing her, and never being able to touch her, surely would.

"I'll contact Juliet and Miranda to see if they can meet tomorrow night." She moved toward the house.

"I am grateful. And grateful for the food ye share with me each night, the books ye leave for me, and the trews."

✧ ✧ ✧

GENEVIEVE PAUSED AT the door and looked over her shoulder. "Thank you for the flowers." The small bouquet of wildflowers he picked for her to show his appreciation sat in a vase on her kitchen table. She'd been moved by the humble gift.

"You are welcome."

Was she being thanked or wooed? Sometimes when he looked at her, the man outweighed the beast. And what did it say about her that she felt less wary of him than she had of Simon earlier this afternoon?

What would she do if this went on for years? By taking

custody of the statue, had she taken responsibility for the man? And how would Finn feel, knowing she was wondering about it?

She had to find someone who could help him and set them both free. And then what? If he survived the transition, if there was one, where would a fourteenth-century man go from here? She couldn't imagine just cutting him loose without helping him find his place.

He was strong, resourceful, and quick to learn. Otherwise he wouldn't have survived this long. But what if he just walked away once he was free? The idea set off unexpected feelings of loss she didn't want to acknowledge. She needed to try to keep her distance. But every time she looked at him, she saw the vulnerable, human man beneath the monster.

CHAPTER 15

GENEVIEVE HUNG UP the phone and stood for a moment in silent reverie. Both women greeted the invitation to dinner with an eagerness that triggered a feeling of premonition. Something had happened. Either that, or both women felt some disturbance in the magic force, or whatever they called what they were sensitive to. Had they heard rumors from some of the other unusual folks who lived in Superstition?

Finn went somewhere whenever he transitioned. She knew he ran with the wolves in the forest, or rather they ran and he flew, but where else did he go?

Probably all over Superstition. He wasn't breaking the law. Otherwise there'd be rumors or newspaper stories about unusual occurrences in the area. And she had no right to try and control his nocturnal ramblings. She might be his protector during the day when he was the statue, but at night he was a living, breathing creature, and free to wander where he might.

But his rambling worried her. What was to keep him from being killed if someone happened to see him? He would make a priceless trophy for one of the hunters in the area, and there were plenty around. She shuddered just thinking about it.

Too restless and anxious to work on the stone carving, she spent the morning gardening. There was a therapeutic release about ripping out weeds and planting a flat of annuals in their place. By midafternoon she'd done as much yardwork as she had the patience for and settled at the kitchen table to sketch.

Using her photographs of the gargoyle sculpture, she did drawings of the creature, then, using her understanding of human facial anatomy, she carved away at the brow to better suit the deep-set shape of Finn's eyes and the width of his forehead. She shaped his roughly shorn locks into a natural order that followed the contours of his head. It took little time to shape his ears into more human facsimiles than the pointy Vulcan forms.

Next she studied his elongated jaw. The added length of his teeth had forced the jaw forward and down, exaggerating the lower half of his face. By drawing human teeth in their place, she was able to shorten his jaw and bring his chin up to its normal position.

For long moments she sat back in her seat and studied the finished sketch.

The face was heavily masculine and heartbreakingly handsome. It was a face that would have inspired great interest from the women in his world. Women from any time period.

Her eyes flooded with tears, and she pushed away from the table. Cinead MacLeod could not have done anything more devastating to Finn than to take his looks and turn him into an ugly creature, reviled by humanity, and feared by women.

She'd never wished to be anything more than what she was, but at this moment she wished she had the power to help him.

She wandered outside to the patio, and pulled a chair up beside the stone gargoyle. Butterbean jumped down from front porch and sauntered over in his slow, meandering way. When he leapt into her lap and rubbed against her, she stroked his back while he arched into her touch.

The cat was the first creature to seek Finn out for attention and affection. "You're a good cat, Butterbean." She rubbed her cheek against the top of his head and earned a head-butt for her praise.

"I'm going to see if I can convince Miranda and Juliet to break this curse, Finn. But you have to try not to scare them half to death when I introduce you tonight. And you have to wear the sweatpants I bought you." She liked talking to him this way. He couldn't argue if he didn't agree with her. But he could fly off as soon as he changed. "Miranda's been doing some research about you. We're going to share our research before I tell them you're alive. So please don't go off with your wolves until we've talked with Miranda and Juliet.

"They're concerned about the magic that surrounds you. They may need you to do your best to remember how all this happened. Not why, but *how* Cinead did it. What he said when he made you into the gargoyle, the spell he used. I know it's been a long time since it happened...but give it some thought."

She rose from her seat. "I'm going to order pizza for all of us. It's like bread with meat, vegetables, tomato sauce and cheese on it. I'll fix a salad to go with it, and I'll order yours with extra meat." She stood, and cuddling Butterbean close, went back into the house.

At eight o'clock Juliet arrived with wine. There was nothing festive in her expression as Genevieve greeted her and led her into the kitchen.

"I've been having dreams, Gen." She set the bottle on the marble island top. "They're terrible dreams, about a man being beaten and tortured. I believe it's your gargoyle."

Before Genevieve could respond, the doorbell rang, and she went to let Miranda in.

"There's something going on with your gargoyle, Gen. I'm hearing rumors at the college. The other night one of our security guards shot at a large bird, but I don't think it was a bird. The *special*"—she made quotation marks with her fingers—"students are all talking about it."

The two of them joined Juliet in the kitchen. "Have a seat. I've got some drawings to show you." Genevieve strode to the pantry and returned with the rolled-up sketches she'd worked on all morning. She straightened the drawings out on the table and set a salt shaker on one side and the pepper shaker on the other to hold it down. "Is this the man you're seeing?"

Juliet eyed the sketch she'd done. "In my dreams, his features are distorted because he's been so badly beaten, but that could be him. In my dreams, he's covered with blood, and he's in great pain. I sense he has a head injury. He may have bleeding in his brain. And he was definitely dying."

"I'm sorry you've been having such terrible dreams. I've been dreaming too, but it's because I look at him and see the man he was."

"What do you mean you look at him?" Miranda asked.

She'd hoped to ease into the announcement. "He's alive."

Juliet and Miranda stared at her with identical blank expressions of stunned amazement. Their reaction mirrored exactly how she'd felt since seeing Finn in the flesh that first night.

Genevieve scooted her chair closer to the small kitchen table and folded her hands on the lace-edged tablecloth. She waited until Miranda took a seat to continue. "He's alive, but only at night. As soon as it's daylight, he reverts to stone."

Juliet's toffee colored eyes widened. "You didn't just dream this?"

"Don't you mean hallucinate? No. I talk to him, Juliet. We eat dinner together. He has a gravelly brogue, thick as Scottish granite, and you have to listen carefully until you get used to the rhythm of his speech. And he's completely oblivious to his nudity. I suppose being naked for an eternity has that affect. I've given him pants to wear. And he's scary ugly. But he's so…human. And has better manners than most of the guys I've dated."

"Dear Goddess," Miranda breathed.

"He's been trapped in the form of the monster for six hundred and sixty-three years. He said if the curse can't be broken—" Every time she thought about it, emotion choked her. "—he wants you to help him die."

Miranda shook her head. "We can't do that, Gen." The two sisters glanced at each other, their expressions conveying something she couldn't read.

"Whatever you put out there comes back threefold," Juliet explained. "To take a life…" She shook her head.

"He didn't say he wanted you to kill him. He said he wants to be allowed to die." She drew a deep breath. "We have to convince him there's hope. He's been alone all this time. I mean how many creatures like him could there be? And how horrible would it be to be totally alone for more than six *hundred* years?"

Juliet got up and opened the wine bottle. Familiar with Genevieve's house, she went to the correct cabinet, returned with wineglasses, and poured each one of them a glass. "It would be beyond agonizing. And there are probably no others like him. This was the work of only one witch, not a group." The bottle shook ever so slightly as she set it down. "The magic around him is very distinctive, and very old. Since the witch who created this spell is dead, it will be doubly hard to break."

"Did you find out what he could have done to be turned into the sculpture? Miranda asked.

"That's a story I think Finn needs to tell you himself. But I have some information Jonathan Brown emailed me from the auction house about Ian Ciar, the MacLeod laird who owned him at the beginning. I also have some information about a young boy who befriended Finn during the Second World War." She rose and went into the living room to get the paperwork from the desk.

When she returned with it Juliet said, "Finn?"

"Yes, that's his name. Finlay MacLeod." She hadn't realized what a relief it was to share all of this. She raked her fingers through her hair, then dropped her hands. "Part of the time I've been stuck in this fog of 'I can't believe this is happening,' and the rest of the time, it's been 'This can't be true.'"

"Welcome to our daily lives," Juliet said with a dry laugh. She seemed to be calming a little, though she continued to clench and unclench her hands. "What you're asking us to do,

Gen… It could be dangerous—for him, and for us. This is a very old and evil magic. It may have some built-in protections that could boomerang back to us."

She couldn't ask her friend to risk her life on Finn's behalf. "I understand. And if you can't help him…" She shook her head. "I'll make him as comfortable here as I can. I'll continue to try and improve the quality of his life. Clothing, food, shelter, that kind of thing, during the times he's a living creature."

Miranda leaned forward to touch her arm. "You realize the commitment you're taking on? This is a magical being. There could be repercussions."

"What else do you recommend I do, Miranda?"

"Send him back to Scotland."

He'd be alone again. She couldn't do that to him. She shook her head. "He isn't my possession. I can't force him to do anything. He's a sentient being. I can talk to him and ask what *he wants to do*. But I can't and won't make decisions for him."

"But he could be dangerous. And the magic around him could be as well," Miranda pressed. "That may be why he was sold. His current…*guardian* may have decided he was too dangerous to keep."

"Or just too much of a burden," Juliet added. She shook back her long hair in an impatient gesture. "Look, we can debate this all day, but until we talk to him, we don't know enough about the magic behind his transformation to make a decision."

The coil of tension across Genevieve's shoulders relaxed somewhat. Leave it to Juliet to take the bull by the horns. "So you're open to talking to him?"

The two sisters exchanged a look.

Juliet leaned forward. "I don't want Chase to know about this until we have more information. He'd be more inclined to put a bullet in him than strike up a conversation. He'd look at it as preserving the public safety. He's already somewhat freaked out about some of the other folks he's discovered living here."

Genevieve paused wrap her mind around that statement. They had suggested something similar the other night. So there were more than werewolves? Shit!

But she felt compelled to come to Finn's defense. "Had he been preying on humans, Juliet, I believe we'd have heard about it. In this day and age of true crime, forensics, and police shows, news of any kind of strange animal attacks would be broadcast on every station. Even from Scotland."

"I agree." Miranda jumped into the conversation. "But what if he's been picking off the homeless or something? Those people disappear without notice all the time."

"He doesn't eat people, Miranda. He runs with the wolves in the area, and hunts small game and fish with them. He's spent his whole life hiding. Otherwise, someone would have captured him and turned him into a circus exhibit, or tried to kill him."

The two exchanged another look.

"Just meet him. You'll see what I'm talking about."

CHAPTER 16

FINN CROUCHED AROUND the back side of the studio. He tugged up the sweatpants. The fabric was soft, but felt odd against his skin. And finding a place for his tail had presented a problem. He had been forced to make a hole in the garment and pull it through.

He supposed he could tolerate them to protect the women's idea of propriety.

If they ever came out of the house.

Genevieve had been inside with the two witches for over an hour. If they didn't come out, he'd know they had decided they couldn't or wouldn't help him.

Then the patio light came on and the breezeway door opened.

Genevieve descended the three steps carrying two large, flat boxes. The other two women followed, carrying other things for the meal, setting them down on the table.

"Finn?"

"I'm here." He moved slowly, so as not to startle the two witches. As he approached, he watched them carefully. Magic had made his life miserable for the past six centuries, and he wanted no part of it now, but there were no other options open to him.

"Dear Goddess," one of the women breathed as he came into the light.

He stopped some twenty feet away. Every muscle tensed as he waited for them to attack.

Genevieve approached and offered him a hand, her gaze steady on his face. She had more compassion and courage in her little finger than any woman he had ever known, for in a matter of days she had decided to trust him and shed her fear. His mouth was dry as he clasped her hand, careful of his claws. She tugged him forward.

"Let me introduce you to Miranda and Juliet Templeton. They're two of my oldest and best friends, and we went to school together."

He cleared his throat and kept his voice low, though it didn't improve its gravelly quality. "Good eve to ye both."

"We can talk after we've eaten. Why don't we all sit down and get acquainted?" Genevieve urged. "I'll get the salad dressing." She rushed inside.

Left alone for a moment, Finn pointed toward the concrete bench with an open palm where he often sat. "If 'twill make ye more comfortable, I can sit over there."

The sisters were very alike in looks, but the one Genevieve had introduced as Miranda pulled a chair out to sit down. "I think you should join us. Genevieve has just spent the last half hour assuring us we can trust you. But be forewarned, you try anything, and my sister will fry your ass, and I'll blow your ashes all the way to the moon."

He took a deep breath. If he wished to be free of the curse, he needed to remain calm in the face of this witch's threats. "Ye have nothing to fear from me. Just because I look like a monster doesna mean I behave like one."

He pulled out a chair for Juliet and waited for her to sit, then stepped away from the table. He stood quietly until Genevieve appeared with the salad dressing. He pulled out her chair, then removed the seat reserved for him, lifted the heavy concrete bench and carried it to the table. When he noticed the three of them watching him with big eyes, he shrugged. "The back of the chair leaves no room for m'wings."

He waited for the three women to serve themselves before reaching for a slice of the pizza. The scent of garlic reached him before he bit into it. He savored the mixture of flavors, tomatoes and onions, meat and cheese.

"What do you think of it, Finn?" Genevieve asked.

"'Tis fine. Like nothin' I have ever tasted." He reached for the wineglass, aware that it looked like a child's cup in his hand as he took a sip. He set the fragile glass down with care.

They ate in silence for several minutes. "I know some of the wolves you travel with," Miranda said. "Would you mind if I ask them about you?"

"Nay, I dinna mind. I kenned they were more than wolves, though they have never shown their other forms to me." He enjoyed their company because they understood his difference and accepted him. "They have welcomed me into their pack, and we have hunted together several nights since I have been here."

"And what else do you do to pass the time at night?" Juliet asked.

"Genevieve brings me books to read so I may learn about all manner of thin's."

Miranda's brows rose, and she looked to Genevieve. "I

wondered why you were checking out books about medicine, machines, politics, and technology. I thought you were looking for inspiration for a sculpture."

Genevieve flashed her a smile. "I have been doing a sculpture. I'll show you my latest before you leave."

Finn had never watched her work, though he often heard her hammering and running all manner of machines inside her studio. By the time he escaped his prison at nightfall, she had stopped for the day. Despite his condition, it would be a wonder to see her create a human form from stone.

Why she had never offered to show him her work? Did she perhaps think it would be hurtful for him to view something so close to what he was most of the time?

Juliet picked up her wineglass and concentrated on it for a moment. "How do you feel about a stone carver acting as your guardian, Finn?"

Had she read his mind or his expression? He finished chewing the bite of pizza and swallowed. "Since I wasna carved, but formed by magic, I dinna harbor any ill will toward Genevieve or her work."

After a moment she raised her glass and drank from it. "Not all witches are bent on using their magic for destruction or harm. Not least because, when you put out anything negative, it comes back to you threefold."

"Does that mean if ye fry my ass, yers will be fried as well?" he asked.

"Finn," Genevieve breathed, her eyes wide with shock.

Juliet laughed. "Miranda started it." She flashed her sister a look. "Things have a tendency to boomerang back to you in the magical world. Nothing is free. There is always a price. Just as your maker discovered, I'm sure."

"Aye. He was bound and gagged and burned at the stake. Once the villagers knew what he was capable of, they feared he might turn his power on them."

"Tell us your story, Finn," Juliet encouraged.

He had prepared himself to do so, but it didn't come as easily as it had with Genevieve. It was hard for a man to bare his mistakes and his shame to strangers. He told them everything, sparing himself nothing. When he fell silent. Miranda leaned forward. "Do you remember the spell he used to turn you?"

"Some, but not all." He hesitated to go back to that time. Would speaking the words give them more power? But what choice did he have? He took a final drink of the wine, then closed his eyes and recited what he could remember of the spell,

"Yer heart has hardened to stone,

"And for that ye shall remain alone,

"Trapped in yer own hardened shell,

"Until ye learn to tell

"Respect and affection, from lust,

"Or until ye crumble into dust.

"No sunlight will ye feel…"

He fought to recall more, but finally shook his head.

"'Tis the last lines I canna remember. I was changing, and the pain was beyond anythin' I had ever known. M'bones were breaking and reforming. And m'wings ripped out of m'back. I thought I would die before it ended. There was a wind that swooped through the castle great room, and raised me to m' feet when I couldna stand on my own."

Juliet's gaze was intent as she leaned forward. "It's important you try to remember those last few lines, Finn. They could mean the difference between successfully breaking the curse or not."

For the first time, hope sang within him. "I will do m'best to remember."

Miranda spoke for the first time in a long while. "In the meantime, we both need to do some research on black magic and how to overcome it." She studied Finn's face, looked directly into his eyes. "We can't promise we'll be able to break the curse, only that we'll study and research the problem, to find out whether there's a safe way to break it."

"I understand." He couldn't expect them to put themselves in danger to help him. They were not friends to him, but to Genevieve. They were acting for her, not him.

The sisters rose to leave and he stood. "I am grateful ye're willin' to try."

FINN MOVED THE concrete bench back where it usually sat, and leaned back against the exterior wall of the studio, one foot propped upon the bench. She had only touched his wings when they were stone, but now with them spread so he could take on his current position she fought the urge to approach him and ask his permission to explore their texture.

"I didna frighten them at all."

"Maybe a little at first."

He snorted his disbelief.

Genevieve laughed at the sound. "They're hard to surprise."

"Aye. I kenned that. And they are more dangerous than they appear."

She couldn't argue that. She had witnessed a small, very impressive demonstration of what Juliet could do. "They will try to find a way to set you free, Finn."

He nodded. "They are protective of ye."

"Did Juliet threaten you?"

"Nay. 'Twas the other one."

"Miranda?" Miranda was usually the even-tempered one. But she was really spooked by the magic around Finn. "Now she's met you and sees you aren't a threat to me or her, she'll do the right thing."

They needed to prepare in case Juliet and Miranda were able to free him. "Are you ever ill, Finn?"

"Nay. I have never been ill."

"Not even as a human?"

"Aye. I had a few fevers, and I was sickened once by some meat we ate while on patrol. But never anythin' serious."

"You do realize the magic holding you prisoner is probably protecting you from illness. There are many diseases you could contract once it's gone, diseases you have never been exposed to, so your body isn't prepared to fight them off. It might be a good idea if you are immunized against some of them before you are freed."

"Was it for that reason ye got the book on medicine?"

"Yes. I want you to be prepared in case you need treatment."

"Have ye lost someone to one of these ills?"

"Not to infectious diseases. We have vaccines against them. But none of us are immune to other diseases, like cancer, heart disease, or diabetes. My grandparents raised me after my mother left me with them while she went to work in another city. She met a man there and married him, and never came back for me."

"I am sorry. It often happened the same way in my time. I was raised in the household of my uncle because my *athair* died and my *mathair* married another."

They'd found a common experience. "It was Pop who taught me to sculpt."

"That is your grandfather?"

"Yes."

"What sort of name is Pop?"

She laughed. "It was just what I called him as a toddler, and it stuck. I suppose it is short for Papaw. I called my Grandmother Gran."

"Names laced with affection." He tilted his head back and studied the overhead light. It reflected in the yellow iris of his eyes.

"Yes. What did you call your uncle?"

"Uncail when he wasna beating me. Ridre when he was."

He said it with such acceptance, pain cramped her stomach. "Oh, Finn."

"It was a long time ago, and I have no lasting hurts from it. At the time I was full of mischief and needed a stern hand. He was glad to give it to me."

"We don't beat our children now, Finn."

"Aye, I know." He raised a brow. "Although from some of the stories I read in the paper, 'twould do some of them good."

Genevieve put a hand over her mouth to stifle her laughter. For all he'd survived so many centuries, he was still a fourteenth-century man.

"'Twouldna do them harm to work a bit, either. Idle hands are the devil's workshop."

So he was quoting the Bible now.

"And what punishment would you think fair for the women of today, Finn?"

"I know naught of the women of today, other than ye. But I knew some men who raised their hand to their lasses when they spoke their minds. I saw no reason for it. I always enjoyed a woman with spirit. There were ways to sooth their temper that didna cause any hurts and deprive either of us..." He paused, an expression of embarrassed amusement on his ugly face. But when she looked at him now, she saw the man, not the beast, and his expression seemed all too masculine.

Genevieve raised one brow and worked hard to keep her face expressionless, though she was tempted to smile again. He clearly had charm then. He still did.

"Women of my time didna have as many choices or as much freedom as ye do. Marriage and children were their duty. A few ran alehouses, wove fabric, or had other businesses, but they didna look for a way to be apart from the men."

She supposed things were a little more straightforward back then. "We don't look for ways to be apart from men, Finn. We look for ways to be independent, because in today's world, a woman must support herself and her children, should her husband die or leave her. We want to be prepared, to make certain we are secure even without them."

"The clan would have taken care of ye."

"In today's world, when you're like me and have no family left, you have no clan. I can't depend on anyone but myself. And there are more reasons for me working than to feed myself. My work fills a need that has nothing to do with the other relationships in my life."

"Do ye na want a husband and children, too?"

"I wanted them." She swallowed, the pain of loss still deep, but not as sharp as it had been. "The man I was going to marry was killed in an accident two years ago. Without my work, I don't believe I could have survived my grief."

He dropped his foot from the bench and straightened, his frown hardening the already dominant planes of his features. "I am sorry, lass."

She folded her sweater tighter around her. "I knew Andy my whole life. I loved him as a friend before I loved him as more. We were building a life here together…" She conquered the tears by will alone. "He was a fireman."

She started to explain what that was when Finn made a dismissive gesture. "I know what that is, lass."

"He'd just finished his shift and was coming home. Someone shoved his car off the road and left him to die. There was dark blue paint on his bumper and the left rear quarter panel of his car. They rear-ended him and forced him off the road into a ravine. He was found the next morning. Someone noticed the skid marks and contacted the police."

"'Twas done with intent, then."

"Yes. But the police couldn't find anyone who had reason to do it."

His silence stretched for a long moment. "In my time, there were reasons to kill. Because ye had no other choice. To protect yerself or others, to seek retribution for an insult or injury to yer honor, or to defend the clan's territory. But murder... that was usually done to gain possession of something owned or held by another. Wealth, power, land, or a woman." He canted his head. "What did your Andy have that another might covet?"

"I wish I could say things have changed, but they haven't. We just have more lethal weapons now." She propped her feet on the bench beside him and paused to give the idea some thought. "He owned some property and a house, which he rented out when he moved in with me. That went to his brother. But Bryan was just as devastated by his loss as I. They were very close. He didn't own anything else but his car, which was totaled—completely destroyed. And he didn't owe anyone any money, and didn't have any."

"He had ye, Genevieve."

She shrank away from the idea she could have been the reason behind Andy's death. It was a moment before she could think about it. "None of my ex-boyfriends could be involved. There hadn't been anyone steady for a long time. At least four years."

"Then for what reason did this thing happen?"

"The police think whoever hit him must have been drunk. The driver would have been afraid to come forward or call nine-one-one because he'd be charged with vehicular homicide."

He nodded, but his pale yellow gaze still rested on her face. "Drink causes some men to behave without reason or conscience."

"Yes, it does." It had cost Andy his life. And where was the justice she and his family deserved? Even if they got it, it wouldn't bring Andy back.

"Ye had the time with yer Andy. Ye enjoyed one another, cared for each other. Ye shared precious moments of humor and affection."

"Yes, we did. When Juliet and Miranda free you from the curse, you'll have precious moments of your own."

"I already have them, Genevieve. Sitting across from ye, talking as two people. Sharin' a meal and a glass of wine. Having ye look at me as ye would any other man without fear in yer eyes. Having ye touch m'arm without hesitation."

Her heart turned over at the look in his eyes.

"All those are more precious than ye know." He rose to his feet and took two long paces across the patio. As though timed, the wolves howled in the distance. "I must go." His gravelly voice shattered her composure and brought tears to her eyes. His wings spread and, with two long leaps, he took to the sky.

Her breathing caught on a sob, but she swallowed it back. What was it about him that touched her so? It was more than pity. More than empathy.

She turned her thoughts away from her questions, afraid of where they might take her.

CHAPTER 17

LIGHTS ILLUMINATED EVERY room of the library, casting a golden glow on the wide stairs leading up to the building. The parking lot was near capacity, and cars were already starting to accumulate in adjoining lots behind the gym and the art building.

Simon parked the Jaguar and sauntered around the front of the car to open the passenger door for her. Genevieve grasped the hand he extended, and he tugged her free of the low-slung leather seat, the hem of her high-collared black silk sheath sliding back into place at her knees. She tossed her red lace shawl around her shoulders to ward off the moist summer night air and gripped a small black purse just big enough to carry lipstick and her cell phone.

She had played up her eye makeup, knotted her dark brown hair atop her head, and stuck black lacquered chopsticks in to hold it in place. The ballet pumps felt strange on her feet. She'd grown too used to work boots or tennis shoes, or even going barefoot around the house.

"I like your hair like this, Genevieve." Simon gave a gentle tug to a curled tendril lying against her cheek. "I've never seen you wear it in this style before."

"Thank you. It isn't comfortable for work with it twisted

up like this, but for an evening function, it's quick and easy."

This new, attentive Simon was a little disconcerting. She was hyperaware of the possessive hand he placed against the small of her back as they walked across the parking lot and up the side steps to the front of the building. She hadn't made up her mind how she felt about the change he was encouraging between them. He hadn't said anything more, but the subtle touches, the lingering grasp of her hand, signaled the change he wanted.

She turned her attention away from what was making her uncomfortable to a subject she understood, the staid architecture of every building on campus. Each was constructed of red brick, had white columns across the front, and sported cupolas atop the roofs. "I wish they had experimented with a different type of architecture for the art building."

Simon shook his head. "Fat chance. It would have ruined the symmetry of the entire campus. Not my words, President Connor's. He's guided everything toward the same style. He's all about tradition."

"Oh, you know him?"

"Yes."

"I suppose one of my sculptures for the library would be totally out of the question."

"Yes, unless it's a traditional image of someone reading a book." He reached for the door and opened it for her. "I didn't realize you were interested in doing a sculpture for the school."

"It would be good press for the community, and for me."

They paused in the large, open foyer where small clumps of people stood talking. "Miranda loves my *Water Baby* so much she wants to put a proposal before the library board for a sculpture to go here in the foyer. Not a nude, but something unusual."

She paused for a moment, scanning the area. "She wants to add some display cases for the art department, too, but I think it would be more natural to display artworks throughout the space. Place them so, while the students and other patrons move through the stacks and use the computers, there's a point of interest to look at. Since the general public uses the library too, the art students could put prices on their works and possibly make some sales."

"I think it would be wonderful for the school and the community. But I happen to be on the library board, and since you're my client, I'll have to recuse myself from the voting on the proposal." Simon's expression was apologetic.

"It's okay. If President Connor is so traditional, I doubt I'd get the commission anyway. But I may do something for them to auction off to raise money for more books for the new wing."

"A small sculpture, perhaps in wood," he suggested.

"We'll see." It was so easy to razz him when she knew he'd want to have complete control over what she donated.

His raised brows had her grinning.

"Why do I get the idea I'm being teased?"

"I wouldn't do that, would I?"

"Yeah, you would. I know you think I'm Ebenezer Scrooge because I steer you away from unprofitable projects, but I'm just trying to keep your career on a straight trajectory." He guided her through the small clusters of people to the sprawling open area in the large reading room. Between the stacks on each side, tables had been arranged for the dinner part of the fund-raiser.

"I don't think you're Ebenezer Scrooge. I know you push for top dollar every time you sell a piece, and you're meticulously honest about making sure I get every dime I'm owed. But mass viewing of what I do will bring me more sales."

"Not from college students."

"No, but Miranda hosts meetings here for visiting alumni and local corporations. She held one for the canning corporation that processes the mushrooms from MM Mushroom. Those will bring me word of mouth sales. There's Miranda." She waved to her and got a wave in return. "She looks like she's got her hands full right now. I think that's the mayor who's bending her ear. I'll let her catch up to us later."

She took in the perfumed and primped women, and the men dressed in their dark, distinguished suits. The cost of the meal was five hundred a plate, ensuring only the very wealthiest in the area could attend. With the large chandelier alight in the foyer to emphasize the glitter of jewelry and the occasional sequin, it looked more like a state dinner than a library fund-raiser.

A student dressed as a waiter and carrying a tray of smoked salmon hors d'oeuvres on toast points paused beside her. Right behind him followed another student with flutes of champagne. She passed on the salmon, but reached for a glass of champagne.

A couple paused to speak to Simon. The woman's blond hair was beautifully done, and her dress a pale shade of green that nearly matched her eyes. "Oh, you're the artist who did the drawings we just acquired." the woman gushed. "I'm Tina Richards. We're so thrilled with the drawings. These will be our first original pieces. And so special, since they're the first drawings you've sold. We're hanging them in our study. They're going to be just beautiful there."

Her husband William was nearly his wife's same height of five six, or so but appeared a little older. "You're a talented young lady, Miss Warren. Sculpture and drawing. Like a female Michelangelo."

"Wow. I'm flattered," Genevieve managed. "I'm delighted you're so pleased with them."

Once the Richards wandered off to meet with a couple waiting for them, Genevieve said, "You didn't tell me you already had them framed."

"I haven't. They saw them and wanted to choose the mats and frames themselves."

"That was fast."

"Your work speaks for itself, Genevieve."

She felt both pleased and a little embarrassed by the compliment, and she turned the conversation back to the student work. "With local art being exhibited here, it might give you an opportunity to discover the next Matisse or Picasso."

"I'm having a hard enough time with my Michelangelo," he replied as he found their name tags and pulled out her seat. "Not really," he said close to her ear, and slid into the seat beside her. "You're not the typical temperamental artist. With some I have to do a lot of hand-holding through every show, vet their stuff, and oversee packaging it for shipment. You're pretty self-reliant."

"As my grandparents raised me to be."

"That's admirable, but you don't have to carry the whole thing alone. That's what you have me for. One day you may decide you want to share more personal thoughts and feelings with me too."

All the ease she'd felt with him dissolved. "You just sprang things on me the other night, Simon. I haven't had time to absorb it yet."

"I know." A tall man, vaguely familiar to her, paused beside him and spoke, saving her from her discomfort. "Have you met Frank Fischer, Genevieve?"

"Yes. I believe we met at the gallery once."

"That's right. You had that beautiful sculpture of a woman kneeling on a bed of fall leaves with a basket beside her. She looked like she might rise and go into the house at any moment. It was unbelievably lifelike. I was so disappointed to learn it had already been sold before I had a chance to enquire about it."

She heard the empty flattery behind his words. Why did people do that when they had no real interest in what she did, or in owning anything she created? "I'm sorry. Maybe you'll have better luck next time."

"The next time she has a piece for sale, be sure to contact me, Simon."

"I'll be sure to do that, Frank." She could practically see the eye-roll Simon suppressed, and bit her lip to keep from smiling.

The two men went on to talk about a meeting they had next week at the chamber of commerce, leaving Genevieve to study Simon surreptitiously. His dark hair lay thick and soft against his head in perfect layers. His jaw was perfectly shaven. His suit perfectly fitted to his tall, lean body. Would he expect her to be perfect, the way he did with his appearance and his gallery?

Her work was dusty and dirty, and sometimes she was, too. She couldn't picture him with someone like her. There were days she stood at the kitchen counter covered with stone dust and ate lunch. If she tracked a little grit into the house, she swept it back out as soon as she was finished for the day, but she didn't stress over it.

Simon picked at small things in the gallery to make presentation as flawless as possible. And his house was spotless. Everything had a place, and it stayed there. She wasn't a pig, but if her clothes didn't reach the hamper in the downstairs bathroom at the end of the day, she didn't sweat it. She'd pick them up to wash later.

Andy had never had an issue with it. He'd added his to the pile, and even put a couple of loads in now and then when the pile had turned into…well, more than a pile. She couldn't picture Simon doing a mundane chore such as laundry.

The client moved on and Simon turned back to her. "I'm sorry for the interruption."

"No worries. Do you cook, Simon?"

"Yes. I'm quite good at it. I ran a restaurant for a time in Lexington before I moved here to open the gallery, and learned a thing or two while I was there. I'll have to fix you dinner one night."

"That sounds nice."

"Do you cook?" he countered.

"When I'm not consumed by my work. When I am, I order pizza or run by and pick up Chinese takeout. Or fix a gallon of vegetable soup and eat it every day until it's gone."

"Next time, call me and I'll cook you some egg drop soup

or baked potato soup with cheddar cheese. It takes next to no time and it will give you a little variety."

"Sounds tempting."

She straightened in the chair. It was time to tell Simon about her new model now, so he wouldn't think it strange when the next sculpture was complete and she hadn't mentioned anything about it. "I've found my male model for the next piece."

His brows crashed together. "Who is he?"

The sharp demand in his voice took her aback for a moment. His movements stiff, he shifted and rearranged the silverware next to his plate.

"He's someone local, but he wants to remain anonymous, like the women I hire to pose for me."

"Has he posed for you yet?"

"Yes. But only partially unclothed. I took your advice about the nudity making it more difficult to sell the pieces, and decided to use a drape." She felt protective of Finn's privacy. After having been naked before the world for nearly seven hundred years, he deserved to have his dignity preserved. He hadn't seemed bothered at all by her request.

"He's okay with that?"

"Yes. And I've done a couple of preliminary sketches already. He's large and muscular, but no bodybuilder. And, as usual, I'll change his facial features to conceal his identity."

"He's behaving himself?"

"Yes. He's very courteous and polite. His body has the perfect symmetry for the piece, and he's flexible like an athlete, so he can hold the pose so I can get both photographs and drawings. Once I get a few more done, I won't need him to pose any longer."

"I thought you were going to let me come out to keep an eye on him."

"There isn't any need, Simon. He's behaving."

"Those are the ones you have to watch out for, Genevieve."

She laughed like she was supposed to, but at the same time recognized he could be placed in the same category. His attitude and the adamant sharpness of his voice made her wary.

She'd been alone a long time before Andy, and her grandparents had trusted her to look out for herself. Andy never questioned her ability to do so either. To have Simon suddenly go all... Was it possessive or protective? She didn't know which, but she wasn't buying into it.

President Connor climbed the steps to the dais set at the head of the room, successfully deflecting her from saying what she was thinking.

"Ladies and gentlemen, if you will all take a seat, please. We want to start the meal while it's hot. But first, let's all thank our students, who are acting as our wait staff tonight."

Applause followed while people went to the tables to get settled.

Connor continued, "And our cafeteria staff, who have catered the meal under the supervision of Chef Ryland Parker. He is the head chef for the Meyer's Restaurant de Famille. There will be four courses. An aperitif, a soup or salad, an entrée, and a dessert. Our first course will be jumbo shrimp cocktail with freshly made cocktail sauce, our chef's secret recipe. You're welcome to visit with the people at your table while our food is being served."

A herd of students began serving iced tea or water, while others placed shrimp before each of the hundred and fifty guests. The man beside her turned to say something. She was grateful for the others at the table, because they kept the conversation going, and filled the void that followed Simon's territorial behavior.

The salad, grilled peaches atop a bed of spinach with English walnuts, feta cheese, ham, and a sweet and sour vinaigrette dressing, was a work of art, and delicious. "I wonder if they'll give me a box to take food home," Genevieve teased.

"I had an aunt who stuffed food in her purse every time she went to a buffet," the man across from her said with a grin.

She held up the tiny flat bag she'd brought.

"Not even room for a chicken wing in there," he commented.

"What do you think, Simon?"

"For five hundred a plate, I think you could probably talk them into giving you a plate."

Leave it to him to come up with a practical solution, as always. "Good idea."

She dug into the entreé of grilled yellowtail tuna, pasta blended with sun-dried tomatoes and asparagus with a divine sauce, and a carrot dish with raisins and nuts. The food was delicious, and now that he was distracted from her sculpting model issue, Simon had decided to be charming to everyone around them.

But she couldn't get back to the easy, stress-free moments they had enjoyed for thinking about his reaction. She wished he'd never said anything to her about his change of feelings.

It was going to ruin their business relationship when she

told him she couldn't return them.

✧   ✧   ✧

Finn watched from the shade of the cupola as the crowd trickled out of the library. Simon and Genevieve were surely not far behind. If she saw him, she would be angry with him for following them, but ever since he'd tracked the man to his house, Finn was suspicious of him. If he was her friend, why had he remained in his car and watched the police search Genevieve's yard and not gone inside to secure her safety?

And though she hadn't treated Simon as a lover, he'd seen the glint in the man's eyes, and the possessive way he handled her while he guided her to his car and helped her in. Was that a normal part of courtship now? He'd handled enough women in his time to understand what Simon wanted. But Genevieve was still grieving her betrothed.

She kept Finn well-fed, entertained, and safe. The least he could do was to keep her safe as well. Beneath the streetlights, he caught a glimpse of the lace shawl draped over her arm, its rich red standing out like blood against the black of her dress. She looked fragile and feminine, very different from when she wore her bulky coveralls while working, or her shorts and T-shirt. He did enjoy the sight of her long, bare legs and slender feet. Her painted toenails... He jerked his thoughts back, but he couldn't ignore the hardening of his cock or the heavy beat of his heart.

Was he any better than the man he was here to protect her from? Yes, he was. He knew his own intent. He would never harm her. He was here to make sure this man wouldn't either. But every time Simon put his hand on her back, or grasped her arm, Finn's stomach muscles tightened and the blood rushed to his head.

As soon as Simon's car pulled out of the parking lot, Finn flew up, then toward home. He hovered just above the vehicle, keeping it in sight until it pulled into the driveway. He perched in the tall oak shading the porch and waited for the man to say good night. When he leaned forward and pressed his lips to Genevieve's cheek, it took every ounce of Finn's control not to fly down, snatch the man away, and hurl him off the porch.

"Thanks for this evening, Simon."

"You're welcome. Maybe next time it won't be business when we go out, but pleasure."

"We'll see. When do you think the drawings will be framed? I'd like to see them before the Richards pick them up," Genevieve said.

"They should be done by next week. I'll call when they're ready."

"Thank you." She unlocked her door.

"May I see the drawings you've done of the model?"

"Not yet, Simon. When I get them just the way I want them, I'll share them with you."

He nodded. "Another time, then." He stepped back. "Good night, Genevieve."

"Good night." She slipped inside and closed the door.

Simon stood there for a second or two, staring at the door. When he turned, the porch light shone upon his features, which were set in a mask of rage. When he pulled out onto the main road, gravel pinged against the underside of the vehicle as the wheels spun hard to keep up with the revving engine.

It would seem Simon was displeased because he hadn't been invited into the house. Finn chuckled and swung down the branches of the oak tree. His feet hit the ground, and he sauntered up the steps and, stretching his wings out, sat down in one of the rocking chairs on the porch.

It would seem she had discussed her drawings with Simon. But he had called him a model. Was that what he was?

With a piece of charcoal, she meant to carve away those areas that made him a monster and turn him back into the man he had been before. She meant to show the sketches to Simon when she finished.

There was an intensity in the way she studied him from the very beginning. He first experienced it when she knelt and rested her palm against his face that first day, inside the storage room. She really looked at him. Really saw him.

It wasn't horror or distaste she felt. He'd seen those reactions on many tourists' faces when they came upon him on the castle grounds. Hers was more a sharp, focused consideration, almost as if she could see beneath his skin to his bones.

Did she look as fierce when carving stone as she did drawing him that afternoon? An idea occurred to him, and he stopped the rocker's gentle motion. What if she carved away his tail and the points on his ears while the stone encased him? Would it rid him of those things when he became the real monster? Could he convince her to try it?

But if she took his wings, he could no longer fly. He would miss flying. But he was getting ahead of himself. They could try something small and see if it worked.

He was willing to take the risk. What was the sacrifice of a tail, or two spiny knobs if he could be who he was before?

No, that could never be. He had been irrevocably changed by the curse. By everything he lost. But he could be human again, at least in appearance. He could be a man. At least part of the time.

So many thoughts clamored inside his head, he covered his ears and closed his eyes to block them out. But the most important one pushed its way forward. If he looked like a man, could pursue her as a man, would Genevieve accept his suit?

With that idea driving him to action, he shoved to his feet, went to the door, and rang the bell.

CHAPTER 18

"GODDAMNIT!" SIMON POUNDED his fist on the steering wheel and then yanked so hard it should have wrenched it loose from its column. She'd learn to be obedient sooner rather than later if she knew what was good for her. And he'd damn well know who her model was, even if he had to stake out her house until the man showed up.

If the man touched her, he'd kill him. He'd done it before, he'd do it again.

"Goddamn her!" He'd sold hundreds of thousands of dollars' worth of her sculptures. She should be willing to trust him with everything.

But she didn't. He'd messed up by demanding to know who the model was. And then again by pushing to see the drawings. He had to learn patience with her.

Unless he took things into his hands and schooled her in her proper place with him. But he needed to be careful. If he rushed, he could crush her creative genius...like he did Katelyn's. She never recovered, and he ended up having to end things between them permanently.

The pressure was building inside him. The raw need exploded through him like a tsunami. His cock swelled now, making his pants uncomfortably tight. He needed that taken care of too.

He checked the time and, seeing it was only ten o'clock, mentally flipped through his options. The address he copied from Genevieve's check register lay tucked behind his license in his billfold, waiting to be used. He shivered as a fresh wave of excitement blended with a skin-tightening compulsion. His breathing sped up. She'd be an excellent substitute for Genevieve.

He'd go to the apartment and watch for her. Perhaps he'd run into her by accident. And if the time was right, he'd know. Reaching town, he pulled into a grocery store parking lot and fished his billfold out of his back pocket.

He got out the business card where he wrote the address, and keyed the location into the GPS built into his dash. The woman's voice said, "Calculating." He pulled back out on South Main while she decided what direction he needed to go. "Turn right onto West Wand Street." He was happy to oblige her.

Several turns later, he cruised through a neighborhood of townhouses owned by the college to house the overflow of students from the dorms. He found the address quite easily, and pulled into the lot to park between a large SUV and a beat-up Honda.

He studied the townhouse where she lived. The trash has been set out along the sidewalk to be picked up, and the lights were all off.

Checking the dashboard clock, he saw it might be late for students who had an early class. He would not be seeing her tonight. But possibly tomorrow.

Part of the pleasure was the hunt, wasn't it? He'd scope

out the neighborhood more thoroughly tomorrow, while she and her housemates were in class. Then he'd return on a pretext. He'd use Genevieve as an excuse. That would make things all the more…satisfying.

Tonight he'd watch Genevieve for a time. He still had the panties he stole from her house. That would hold him over until a more satisfying alternative to fulfilling his needs presented itself.

✧　✧　✧

"Is something wrong, Finn?" He had never rung the doorbell before.

Genevieve was slow in opening the door, worried it was Simon returning. Relieved to find it was Finn instead, she relaxed and even offered him a smile.

"An idea has come to me. But I will need yer help to try it."

Genevieve walked out onto the porch and immediately wrapped her arms around her waist as the moist mountain air caressed her bare arms and legs with icy fingers. "What is it?"

Finn closed the distance between them and wrapped his wings loosely around them both. His body gave off heat like a sauna, and she relaxed within the cocoon he'd created.

"While I am the stone statue, I want ye to carve away my tail."

She stared at him for a moment. It was not what she had expected him to say. "Why?"

"I want to see if removing the tail while I am a statue will remove the tail while I am alive."

It was a…she wouldn't say *good* idea…but it was a logical

one. But a dangerous one, too. "Finn. Your tail is part of your spinal column. It may leave nerves exposed if I remove it. You could be in constant, terrible pain."

His features—part man, part creature—set in mulish lines. "I am willing to take the chance."

"I know how desperate you are to be rid of the curse."

He grasped her arms and pulled her closer. "Do ye, Genevieve? Do ye ken what 'tis like to spend sixteen hours a day as a block of stone, locked in the same position and unable to speak?"

It was torture for him. It had to be. "No. I don't know what it's like. But if I deface your statue and you end up in terrible pain, it will make your life more difficult, and it will be my fault, Finn."

She closed her eyes, unable to look him in the face when she said it. "If we can't free you from the curse, you'll be in pain for...." She couldn't say the words aloud. An eternity. It would shatter all hope for him to hear those words.

"I'm in pain now. I dinna know how much longer I can bear being this creature."

Tears blurred her eyes. "I know." She moved in close and put her arms around his waist. His body was large and muscular. But for his wings, tail, and claws, his anatomy was human. *He* was human. She recognized him as human. A man. A man with a horrible deformity. A man worthy of affection and caring.

She rested her head against his chest and listened to the steady beat of his heart. Felt the heat and smoothness of his skin against her own.

Finn stood as still and stiff as the statue, and for a moment she thought she had overstepped the boundaries between them. Slowly he pressed a hand against the small of her back and held her. His chin brushed her hair. "I havena held a woman in centuries, Genevieve."

"You're doing just fine."

He chuckled, his deep voice holding a texture all its own. He rested his palm at the base of her neck, then ran it down her spine to the small of her back, then tugged her closer, until her body conformed to his, and she became aware of how much he wanted her.

An ache of longing sparked deep within her. She hadn't felt those stirrings of need in so long.

He plucked the chopsticks out of her hair, and it unwound and fell to one shoulder. He smoothed it, but one claw tangled in the strands. "I could use some help, lass."

Grateful for a reason to move away, she caught his hand and lifted her hair free. She studied his nails. They were thick, and about an inch long. An idea formed, and she grabbed onto it to get her mind off other things.

"Claws, Finn."

His yellow eyes looked almost green in the dull porch light.

"Aye, I have them."

"Claws. I could try to file down one of your claws and see what happens. I don't think it would cause you pain like a more intricately woven part of your physiology. But we can find out what happens when your statue form is altered."

A slow smile curved his mouth, revealing pointed, lethal-looking teeth...which no longer frightened or horrified her.

"When will ye do it?" he asked.

"Tomorrow. Which claw would you like me to experiment on? Foot or hand?"

"Foot, I think. I only walk on them. I dinna use them to hunt."

"Okay. I'll do just a little reshaping, and we'll see what happens. If it hurts you while I'm doing it, how will I know?"

"You won't, lass. I canna speak or move. But 'twill only be a wee nail. How painful can it be?"

He'd obviously never had an ingrown toenail. "I think I'll take it slow and do this by degrees, and wait to check in with you to see what you experience. It's best we don't rush it."

"All right, lass. But if it works…"

"Some of the other things would be major changes to your structure. Your wings are as much a part of you as your arms, hands, and head. They're flesh and bone. It would be a major amputation, and I'm not a doctor, Finn. If I removed them and you transitioned and bled badly, it could kill you. Or leave you permanently crippled. The bones of your wings are attached to your shoulder blades, and possibly your shoulders."

He fluttered his wings, and they brushed against her. They felt soft—not like leather, though they looked like it—but more like skin.

"Mayhap we can wait 'till the end to remove them. I rather like flying. 'Twill be one of the few things I'll miss."

She couldn't imagine what it would be like for him to be without them after so many centuries.

"Are ye afraid of heights, lass?"

"No."

"Go change into warmer attire, and I will share the experience with ye."

Genevieve opened her mouth to tell him no, but to be perfectly honest with herself, she *had* been curious about his wings, how they worked, and what it was like to fly. "I'll only be a moment."

She rushed to her room, shed her dress, and changed into sweatpants and a sweatshirt.

When she exited the house again, Finn was waiting in the middle of the yard.

"There is no need to be afraid."

She swallowed, though her mouth was dry. Not with fear, but a complex tangle of emotions she didn't understand. "I'm not afraid."

He placed an arm around her waist, then bent to scoop her up and lift her. She might have weighed nothing, it seemed so easy for him. He took two long strides, and his huge wings flared and flapped once, twice, and they were airborne.

As they climbed, a quick frisson of fear struck her, and her arms locked around his neck while the air cooled significantly, making her ears burn.

They glided and swooped down over the treetops, and though they were a safe distance above, she had to fight the urge to lift her feet.

When they flew over an area cleared of trees, she spotted the wolf pack, many more wolves than the four animals she saw the other night in her yard. There were at least fifteen in the group.

They looked up as Finn and she passed overhead, and she heard their high-pitched yips and howls as they fell behind. Finn swooped higher as they reached the edge of town.

"Someone will see us," she shouted above the whoosh of

the wind as it passed.

He shook his head. "They dinna glance up as often as ye might expect. They are too busy looking at their phones."

He was probably right. It had become the way of the world.

He glided in a long swoop around the outskirts of the college, keeping high above the glow of the streetlights. The buildings looked like a model to scale, and the cars like toys. They passed over a cluster of apartment complexes where a group of students walked down the middle of the street. A car came upon them and the driver tapped his horn to urge them out of the way. The vehicle gleamed beneath the streetlights, its sleek lines familiar, even from above. "I think that's Simon's car."

"Aye, 'tis."

The students danced out of the road and up on the narrow sidewalks. The Jaguar rushed past and cut down the next side street on its way back to Main. Finn cut a diagonal path across the neighborhood and flew north. When he wound his way over Simon's house, she frowned.

"How do you know where he lives, Finn?"

"I followed him home the night you thought m' statue had been stolen. He parked on the side of the road beneath the trees and watched the men search."

She frowned. Why hadn't he come up to the house?

Finn circled until the Simon's car pulled into the driveway, and then was swallowed inside his garage.

"Is his house pleasing to ye?" Finn asked.

She thought about the perfect furniture, perfect organization of every piece of art and every painting. "It's nice, but not as nice as mine. But then I grew up in mine, and lived there with my grandparents. It's home."

He nodded.

Was he missing home? But what kind of home could he have after being banned from the castle and hidden in the surrounding woods?

And why hadn't she ever invited him into her home?

Well, for one thing, his wings might create a problem, and he would probably find the space difficult to move around in. But what about the studio?

She'd have to clear an area for him. Perhaps a quarter of the room. Perhaps put in a small television. What would he think of television?

Finn turned back to the outskirts of the town. The closer to the ground they flew, the warmer the air—a relief, because she was feeling the chill through her sweatpants and shirt, and couldn't keep from shivering. Finn glided along the contours of the mountains. She'd never noticed how many streams and cleared fields existed within the ten or so miles just outside the city limits.

When they came upon a small creek, and Finn flew up, then straight down, feet first, and slowly landed along its banks, where he lowered Genevieve's feet to the ground. The crickets' chirps built to a chorus, and the only light was the half-moon overhead, and the million fireflies blinking in scattered synchronization across the field.

"What are those called?" Finn asked, nodding toward the fireflies. "I have noticed them close to water and in the tall grass. And why do they light up?" He rubbed his large hands up and down her back and arms to warm her.

"They're called fireflies or lightning bugs. When we were young we used to catch them in a jar, until we realized how cruel it was to confine them and let them die. They have a chemical reaction in their body called bioluminescence. The chemicals they produce react to the oxygen their bodies take in, and they light up. They use the flashes to identify their species, or attract a mate. The males that light up the longest attract the most females."

"Lucky buggers."

Genevieve laughed out loud and was rewarded with a soft, gravelly chuckle. Curious, she reached out and touched his wings. Finn stilled beneath her touch. "They're not at all leathery like a bat's. They're soft, like skin."

"'Tis because they are skin." There was a huskiness to his tone that heated her cheeks for a moment. She dropped her hands and silently chastised herself for her thoughtlessness. She should have known better.

He stepped away and went to the small stream. "The water here is pure, Genevieve." He knelt and dipped his hand in to drink.

Silence fell for some moments. "They seem to be at home here, he said. "The fireflies."

"Yes, they do." She paused. "Do you feel at home here, Finn?"

He looked up at her face. "Aye. As at home as I can be anywhere. The crags and glens here are different than at home. They are covered with many trees. But I've grown used to them. Though I sometimes miss the sea. There was a loch close to the castle, and the seals lived there."

"I love the sea too. It's like a heartbeat that calls to you."

"Aye." He looked toward the east. "'Tis growing late, and 'twill rain soon. I'd best be getting ye back to the house before the storm hits."

She glanced at the distant horizon for any sign of the coming weather. "How do you know it's going to rain?"

"'Tis like that heartbeat. I can feel it."

Her eyes were growing used to the deeper darkness, but he was still just a shadow moving toward her. She shuffled forward and collided with him, and he looped an arm around her waist to steady her.

His taut, muscular abdomen, and the unmistakable maleness of his body pressed against her, triggered a quick, tingling flash of need. She caught her breath and instinctively leaned into him.

He froze, and she heard him swallow. His muscles went as rigid as the erection pressed against her. The ragged intake of his breath gave her a sensual thrill, as did the hard beat of his heart.

Every nerve in her body seemed to bristle with awareness. She trembled with the fierce need to part her legs and let him in.

Oh, God. They couldn't do this. But she wanted to.

His hand moved to the small of her back, and he held her more tightly. "When I am no longer the monster, I would ask ye to remember this moment."

Quick tears stung her eyes, but she refused to allow them to fall. She swallowed, though her mouth was dry.

"We must go back." The gravel in his voice had deepened.

"Yes."

The trip took only fifteen minutes, but it seemed too

short. Within the glow of the porch light, she found it hard to look at him. "I didn't mean to make things more difficult for you, Finn."

"It already was, Genevieve. Since the first time you looked into the eyes of my statue and said I was so ugly I was beautiful."

She looked up. "You heard me?"

"Aye. 'Twas close to sunset, and I could feel the change starting while ye cupped my jaw."

She'd thought his jaw human to the touch even then.

"The rain is here, Genevieve, ye must go in."

Almost as though he'd called them down, fat drops splatted on the concrete sidewalk next to the porch, and she dashed up the steps. She turned to find him standing in the rain below her. He tilted his head back and let the water flow down his body. In moments, his hair was saturated and the hair on his chest dark with moisture. His skin looked bronzed in the dim light, the muscles beneath a play of light and shadow. He was one with the elements as long as he was the creature. And, dear God, he was beautiful.

"Will you try carving away the nail tomorrow?"

"Are you sure you want to risk it, Finn? Miranda and Juliet may come up with a spell."

"And they may not. I've waited so long already, Gen." He strode forward to rest a foot on the bottom step. Once again his eyes appeared green beneath the porch light.

"I'll use a sander, and just reshape the nail a little, then. Nothing drastic."

He nodded. She ached to go back down the steps and hold him. Just in case.

"Ye will do well, lass." There was such hope in his expression, emotion swamped her again, and she had to look away.

At a loss, she murmured. "Thank you for taking me flying, Finn." She turned and went in before her words or actions made the situation worse. She leaned back against the door, her throat aching with the need to cry.

✧   ✧   ✧

FINN STOOD IN the rain and let it wash down his body and cool the fire of need raging inside him. The scent of her arousal had called to him. How could she want him when he was still the monster? But she saw more than the monster when she looked at him. He read it in her face, in the way she allowed her arm to brush his when they sat together, in the way she touched him.

She hadn't just made it more difficult for him by responding to him. She had made it impossible for herself. He could not act on his desire or respond to hers as the monster. He wouldn't. There was always the chance he might lose control and hurt her.

And if he couldn't be human again, how would either of them live with wanting each other and never being able to act on it?

CHAPTER 19

"YOU'RE SURE YOU don't mind posing while I draw you?" Genevieve asked as she opened the large pad of paper and set it up on the table easel.

"I dinna ken why ye wish to draw me, lass. But ye've more than earned the right, since ye've fed and housed me these past weeks."

"You've brought me fish twice this week, and those mushrooms you harvested were perfect in the salad we ate tonight."

Finn looked up, and she caught the slight wrinkle of his nose.

"Man cannot live by meat and potatoes alone, Finn. And don't say you aren't a man because, you're ninety percent man and ten percent stubborn. When you become human again, you'll have to start eating healthier, otherwise you'll have a heart attack before you're forty."

She pointed the stub of charcoal at him. "And don't say you're already older than that." She glanced at him, studying the line of his jaw. "How old were you when you were...changed?"

"A score and eight years. An old man for my time."

"Twenty-eight is young today. I'll be twenty-seven my birthday."

"Ye would have been thought left on the bush if ye were rich. Comin' from a landed family, yer husband would have been chosen for you and you would have been breeding within the year at seven and ten. Had ye had no resources, ye would have been thought a prize because ye have a skill, and the lads would have been hangin' about ye, tryin' to woo ye to the altar for what ye could bring to the marriage and the marriage bed."

"Seventeen, huh?" She felt a wave of outrage for those poor girls, forced into marriage with strangers while little more than children.

His accent always thickened when he spoke of his home. "Aye. Sometimes older, if their *athair* was not in need of a political ally or some other binding situation."

"Why didn't you want to settle down with one of the landed ladies? I'm sure your cousin could have found you one."

"Aye, he did, a widow, but she died of consumption before the banns were posted."

He spoke with such dispassion, she looked up. "I'm sorry, Finn."

"Life was harder then, and there were no medicines to fight disease as there are now. I would have been a better man then, had she lived, and I took responsibility for her property and the needs of her clansmen."

"You're always so hard on yourself, Finn. You patrol my property to make certain I'm safe. You bring me freshly caught fish, mushrooms, wild greens. You make me feel... cared for."

"I am always at your service." He raised his yellow-green gaze to her face. The look in his eyes had heat flaring in her face and an empty ache erupting between her thighs.

"I need to concentrate on this. After you've been stationary all day, I don't want you to have to remain so any longer than necessary. I've been working from photographs, but this will finish off my ideas."

He inclined his head, but continued to gaze at her for several moments.

She focused on the paper before her as though it were the most important thing on earth. After half an hour, she said, "You can get up and move around now if you like." He rose and stretched. The wide, muscular depth of his chest captured her attention, and her mouth dried. He turned to look over his shoulder at her, almost as if he knew what she was feeling, and she dragged her attention back to the drawing. She finished it and tore it off the pad, set it aside, then turned her attention to the portrait beneath.

She had to learn to suppress these feelings. For several days, things had been awkward between them. She was wary of standing too close, for fear of giving away, yet again, how she felt when he was near. Every look seemed awkward.

"Will ye show the drawing to me when ye're finished?" he asked.

"Yes. Of course. Will you mind if I use it for my next sculpture?"

His brows shot up. "A sculptural copy of me like this?"

"No. It isn't. It's as I see you. As you really are." She put several finishing touches to the portrait, got up, and moved back to view it from a distance.

"I would like to see it before I say aye or nay."

"All right." She turned the full-length drawing of him so he could see it. It was of a man fighting his way free from an invisible force. The plan was to add the polymer clay to it as she had Mai's. Mai's was about looking to the future. Finn's would be about fighting against an internal prison and overcoming it. The clay would bond one arm to the base, and the other would reach upward, with tatters hanging from it.

She glanced up to find him studying the drawing. "Ye have left the face blank, lass."

She tore the portrait she'd done off the pad and placed it carefully atop the other drawing.

He stared at the portrait and his throat worked as he swallowed. "'Tis a face I was once familiar with. How can ye see what was in the past?"

"I know human anatomy and bone structure. Yours is camouflaged, but it's there."

"Is it the man you see in the picture ye care about, or the monster before ye, Genevieve?"

"You are one and the same, Finn."

"Nay. The monster is inside me as well as my shell. I have instincts I work to suppress that no human should have to fight. The urge to hunt, the need to pursue."

He limped closer. She had filed on the second nail from his big toe, and she should never have done it. He wasn't healing as he had always done before, because she interfered with the magic.

Why did his yellow irises so often appear green in the glare of the patio lights? Were his eyes changing color?

"The need to take."

The way he said it brought visions of him coming inside her, and triggered an immediate, visceral reaction.

His hands closed over her arms, and he brought her up

against him, the hard heat of his erection pressed against her. He bent his head and nibbled at her throat, using careful pressure while his tongue feathered her skin.

Genevieve moaned his name aloud. She ran her hands up his back to the joint of his wings. Finn shuddered and dragged in a breath. He thrust against her. "If I bite you, if I make love with ye, the magic may pass to ye. I winna let that happen."

He dragged himself out of her arms and took two stumbling steps back, then turned and raced across the yard, his wings spread. He rose into the sky.

Genevieve bent at the waist and braced her hands on her knees. She couldn't drag in enough air. Every muscle in her body jerked and shook with frustrated need. Her empathic abilities seemed to be growing stronger. She read his need, and it blended with hers as soon as she touched him. She bit her lip and forced herself to stand.

As her passion cooled, the urge to weep overwhelmed her. Crying wouldn't help, but now they'd opened this box, there'd be no way to close it.

Miranda and Juliet had to help them.

✧   ✧   ✧

FINN CIRCLED THE house until he was sure Genevieve was inside where she would be safe. Seeing her drawings had only brought back what had been and what might never be again. They were trapped in an impossible situation. He wanted her with an ache that never eased. But he was afraid of losing control with her. The monster wanted to nip her. The man wanted to kiss her senseless. It was too much for him.

And now his blood was cooling, the impossibility of their

situation continued to torment him. To have her so close and not be able to woo her like a normal man… And knowing how she saw him now made it more difficult.

If he had the power, he would leave for a time, stay away until they had their emotions under control. But leaving was not an option. He was tied to the blasted base, which called him home every morn. To destroy it might be the answer, but to do so might unleash things neither of them could control. He could not take the chance.

And even if he could…he would not have the strength to leave her. She had captured him as thoroughly as the magic that surrounded him.

CHAPTER 20

G ENEVIEVE WOKE TO the sound of the phone ringing. She forced her eyes open and winced at the dull ache throbbing behind them. Dreams of Finn, tortured and in pain, had again chased her all night, while he avoided her and occupied himself with the wolves.

It was her fault. If she hadn't responded to him a second time, it wouldn't have left them both exposed.

The phone rang again. She cleared her sleep-clogged throat and fumbled to answer.

Miranda barely said hello before jumping into what she'd called about. "I've been doing some research on Druids, black magic, and creating chimera, which is what Finn is. He's part one creature and part another."

Genevieve struggled to a sitting position and propped a pillow behind her. "Please tell me you've found something helpful."

"I've been concentrating on the reasons behind why he was turned. And the lessons he was forced to learn." She paused, and Genevieve could hear her talking to someone and papers rustling.

"Sorry. I'm at work. With every lesson Finn's learned, he's weakened the curse to some extent.

"If that were true, wouldn't he be changing on his own?"

"In the beginning, he could have been far more monstrous than he is now."

"He told me when he was first turned into the monster he lost his reason. So maybe you're right. But what can he do to speed up the process of reversing it, Miranda? I don't believe he'll survive another six hundred years as he is."

"There's a lesson he hasn't learned or an action he hasn't taken yet that's needed to break the curse."

Her mind rushed with possibilities. "What do you think it might be?"

"I don't know. But Juliet and I have been working hard to create a spell that will reverse the transformation. He might still transition into the stone creature during the day, but he may be a man at night."

Genevieve bent her knees and rested her forehead atop them. "How dangerous would this be for him, Miranda?"

Silence stretched on the line. "We don't know. We can't be sure. We've never tried anything like this before. And it will take more power than Juliet and I have. We'd have to ask some other witches in the area to help us."

The more people who shared Finn's secret, the more dangerous it was for him. What if someone decided to steal and imprison him while he was frozen in statue form? People would flock to see a real gargoyle. And even worse, what if they just wanted to destroy him? Humans didn't trust things they couldn't understand.

What had inspired Cinead to choose such a creature?

Carvings of chimera began with the ancient Egyptians. Then the Greeks and the Romans borrowed from the cultures they conquered, and absorbed the gods of other cultures into their religion, until Christianity put a stop it.

"What if Cinead was Druid, but his beliefs were tied to an older belief or religion?"

"What do you mean?"

"There have been carvings gargoyles of one kind or another since ancient times. To ward off evil, to warn the illiterate masses against the evils of worshiping false gods, and as decorative structures on buildings to redirect rainwater away from the foundations. Some were even used as fertility symbols. Why did Cinead choose this particular creature?"

"I have no idea. It had to be significant to him. Or it could have been the most hideous thing he could imagine."

She didn't find Finn hideous. But he had been terrifying to behold at first. Because it just seemed impossible such a creature could truly exist.

"I've been carving away at one of the toenails of the statue, just shortening it. It did change to his claw when he transforms to the creature, but now it's sore and not healing. At first he suggested cutting off his tail. Thank God I convinced him it needed to be something smaller. Otherwise he'd be in agony."

A thoughtful pause came across the phone. "You should never have tampered with things at all. Even this small thing has come back on him. And it could come back on you, too, Gen. Leave it alone."

Genevieve raked her hair back. "He's so desperate, Miranda. Maybe if he has some hope to cling to…" She didn't want to be responsible for his suffering, not even a damaged nail.

"Juliet and I want to confer with some of the others before we go any further with the spell, Gen. And you need to ask

Finn if he's willing to risk having a larger group knowing about him, meeting him. He's so unusual…amazing, really…it will be a huge challenge for some of them to resist talking about him. And the spell could be extremely painful for him. Or worse."

Miranda's insights set off another round of anxiety. "If he's willing for me to take a hammer and chisel to his statue, chances are he's ready to try anything. Arrange for the ladies to come tonight, and I'll call you as soon as I'm able to check with him."

"That sounds good. I think if they can get a feel for the magic around him, they might have some insights into how we need to proceed."

She wanted to share what she was feeling with Miranda. The words *I think I messed up* kept playing through her mind. The heart-racing, breath-stealing moments between them might make Finn more reckless. It could very well feed his desperation.

Why did she feel this way about him? Why had she wanted the statue to begin with? Were their feelings real, or were they caused by the magic that surrounded him?

After hanging up, she clutched her hair in frustration and gave it a tug. What kind of monster would cast such a spell?

And Cinead MacLeod was the real monster. Finn had been arrogant and cocky. Handsome and charming. And he behaved reprehensibly by taking advantage of a vulnerable young woman and refusing to accept his responsibilities. Had she met him then, she wouldn't have liked him at all.

But he'd more than paid for his mistakes. He was different now. He'd learned from them. His need to protect her from the repercussions of their relationship was proof he'd changed.

He could have pushed for more last night. But it was he who had backed away. And she was grateful. There might be hidden dangers to such a relationship besides the obvious. He was a creature of magic, and she was a human with no mystical powers. He was not completely human anymore. She had to accept it.

What if the curse extended past turning him into the creature? What if it had other properties they weren't aware of? What if there was a punishment attached to getting too close to him physically, emotionally?

It was already too late.

THE BLURRED IMAGE on the computer screen of Genevieve in the shower was too indistinct to give Simon any satisfaction. The light bulb camera wasn't powerful enough. He would have to find an alternative and install it as soon as he got an opportunity. If he could think of something to get her out of the house for an hour or two…

He chose the bathroom block on the screen and clicked on it. It went to full screen. The frosted glass in the shower door distorted her shape. When she turned off the water, he waited for her to open the door, and leaned closer to watch her step out. Her dark hair was slicked to her neck and back. He caught the curve of one pale breast as she reached for a towel and brought it against her, almost as if she was covering her nudity, even though she was alone.

Was she always so modest?

When they were together, he would teach her to be unconcerned with her nudity. He'd have her parade around the bedroom naked for hours until he had his fill.

She brought the towel up and rubbed her hair. The back and forth flopping of the terrycloth kept him from seeing her body, and when she moved out of the frame, he swore. There had to be somewhere he could place a camera so he could watch her, enjoy her naked beauty. He clicked on the screen and the block shrank so he could scan the other camera images, concentrating on the bedroom camera. She walked into the frame already dressed, but was still drying her hair. She'd taken her clothing into the bathroom with her.

That, too, would change after he moved into the house with her. He would teach her to please his...needs. He would touch and taste every inch of her, and he'd teach her how he liked to be touched and tasted. The thought brought his semi-hard cock to a full-blown erection.

He went back to the bathroom camera and rolled back the digital image to freeze it at the point where she stepped out of the shower and leaned forward to reach for the towel. He concentrated on the sweet curve of her breast. They were soft and firm. He'd purposely hugged her close before kissing her cheek so he could feel her body against his. And was disappointed and angry when she didn't press closer or linger. That would change. He'd insist on it.

He opened the top desk drawer and reached for the tiny strip of lace he'd stolen from her laundry basket. His hands shook as he unzipped his black pants, lifted his hips and tugged them and his boxer briefs down to mid-thigh.

He shoved his hand inside the panties and wrapped it around his erection. While he stroked himself, he thought of all the things he wanted to do to Genevieve, most of them while she knelt at his feet and followed his instructions. She'd suck his dick until he told her to stop. He imagined her mouth wrapped around him while he pumped his hips, and tightened his grip until his cheeks burned and his heart raced.

After she brought him to the edge, he'd turn her around and take her from behind, hard and fast. He groaned his pleasure as he ejaculated into the panties and rolled his head against the back of his leather desk chair.

He waited for his breathing and heartbeat to settle before tossing the panties into the trashcan next to his desk and standing to rearrange his clothing. He closed the frozen image on the screen.

He wouldn't have to do that again. He'd use the Genevieve substitute next time. Maybe tonight.

This was a very poor substitute for the real thing.

CHAPTER 21

GENEVIEVE CARRIED TWO large mugs outside and sat down beside Finn's statue while she waited for him to transform. She sipped her coffee and studied the statue's face. It hadn't changed at all, but the live creature had. His ears were becoming more human. His brow ridge was less exaggerated.

He was going to be upset when he saw she hadn't tried working on the nail again today.

In fact she'd gotten precious little work done at all because she'd been busy stewing about him. Especially about her response to him.

She should never have acknowledged it. Should never have encouraged his advances. It only put more pressure on Finn to solve the problem, and it tempted him with something they might never have together.

She'd been celibate for two years. Maybe she was just sexually frustrated.

How could she want him when he looked like a…a monster?

Because she'd seen what he looked like before he became the creature. That image was firmly implanted in her head. And her heart. It was like looking at a burn victim. She saw past the disfigurement to what was supposed to be. But this was much worse.

She felt Finn's transition before she saw it. Heat wafted off him, and the stone began to shimmer and take on a more pliant texture. She stumbled to her feet, uncertain about being so close to him when it happened.

When he staggered to his feet, she took another involuntary step back, trying to ignore the response she had to the sight of his broad, muscular chest and taut abdomen.

He was so…virile…standing naked before her.

HE HAD WAITED for her, making an effort to prepare himself for the pain while she worked on the nails while he was trapped in the stone…but she never came. He didn't know whether to be angry or relieved. "Why did ye not try t'carve away some more?"

"Would you get dressed before we discuss this?" She handed him the sweatpants and wandered to the edge of the patio with her cup.

He studied her back. She could try to hide her response to him, but he could sense the heavy beat of her heart and smell the changing scent of her arousal. Having her this close after a few nights without her only made his need sharper.

"I poured you a cup of coffee. But I put some water on the table too."

He pulled on the pants, but was more interested in the water than the coffee. The long hours of being confined to the stone made him nearly mad with thirst. He took several long gulps of water, and used the back of his hand to wipe away the drop or two that ran down his chin. He brought the glass, which was sweating with moisture in the warm evening, when he went to stand beside her.

"Miranda thinks that if I do anything more to change your statue, there could be worse repercussions. She wants to try a magical solution before we carve anything else away."

So there was a reason behind her hesitancy to cutting into him when he was in his stone form, other than her fear of causing him pain. "What sort of backlash?"

"I'm not sure. But your foot isn't healing, and that was just after very shallow changes to a nail that normally can be trimmed without danger or pain. I think it's proof enough we shouldn't attempt anything more."

'Twas true. His toe throbbed like a heartbeat and had begun to fester. He moved to the cabinet and removed the peroxide and salve she'd given him to treat the wound, then moved to the edge of the patio and knelt to pour some of the liquid over the injury. It burned and sizzled when it hit the wound, and bubbled madly. He doused the wound twice more before patting it dry and putting the antibiotic salve on it.

"She and Juliet are cautious." Genevieve said as he sat on the concrete bench. She handed him his glass of water. "They're flying blind regarding the magic around you, Finn. They've never seen anything like it."

He nodded. "Cinead was an evil bastard." He focused his attention on the cubes of ice floating in the glass. It was hard to trust the witches. He did not know them. "Are ye sure they intend to help me? Or are they stallin', hopin' I'll give up?"

"They're not stalling, Fin. She's worried your magic might rub off on me if I disturb your shape any more."

God's blood, why had he not thought of that? "'Twouldna be what I would wish for ye, Genevieve. Or anyone else."

"I know." She frowned. "Miranda and Juliet need help with the magic, Finn. They have several friends, fellow witches, they'd like to bring on board to boost the power of the spell they're formulating. But the more people who know about you, the greater the danger that others will find out about you."

He wasn't surprised. He hadn't exactly been hiding away when he prowled above the town and climbed about the rooftops every night. He knew it was partly because he was tired of hiding. Tired of being alone. "How much longer do ye think I'd be able to hide, lass? This isna the wilds of Scotland."

"They want to come tonight and meet with you, Finn."

He fell silent for a moment. "How many?"

"I don't know. I'm assuming there'll be thirteen altogether."

What other choice did he have? It seemed he was being pushed in one direction.

He nodded.

"So, you'll be okay with the other witches helping them?"

"Aye." He paced away from her to sit on the steps leading into the breezeway. He drank more of the water.

"Would you like something to eat before they come?"

"Nay, lass, thank ye. Mayhap later."

When she sat down next to him, he breathed a quiet sigh of relief. She'd been keeping her distance. He didn't have to be hit on the head with the flat of a broadsword to tell she was worried about what happened the other night.

He couldn't blame her. How else was she supposed to feel

when a monster showed her he wanted to do a bit of swiving? Wanted to bite her, too.

He raked his fingers through his hair. He wanted more than that. "Ye should call them."

He watched the battle of emotions on her face. She reached for her phone and dialed the number.

He refilled his water glass and nearly drained it again. The glass rocked a little when he set it down on the patio table, and he steadied it.

He needed to get away from this situation for a time. Away from her and the emotions she stirred. He opened the small outdoor cabinet and reached for the towel and the small basket with the soap, hairbrush, toothbrush, and toothpaste she'd placed inside.

She treated him like a guest. But she also worried about him. He took some comfort in that.

He gathered the things and went around the side of the studio to strip off and bathe before the witches arrived. He heard the engines of several cars arrive as he was finishing up, and turned the water off.

A quick burst of impatience bubbled up. He was tired of tiptoeing around the humans. He had been a slave to magic for six hundred and sixty-three years. He was done with it.

He took two long strides, and his wings lifted him. He circled Genevieve's property for several moments while he watched from the distance to see two more cars arrive. Would they try to break the spell tonight? Dread lay in the pit of his stomach like a fist, warring with hope.

What more could they do to him that Cinead hadn't already accomplished? If they killed him, he'd at least be free. He turned into the wind and came in for a soft landing, twenty feet away from the crowded patio and approached the circle of women. Their identical looks of shocked amazement might have amused him any other time, but he was too busy bracing himself for what was to come.

Silence stretched, and he cleared his throat.

"Good eve, ladies."

"Nice entrance, Finn," Juliet said, her tone dry.

The comment triggered a chuckle, lightening his mood. "Thank ye."

The banter between them seemed to break the ice, and Juliet went around the circle, introducing each woman. The group varied from young to old, and small to large. One woman in particular stood out because of her flaming red hair, and another because of the tattoos of symbols and designs coloring her arms and hands. Each had a varying degree of power radiating from them.

Their reaction to him ran from fearful fascination to excitement. Each witch circled him with palms out. He stood patiently while they conducted their examinations, watchful of their reaction. His magic had been a part of him for so long he didn't notice it, but they each reacted to it, strongly.

Once they finished and began their discussion, he moved away to sit on his block. It was a relief when they took the meeting into the house, leaving him in peace.

After a time, Genevieve came out, Butterbean at her heels, and pulled a seat up next to him. "It's like a war room in there. I can't help, so I'm leaving them to it. How about some food?"

"Nay, lass." The cat gave him an affectionate head bump and rub against his thigh, inviting some petting. Finn obliged, and picked him up and held him against his chest.

The yap and howl of the wolf pack came from the north.

"They don't come close to the house anymore."

"I bid them not to. There are younger wolves in the pack who dinna have the control of the older ones." The cat stood on his hind feet, braced his front feet on his chest and rubbed his head against his cheek.

"Like the one who tried to eat Butterbean."

"Aye."

She got up and wandered from one side of the patio to the other, her movements restless and sharp.

"Thank you for looking out for him and me, Finn."

"As a soldier, 'twas my duty to protect the clan and the laird's property. 'Tis my duty to protect ye and yer home now, when I can. 'Tis good to have a purpose."

She came to a halt beside him. Her expression in the patio lights was both worried and intense. "I want you to be able to walk in daylight among us again, Finn. I want you to be able to have a normal life. Go to the library and chose your own books. Go to the grocery store and chose the food you like. I want you to be free to choose your own way, instead of being tethered to me as though I own you. You are still your own man, despite all the magical bullshit forced on you."

"I was owned by my laird before ye bought my statue, Genevieve. But if it makes ye feel any better, I dinna feel *owned* by ye, lass."

"I don't ever want you to feel as though you are obligated to do anything because I give you food or...or anything."

"There is no sense of obligation, lass. Only what is right. It suits me to earn my keep in some way."

A quick, relieved smile finally flashed across her lovely face, but she remained on edge.

"What has brought on this sudden concern about owning me?"

"Miranda said you may be programmed through the magic to be loyal to those who take possession of your statue."

He thought about it. "I didna stay on the castle grounds because I was loyal to the lairds, lass. I stayed because I had no choice. I have to stay where my base is. I've tried to fight the pull when the sun rises, but I canna resist. I have to return to it.

"I dinna feel loyalty to ye because of magic, but because ye have been generous and kind to me."

And because he found her irresistible. He found it impossible not to look at her if she was anywhere near. The expression of determination on her face when she was about to tackle a job, be it cleaning his statue or weeding the flowerbed, fascinated him. He was enslaved by the length of her legs and her delightful polished toenails. Her hair was a hundred different shades of brown, and he wanted to memorize each and every one of them.

Was she doing this because of what had happened between them? His pride rose up, smarting at the thought.

He gave Butterbean a final stroke, set him on his feet and then stood, looming over her.

"Ye dinna have to be saddled with me out of a sense of obligation, lass. Ye can move the base wherever ye wish, and I will, of course have to stay on it during the day, but at night I can see to m'self and never bother ye again."

She stared at him, her expression changing to the focused one he'd just been thinking about. Instead of addressing the issue she grabbed his arm. "Come into the studio for a minute,

Finn."

She tugged at him as she strode toward the exterior door. He followed, even though anger, triggered by his hurt pride, still burned inside him. She hit the numbers, the door rose, and she flipped on the lights. "Come in."

He stepped inside the wide entrance and paused. The interior of the studio was at least half the size of the great hall of the castle, though the ceiling was not as high, and the walls were made of sheets of metal.

A sculpture, as tall as he was, stood midway across the large space. The shoulders and head were roughly cut, but still retained a block-like structure, without distinct features. But based on the muscular forearm pressing to break free of the marble, he recognized the figure as male. The limb thrust through the stone as though it had punched loose.

Genevieve picked up an odd object and descended on him. The orange cord strung from it was for electricity. She raised the cone-shaped thing and pushed a button on the side. The bulb flared, blinding him, and he blinked.

He threw up a hand to shield his eyes. "What are ye about, lass?"

"Look at me, Finn."

She had never spoken to him in such a tone, with a strong undertone of command. He glared down at her.

"What color are your eyes, Finn?"

"Yellow. Brighter than a wolf's, but not as bright as an owl's."

She smiled, excitement radiating from her. "No, they're not. They looked green the other night. I thought it was just the light, but now they've turned blue."

CHAPTER 22

S IMON WATCHED THE girl, Mai, as she turned pages in the book. She rarely looked up, but when she did, it was with the distant concentration of someone committing information to memory. She had yet to notice him, but that would change as soon as they left The Dish.

The aroma of baking pastry lingered in the air. They said the sense of smell triggers the strongest memories. It certainly would for him when he thought of this moment in future. Mai was lovely. Slender, high-breasted, with rich brown hair and brown eyes tilted up at the corners. Perhaps she had some Chinese in her heritage. He preferred blondes, but she would do, just as she was.

The waitress brought him his blueberry pie à la mode, and he thanked her. The pie was excellent, and the ice cream fresh, with black specks of vanilla. He lingered over it and his coffee.

When it looked as though Mai was preparing to leave, he slid out of the booth and went to the counter, laying a ten-dollar bill on the register and waving away the change. The waitress's face lit up, and she thanked him as she tucked the five into her pocket. She'd remember he left before Mai, and that he had no interaction with the girl.

He strode down the steps, automatically searching the

parking lot and street. It was almost ten, and the street was deserted. He slumped into the passenger seat of his old dark blue truck, flipped a baseball cap onto his head, and hunkered down. She'd have to pass by on her way to her car parked two slots further down, and she'd never associate him with the beat-up vehicle. He'd take her as she passed.

From the glove compartment, he retrieved rubber gloves and slipped them on. In the cup holder between the seats waited the hypodermic, which he picked up and held ready while watching for her to appear around the corner.

She had a distinctive walk, full of purpose and confidence. He liked that. He tugged the cap off the needle with his teeth and waited. The summer heat had soaked into the vinyl seats and the fabric stuck to his wrist as he shifted sideways.

Through the open window he heard her steps coming close and waited for her to pass. His heart drummed inside his chest, heavy and fast. His cock was so hard it was almost painful. He eased up as she passed, shoved the door open, and leapt from the vehicle. She was carrying a cup in one hand, and with the other held her backpack in place over her shoulder.

Simon slapped a hand over her mouth and jerked her back against him with such force she lost her footing. A squeak of fear vibrated against his fingers. The cup flew to one side, hit the sidewalk, and splattered dark liquid across the concrete. He jabbed the hypodermic into her shoulder and pushed the plunger.

Seconds later she went limp, her hand fell away, and the backpack slid off her shoulder, falling heavily to the ground. He lifted her easily, placed her inside the truck, looped the seat belt around her, and bent to retrieve the backpack. He tossed the heavy, book-laden bag into the bed of the truck and rushed around to climb into the driver's seat.

He grinned as he pulled away from the curb and drove slowly south to the end of the street and cutoff for the lake.

✧ ✧ ✧

GENEVIEVE WATCHED WHILE each witch examined Finn once again. Juliet was so close, she was almost nose-to-nose with him. "You've done something to weaken the curse, Finn."

"What could I have done?" he asked. "Tell me so I might do it again."

Genevieve bit her lip and smiled. He was being a smartass, but serious, too.

Juliet narrowed her eyes at him. "Has anything different happened in the past few days? We were here just about a week ago, and your eyes were as yellow as a cat's."

"I havena seen my eyes in at least a century. I wouldna know if they have changed or not. I have been eatin' and drinkin' better than before, and have had a bath nearly every eve."

He was skirting the obvious thing that had happened between them. And avoided looking in her direction. Was it to save her from embarrassment? Or was it because if he said it out loud, they'd both have to acknowledge it?

How would the ladies react to their attraction?

Beatrice Stone's natural red hair and pale white skin set her apart from the others. "Were your eyes this color before you were cursed?"

"I dinna know, I havena seen them yet."

"Do you have a mirror in here, Genevieve?"

Genevieve crossed through the studio to the office and opened one of the desk drawers. She scooped up the small compact, but hesitated. Had Finn ever really seen his face? The reflection in a window, in water perhaps, but had he seen himself clearly?

"Have you found one, Genevieve?" Beatrice asked from the door.

Genevieve shoved the compact under some papers. "No."

She closed the drawer and turned to say something, but Beatrice was gone.

She returned to the group to find Beatrice had found the white ceramic bowl she used to hold water to moisten clay. She'd filled it, and holding her hand flat over the surface, she spoke some words in Latin. In an instant, the surface congealed into a bright, unblemished mirror.

Finn held out his hand, and she gave it to him. He gazed into it for long, silent moments, features frozen. His throat worked, and he handed it back to her. "Aye. They are the color they were when I was a man." Despite the careful tonelessness of his gravelly voice, pain layered every syllable. He clenched and unclenched his fists, his body stiff.

Genevieve looked away, trying hard to maintain her composure.

"Can you think of anything else that has changed since you arrived, Finn?"

"Butterbean shows me affection. And I have been accepted into the area wolf pack."

"So you're experiencing more social interaction than you did before," Beatrice commented, her tone so falsely upbeat,

Genevieve flinched.

Finn's mouth thinned, and he folded his arms, his biceps bulging.

Miranda sauntered close. "You may be able to break the curse by simply continuing to do the things you're doing now."

"For how long, lass?" There was a painful dignity in the way he met her eyes.

The group fell silent again.

"I've waited long enough. I need this to end, one way or another." Finn scanned the group until his attention settled on Juliet.

Once again he avoided looking at Genevieve. She swallowed against the thick emotion clogging her throat and wove her way free of the group to stand close beside him.

"Finn…" Juliet swallowed. "The spell will be dangerous."

"Aye. When can you do it?"

The women shifted, and several exchanged uncomfortable looks. "We need at least three or four days more to prepare," Juliet said. "We don't even know if it will work."

Finn nodded. "I winna hold it agin' ye if it doesn't. But I need ye to try."

He took a step toward the open door, his body language screaming his need to escape from the room, from them. Genevieve placed a hand on his bare shoulder. He stiffened, and she withdrew it.

Pain seemed to expand and stretch inside her chest, and tears streamed down her face.

Juliet glanced away, her eyes suspiciously bright. "Friday night at midnight."

"Good." He nodded to them. "I am grateful to all of ye for yer help."

He strode out of the studio, his wings unfurled, and he flew away.

The high spirits and chattiness of the hour before had ended.

"We need to meet at our place tomorrow," Juliet announced. "This is not an unusual creature, or a freakish anomaly. This is a man in great pain. He's survived for six hundred and sixty years alone, shunned, feared. It's time it ended. We need to help him end it."

Genevieve brushed the tears away with the back of her hand. "I have something that might help."

She went to the drawings on her worktable, and choosing one of the full facial views of Finn she had drawn, returned with it. "You've seen what he looks like now, but I know what he looked like before. I've studied his bone structure, and honed it down to human again. I thought it might give you a visual to concentrate on." She handed the drawing to Juliet.

The women gathered close and silently passed the drawing from one to the other. She read the same stomach-dropping shock of loss on their faces as she'd felt.

"How do you know this is what he looked like, Genevieve?" Miranda asked.

"I thought at one time I was going to be a forensic artist, so I studied human anatomy and took some classes. My first assignment was to draw a man who had been burned in a fire. I was able to reconstruct his face, but the experience... I couldn't distance myself from his suffering, and I had to switch over to sculpture and a studio degree. I transferred to the foreign exchange program right after that."

"You know that empathic thing we talked about before," Juliet said.

"Yes."

"That's why you couldn't distance yourself, and it's probably why Finn was able to reach you, even while he was encased in stone."

It made sense. But it still didn't change the way she felt about him. If he couldn't be wholly human again, what kind of relationship could they have?

The witches left, and the silence they left behind seemed that much more profound because of Finn's absence. Genevieve wandered to the statue she was working on and ran her hand over the forearm that strained to escape the stone. The blocky face had few features so far, but she could already see the face clearly.

She shouldn't wander around the house waiting for Finn to return, but she knew she would. She had to know he was okay.

So she reached for her coveralls and went to work.

✧   ✧   ✧

SIMON STEPPED AWAY from the bed and disposed of the condom in a bedside canister. It had been a shock to discover Mai was a virgin. Blood stained the bed and the inside of her thighs. How many girls hadn't at least experimented by the time they were a junior in college? Obviously one more than he'd thought.

Mai had stopped struggling, stopped screaming from beneath the pillowcase when he took her the third time. He liked them to scream and fight. Genevieve would have to learn to play the game so he could get what he needed. Or maybe things would be different with her, and he wouldn't need any of this.

The girl's wrists and ankles were red and raw from pulling at the leather cuffs binding her to the bed. A shame, because he couldn't get enough of her skin. It was firm and soft, flawless, with just a hint of her Asian descent, her body slender and perfect. Genevieve's sculpture had done her justice. He trailed his fingers up her thigh. She didn't flinch or react in any way. Perhaps she'd worn herself out.

He placed his hand on her midsection to check her breathing. Nothing. No movement at all. Perhaps she'd fainted. He tugged up the pillowcase he'd put over her head and saw a blue ring about her lips. Jerking the case off her head, he pounded on her chest and was rewarded when she gasped for air. He quickly pulled the case back down so she wouldn't see him when she opened her eyes.

"Shit!"

He backed away, nearly tripping over his feet. His heart beat high in his throat, and his breathing wheezed in and out in gulps. Pacing around the bed, his hands fisted, he continued to swear.

As his panic eased, rage began to build. He leaped upon the bed and straddled the girl. "If you hadn't fought, you wouldn't have nearly suffocated, you stupid bitch. It's your fault." He gripped her shoulders and shook her, her head flopping back and forth like it had been disconnected.

"I'm not through with you yet. Don't you fucking die on me, not yet."

CHAPTER 23

G ENEVIEVE BACKED AWAY from the sculpture and set aside the air hammer fitted with the chisel bit. The tool made the work go faster, but she had to take more care. It was good for large areas, but the finer details had to be honed with smaller instruments and sandpaper.

She worked on the face for nearly two days while she waited for Finn to come to grips with things. He'd been quiet, distant. It was probably the best for them both, but knowing didn't make it hurt any less.

Her shoulders ached from holding the tool and she rolled them. Time to stop. She was tired enough that she'd probably make a mistake.

Taking off her work clothes, mask, and goggles, she carried them outside to shake off the dust and hung them on a peg next to the door. After securing the studio, she went into the house. With a cold drink in hand, she wandered into the living room and flicked on the television. Leaning back on the couch, she propped her feet up on the coffee table, and allowed her mind to wonder while an endless stream of commercials played.

What would happen to Finn if the spell didn't work? She feared what he would do, not to others, but to himself. How could he go on like this?

The news came on, and she half listened to the broadcast. If the spell didn't work, she had to find a way to make things easier for him, to give him a reason to go on. Tears welled, and she covered her face with her hands.

The word Superstition spoken in the news anchor's generic accent caught her attention. "A college student enrolled in Superstition, Kentucky's community college has disappeared. Her roommate reported her missing on Wednesday night." A picture flashed on the screen. Genevieve caught her breath, recognition immediate. She'd done drawings of Mai for several days before starting the sculpture. Her eyes wandered to the figure before the window.

The news anchor continued, "Mai Chen left a local restaurant, The Dish, around ten o'clock, carrying a drink and her backpack. Her car was found just down the street from the restaurant. It did not appear to have been disturbed, and no personal possessions were inside. No one has seen or heard from her since Tuesday night. If you have seen this young woman, or have information about her whereabouts, please contact the Superstition Police Department at...."

Genevieve's breathing came in labored gulps, and her heart beat heavily in her ears. Mai would never just go off without contacting her roommate. And she would never miss classes. She was working hard to get her degree so she could help her mother and father immigrate to America from China. It was all she talked about while Genevieve sketched her.

Her roommate, Silvia, came with her for the modeling sessions, and had teasingly complained about how straitlaced and studious she was. They both were. Mai didn't have a boyfriend, or drink and party. Doing a work-study program and maintaining a 4.0 grade point average left little time for other things. Mai mentioned she studied at The Dish.

Something had happened to her. Someone had taken her.

Genevieve hit the button on the remote and turned off the television. Her stomach churning, her mouth tasting of bile, she paced the room. She had to do something. But what?

She still had some drawings of Mai's face would work well for flyers. She could print them and put them up in town. She needed to call Chase, Miranda's boyfriend, and offer to do that. Rushing into the kitchen, she picked up her cell phone, intent on the call, when an idea struck.

She hurried out the door to the breezeway and sat next to Finn's statue, placing a hand on his arm. "Something horrible has happened, Finn. A young woman I hired as a model has disappeared. Do you think you and the wolves could track her? She disappeared from a local restaurant on her way to her car. I know you have a lot on your mind right now, but I'd really appreciate it if you could try."

She waited impatiently for him to transition from sculpture to gargoyle.

FINN RECOGNIZED THE distress in Genevieve's voice, and fought against the constraints of his form. As soon as the sun sank behind the mountains, he writhed against his prison, but the hold the magic had over him was too strong. Dusk had fallen before the stone melted and he was free. "I can ask the wolves if they will do what ye ask. My appearing on a street downtown might cause confusion, but one of them might be thought just a dog."

Genevieve was so tense, her eyes revealing the shadow of worry and grief held in check. "Can you go now to find them, and see if they would be willing to help?"

"Aye. But we dinna know what she looks like."

She hurried away and entered her studio.

He had barely gotten his pants on when she returned with a paper, holding it out to him. "She's very petite, slender, barely comes up to my ear. Her hair and eyes are dark brown. She's Chinese. She disappeared just down the street from The Dish, a restaurant downtown."

He studied the drawing. "Do you have anythin' with her scent on it? 'Twill help the wolves track her."

She looked blank for a moment. "Yes, I think I do."

He tucked the drawing into the waistband of his pants and followed her to the studio door. She opened a cabinet and withdrew a robe. "While she posed for me, I gave her this to wear when I wasn't taking pictures and drawing her. I gave her all the photographs, and I've sold most of the drawings. All but a few of her face, and the one you have."

Finn didn't touch the garment. "The wolves will find the robe more helpful than the drawing, and I will take it with me. 'Twould be better to put it in something so my scent doesna blend with hers."

"Of course."

She rushed to get a bag, the kind she lined the rubbish bin out back. She put the robe inside, then handed it to him.

"I'll go and find the pack now, and return as soon as I can."

Genevieve pressed a bottle of water into his hand and

hugged him. "Be careful. It's not fully dark yet."

He held her because he couldn't resist the temptation, and because she needed the comfort. He sensed grief in her, tightly controlled. She believed the woman was already dead.

"I'll be careful," he assured her, and, with some reluctance, turned and walked to the edge of the yard.

Gripping the bottle in one hand and the bag in the other, he took to the sky. After some time, he came upon the pack in the field where he took Genevieve a few nights before. They were drinking from the creek, and several looked up as Finn landed close to them.

"Good eve, friends. My mistress, Genevieve, has asked me to approach ye for help. There is a missing woman, just a wee lass. This woman once posed for her as a model for her sculptures. She disappeared in the village at a place called The Dish. I have a bag with a garment in it with her scent. Would ye be after helping to find her?"

The alpha wolf yipped and trotted closer.

Finn knelt down and opened the bag. "The garment has Genevieve's scent on it, too."

The wolf stuck his head inside the garment for several moments. Then jerked back and took off across the field.

Finn paused to breathe in the scent from the bag as well. He knew Genevieve's as well as he did his own—he dreamed of it often enough. Genevieve's was like stone and apples with a hint of vanilla. The other woman's was more musky, with a hint of spices.

Then he laid the bag with the robe in it on the ground for the others to sniff, if they would, and took to the sky to follow the pack leader.

The large wolf loped across the field in long, graceful strides. He came upon a truck parked within a stand of trees and leapt into the bed. A man sat inside the vehicle. He started the truck, pulled out onto the road, and turned in the direction of town, leaving Finn wondering how he knew where to go.

Finn rose high in the sky, above the glow of the streetlights and signs, following the truck easily. It came to a stop in the parking lot of a small building with a large sign shaped like a pie atop it.

Why had the woman not parked there in front of the building? She would have been safe in the brightly lit lot.

The man got out of the truck and came around the side. Sliding a leash over the wolf's head, he waited while it jumped out of the truck. He walked the large animal down the street like a man walking his dog.

Yellow ribbons blocked off the sidewalk where the car had been parked. Finn landed on a building above the two to watch.

The man walked around the area with the wolf. The animal kept its nose to the ground, but stopped at a spot where a dark stain marred the sidewalk. The wolf trotted past the tape and moved down the street, following a scent. Finn leaped across the roofs of the buildings, following him. The animal stopped at the corner, and tilting his head back, scented the air. Finn did the same, but the odor of car exhaust disturbed his sense of smell. He longed to jump from the building to the street below, but there were still people moving about, on foot and in cars.

When wolf and man headed back down the street toward

the truck, he followed. Finn ran across the roof and used the side of the building as a springboard to leap into the air. He rose high again, and circled until the truck pulled out of The Dish's parking lot.

If need be, he'd return later, when everything was quiet, and see if he could pick up a sign or scent the wolf had missed.

He followed the vehicle back through town and landed in the stand of trees. The driver got out of the vehicle and walked toward him, nodding in greeting and extended his hand, "Braxton Myers. We've hunted together."

Finn clasped hands with him. "Finn. I'm glad to know ye."

The wolf jumped out of the back of the truck and stretched forward. His spine bowed, and the bends in his back legs straightened.

The sound of bone and joint being reformed into human triggered memories of Tearlach pounding him with his ham-sized fists. Finn swallowed against the rush of nauseous pain the memory evoked.

The wolf, now a man, stood a little more than six feet, with dark chestnut hair and a square-jawed face. He walked naked to the side of the truck, reached inside, and retrieved a pair of sweatpants, pulling them up while he joined the driver and Finn.

"Henry Sutton," he introduced himself. "She was put inside a vehicle and driven south. The scent was faint, since she was inside a car or truck. Her vehicle was one car down from the one she was placed in. I could smell her on the sidewalk in both places."

"What lies south of the village? I have not traveled there."

"The lake. There are empty cabins down there. She could have been taken anywhere. But the pack and I will have a look around. Want to come with us?"

"Aye, I do."

✧   ✧   ✧

FINN CAUGHT GLIMPSES of the pack as they streaked through the woods. Seeing the direction they were traveling, he flew ahead. For miles, all he saw was forest, until suddenly the trees fell back, and he came upon a huge body of water, the moon's glow casting a glittering path across its surface. Though it didn't have the same smell as the ocean, nor any waves, it was just as beautiful. He would enjoy fishing here another time.

He'd retrieved the bag with the robe in it so the wolves could get a fresh whiff of the woman's scent before searching, and flew along the bank to get a feel for the area. Houses of every size and shape were staggered along the water. Docks long and short shot out from the banks. Other houses were built deep into the woods. He began to get an idea of how huge an undertaking this would be. They could search for days and never reach them all.

How might they cover more area and search? They would have to divide each area of the lake into sections. It would work better if they looked at areas reached by the main roads leading into the lake.

Finn flew higher to see where those roads converged. He saw only two branching from the main highway. On one a truck wove its way toward the lake. It was Braxton, arriving ahead of the pack.

Every occupied house had a car in the driveway, while

others that appeared empty didn't. They should probably check the houses that appeared empty first.

The wolves emerged from the forest a long distance from where he was, and he turned back to meet them. The pack leader was standing, once again human, waiting for him when he landed.

"'Twill take weeks to search here unless we divide each section up and allow two wolves to search each area," Finn said.

"Braxton has a map in the truck. Let's section the areas off and spread out in grids, using the lake as the reference point."

"The driver would have to come into the area from the two main roads. Mayhap we can use the roads as a reference as well."

After a five-minute wait, Braxton pulled the truck up close to the dock on which the pack milled around. There was tension and excitement in the air. The wolves bunched together, waiting for their alpha to give the order. Braxton got the map out of the glove compartment and spread it on the hood. He raised a large flashlight high and pointed it at the map.

Henry leaned naked against the vehicle as he pointed out the landmarks. "Here's the river, here's the road. We can concentrate on this pie wedge right here until we've checked all the houses and cars in this area, then move over here to the wedge between the roads."

Finn nodded. "I'll search for disturbed areas on the ground around the lake, anything floating in the water, and the house boats."

"Be careful on the boats. Some of the people who own

them have weapons on board. Should anyone find who we're looking for, dead or alive, you'll hear the howls."

"Or my roar," Finn added. He handed the bag with the robe in it to Braxton, left Henry to direct the wolves, and took to the sky.

Pinpointing the edge of the wedge Henry had designated, he flew up the mountain to the top, then glided back down. He searched for any disturbed soil around the houses, but every house had bushes, trees, and flowers planted like Genevieve, making it difficult to decide which was decoration, and which disturbance. He paused at some of the empty houses, scented the areas around the doors and windows, and spied inside.

He moved further downhill and flew out over the water. He checked every dock and small craft that fell into the wedge, then suddenly realized how many houseboats there were. He was of less use on land, so he would concentrate on the boats.

He glided over the first one and circled it.

If he landed, it might rock the boat and alert anyone inside.

If he landed in the water, he'd drown. His wings became a weight, and would drag him down.

He chose a houseboat that was dark and seemed deserted, somewhat separated from the rest, and landed as lightly on the roof as he could. He climbed down the ladder at the back of the structure and walked around the deck. The smell of fish and burnt charcoal blended with that of the humans who used it, but there were no traces of Mai.

He moved on to the next one, also separated from the rest, then the next. He had soon checked nine of the boats. The tenth was much like the rest. No boat or dingy was tied to it. He landed on the roof and climbed down, as before.

As he passed a window on the port side he caught the scent of blood. He moved cautiously around to the foredeck and paused before the front door. Again he smelled blood—not animal blood, because it didn't have a wild, earthy scent.

Yes, this was human blood. He hooked a claw in the door handle and tugged it sideways. The door would not give, so he gripped the handle and pulled. The lock sprung, and the door slid open on its runners. Hesitating, he debated whether or not to enter, and settled on sticking his head into the opening and breathing in the smell. Urine, blood, and sickness flooded his senses, along with a faint whiff of spice.

He stepped inside, and the size of the tiny, enclosed space had him pausing to take in a deep breath. The faint light from other occupied boats penetrating the narrow blinds did little to guide him. He concentrated on the dim glow of a small light down a narrow hall and took measured steps toward it. His lowered wings brushed each side, and he folded them as tightly as he could.

The light came from a small camping lantern next to a bed. In an instant, he took in the naked female body lying prone, manacled to the corners of the bed frame. Her eyes were covered by a strip of fabric, her hair tangled in the strip as well.

A metal pole stood near the bed with a bag of fluid. There was a tube running from it to her arm. Breathing, deep and labored, filled the room. Even from the doorway he could see the raw swelling of her wrists and ankles. Pity struck him, and outrage gathered and expanded in his chest. His first instinct was to cover her nudity, then free her, but if she woke and saw him, it would terrify her. She needed care and help.

He crept back down the hall to the front door. He knew nothing of the modern engines on boats, but he might be able to tow the boat to shore. He circled the deck to see what was holding the vessel in place. An anchor and a heavy rope attached to a float of some kind held it stationary. He pulled the anchor up, and rushing around to the rope, he ripped at it with his claws, shredding it and freeing the boat from the float.

Taking off from the edge of the railing, he strained against the weight, his wings sounding like the sails of a boat caught by the wind. He threw his weight into it, pumping his wings as hard as he could, until he got the vessel moving toward one of the empty docks. The weight of the vessel made it difficult to maneuver, and stopping it would prove a challenge, so he spent the rest of the journey plotting how to stop it next to the dock safely.

Fifteen feet from the long wooden dock, he pulled the rope sideways and turned the vessel parallel, hoping it would bump hard against the structure. When it didn't, he released the rope and gripped the metal railing that ran along the edge of the deck. With a push and pull movement, he eased the houseboat in against the dock. Then he climbed the ladder and, standing atop the roof, let loose a roar that echoed across the lake.

Lights came on in several houses and some of the houseboats nearby.

When he heard a heavy engine start up from down the lake, Finn flew toward it.

CHAPTER 24

WAITING WAS AGONY. And sleep was impossible.

Genevieve paced the floors while visions of what Mai might be going through filled her mind, growing worse as the minutes passed. What if they never found her? They said the first forty-eight hours were the most important in solving a crime, and if they didn't find her within that time, what then?

As the hands of the clock crept closer to dawn, anxiety gnawed at her, tightening the muscles across her neck and shoulders until they ached.

A sound much like snapping sheets alerted her to Finn's return. She rushed to the breezeway door and down the patio steps just as he landed on the lawn.

She threw herself against him with a grateful embrace. "I've been worried. You've been gone all night, and it's almost dawn."

He held her away to look into her face. "I found her on one of the houseboats on the lake. She is alive, but she is badly hurt."

Quick tears rushed down her cheeks. "But she's alive."

"Aye."

The sleeves of her T-shirt were smeared when he dropped his hands, and for the first time she realized he was bleeding.

She grasped his hands and turned them palm up. They were scraped and raw.

"'Tis from towing the houseboat to shore."

She rushed to the cabinet where she'd stored the supplies he used that first night and returned with the peroxide and cotton balls.

"They will heal when I change to stone, Genevieve."

Maybe not. "This will soothe them until they're healed." It helped her to care for him in some way. There seemed so little she could do for him, or for Mai.

He saved a woman's life tonight.

Though his comments were vague, undoubtedly an attempt to shield her, from Finn's description it was clear that Mai had been taken, imprisoned on the houseboat, drugged, and raped. Braxton Myers and Henry Sutton called the police and told them they found the houseboat drifting and the door broken open.

It was easier for the community to accept that local men discovered Mai, rather than a mystical creature.

In fact, Genevieve marveled at how surprisingly easy it was for her to accept that Henry and Braxton were wolves at night and men during the day. Why not? She was already living with the impossible.

She had to know more. "How did Mai seem?"

"She would not awaken. There was a tube running to her arm, which Henry said was meant to make her sleep."

"Was she beaten?"

"I saw no bruises or wounds, but there was—blood. 'Twas the blood I smelled first."

She bit her lip, her eyes burning. Mai's life would be forever changed by this. She shook her head and closed her eyes against the images that flashed through her mind of what Mai might have endured.

Finn wrapped an arm around her waist and held her against him. She leaned into him, grateful for his comfort.

"She's never had a boyfriend. She said she wanted to wait until her parents were here in this country. She said she didn't have time for one. I don't think she'd ever been with a man." She curled her arms up over his back and buried her face against his shoulder. "That seems somehow even more tragic and disgusting." Tears slid down her cheeks.

Finn stroked her hair. "She will be whole again, but 'twill take time."

His fingers caressed the nape of her neck, and she relaxed against him.

"How did women of your time deal with this?" she asked after she calmed a little.

"If they went before the laird, the man would have to pay for the harm he had done her with coin or property. Sometimes the man was forced to wed her. More oft her *athair* or *bhràithrean* exacted justice."

Genevieve shuddered. "Marriage to your rapist would be the worst kind of hell. How could they do that to her?"

"It was a different time, lass. A woman was looked at as her *athair's* property then. He could demand recompense for her maidenhead through marriage or property or both."

"Dear God. It would be more just if the man was tied down and she was allowed to exact her revenge with a belt and blade."

"Aye, 'twould, to be sure. I canna understand why any

man would have need to tie a woman down and treat her with such violence. I wanted very much to set the lass free, but feared I would frighten her if she awoke."

She leaned back to look up at him. "You did the right thing. Did you wipe the door handle clean of prints?" she asked.

"Nay. Braxton did, and the ladder as well. Is it true they can search for the villain using the markings from the pads of his fingers?"

"Yes." She studied the loops, arches and whorls on his fingertips. They looked so human. He still looked like the beast, but a change had occurred. She reached up and brushed the shaggy hair from his forehead. Your hair's growing. Has it grown before?"

"Nay, it has stayed the same since... I canna remember."

"It's longer now." She looped it back behind his ear. Was the tip less pointed than usual? But when he changed from flesh to stone, there was no change in the sculpture.

"How can ye look at me as I am and want to touch me in any way?"

His gravelly voice sounded husky.

The intense longing in his sky blue eyes crashed right through her defenses, triggering a dropping sensation in the pit of her stomach, and a tingling heat between her thighs.

How could she feel this way after learning about Mai?

Because he had nothing to do with her assault, and everything to do with her rescue.

"If your face had been disfigured in battle, would the women of your time have refused to touch you, Finn?"

"I wasna disfigured, lass. But as I am now, none would

have ever allowed me near. If they had, they would have been damned by the church. I am a beast, not a man."

"You are both, Finn. You have a man's reason. You have great tenderness in you. I've seen it in the way you handle Butterbean, and in the way you treat me. You showed understanding and sympathy in the way you handled the situation with Mai. When are you going to stop blaming yourself for what was done to you?"

He shook his head. "If I have paid enough, why has the curse not lifted?"

"Maybe part of breaking it is learning to forgive yourself."

His throat worked as he swallowed. "I believe 'tis ye who are responsible for the changes I am going through, Genevieve. Ye see me as more than I am. Perhaps more than I have ever been."

"You saved a young woman's life tonight, Finn. If the man who kidnapped her and hurt her had returned first, he would have continued to hurt her. More than likely, he would have eventually killed her and dumped her body in the lake. You can't ever bring back Isabel, but saving Mai has to count for something, doesn't it?"

"I hope it does." He looked toward the horizon. It was growing lighter. "The cuffs she was tied down with were leather. They were stained and worn, and, I have no doubt, well-used."

"So she may not be the only woman he's done this to."

"Aye." His hands worked up and down her back in soothing strokes. "I dinna wish ye to go anywhere alone, Genevieve. You must take care."

"I will."

"Should ye go anywhere at night, I can follow and protect ye."

She was often alone wherever she went. "I seldom go anywhere at night, Finn. But if I do, you're welcome to follow me."

He nodded. His looked again at the horizon. "I canna protect ye during the day. Ye must be careful."

"I will be. I promise."

"The day is coming." His hands tightened on her arms as though he sought to delay the moment when he would be trapped again in the stone.

Dawn tinged the sky with a pale shade of blue-gray. He caught his breath but didn't move toward the block. His muscles bunched as he fought against the call.

The sun rose over the mountains, and for a moment, the light struck Finn's face. His pupils contracted, and his eyes looked silver-gray with the change. He looked down at her, and for a split second, his features seemed to shift from the brutish grotesque to the man.

There were subtle differences, but her drawings were very close. His wings were no longer there, and for an instant he was wholly human. She lifted her hands to cup his face, but he was torn from her in a rush, one second there, and the next he was once again the frozen stone creature crouching on the block.

The black sweatpants lay at her feet in rags. Genevieve swallowed a cry of frustration and pain. Voicing it would only steal his hope.

But she had felt the strength of the magic while it yanked him toward the base. Turning water to a mirror would be a parlor trick in comparison. Juliet and Miranda needed to feel it for themselves.

✧ ✧ ✧

WHY WASN'T SHE sleeping? Simon watched Genevieve bring the cat in and go straight to her room. She set the cat at the foot of the bed then climbed under the covers. She had been up nearly all night, as he had been, watching her go from window to window, looking out as though waiting for something. And now she was finally going to sleep when she normally would be getting up.

Something was wrong. Something was upsetting her. But what? He needed to go out today and find out. She might talk to him about what was keeping her awake, and why she kept having that odd group of women at her house at all hours. If he could figure out a way to ask. The women had been all over the studio the other night while he'd been occupied with Genevieve's protégé, Mai. Watching it on the recorded video, it seemed to him their presence at her house was odd. They seemed to be having some kind of meeting.

It was Juliet and Miranda Templeton's fault. They were getting Genevieve involved in something. Well, he'd put a stop to that soon enough. Genevieve would soon have no time for anyone but him and her work.

He had never known her to sleep during the day. Never. But he'd have to give her some time to rest before going out to check on her. He turned the camera app off and wandered into the gallery.

Keith stood at the door, looking out onto Main Street. He turned to speak over his shoulder. "Genevieve's framed drawings arrived, and I unboxed them and hung them in the green room. They're stunning."

"Good. I'll go look at them before I call the clients who bought them."

"The young girl in them…She's quite extraordinary."

"I thought so too." He hardened just thinking about Mai as he wandered through the many rooms to the area they called the green room to stare and gloat over the two hung drawings. Framed in sleek black frames, the deep red mats were a brilliant choice to display the charcoal sketches.

He shoved his hands into his pockets so he could caress the aching length of his erection while he looked at them. Pity he'd have to wait until dark before going back out to the houseboat to see her.

At least the medication he'd given her would keep her asleep for at least eight hours.

He'd been a little wary about giving it to her, but he couldn't leave her unattended without putting a gag on her, and after her close call, he didn't want to cover her mouth. Keeping her sedated was his only option. She'd be fine until he returned, and if she wasn't…it would be a pity, but he'd weight the body and dispose of it in a nearby cove. She'd never be found, and if she was, the water would have destroyed any evidence.

"What do you think?" Keith asked.

"I think your assessment was correct. They're gorgeous."

Keith studied him, and Simon smoothed out his expression. "Have you met the real model?"

The lie came easily. "No. But I'd like to."

"I would too."

Simon's brows rose. "I didn't think women were your thing."

Keith's jaw tightened. "I can appreciate beauty wherever I find it, Simon. Speaking of which, I wonder why Genevieve never does self-portraits? She's certainly beautiful enough."

He turned his attention back to the drawings "I believe it's because she's more aware of other people than she is herself."

"I believe she's empathic."

Simon looked a question at him.

"She can sense other people's emotions."

Simon had never thought of that. Could she? A shiver worked its way up his spine. "Why don't you ask her next time she comes in?"

"I think I will, but I believe she is. Look at the emotion on the girl's face. It's as though she's looking through a barrier toward the future."

If she was, she'd never see it. He'd see to it. He couldn't take the chance that she might offer evidence against him. Even if she hadn't seen him, she heard his voice and felt his body. Better safe than sorry.

"Are you going to call Genevieve to come into town and see these?"

"Not quite yet. She called earlier and said she hadn't slept well. I thought I'd give her some time to rest, then call her."

"She's going to regret selling these. She always does. It's like she's giving up her baby."

Simon laughed. "I told her the same thing."

Keith went back to the showroom, and Simon returned to his office to call some other artists whose work was popular, but not as lucrative as Genevieve's. Around three he called and invited her to come in and view the drawings.

When she wandered in around four, dark circles discolored the skin under her eyes, and she looked tired. She stood in front of the drawings and gazed at them with open regret. "I want to pull them, Simon."

For several moments he seemed unable to respond. "They've already been paid for, Genevieve."

"I don't feel right about selling them."

"Why not?"

"Didn't you hear about the girl found in a houseboat on the lake? The one who was missing? It seems the boat broke free of its mooring and drifted into one the docks. Some fishermen found her tied up inside, assaulted and drugged."

Panic like an electric shock raced through Simon's entire body. "When did this happen?"

"She went missing on Tuesday night, but was found very early this morning, about five o'clock."

"Shit!" Simon murmured. He'd discarded the condoms down the toilet, and scrubbed the wastebasket and changed the sheets. Once she had succumbed to the drugs, he even bathed her to remove any DNA. But what about fingerprints? He hadn't wiped down the room yet. *Fuck!*

"I called her roommate, Silvia. She's just now come out of the drug-induced sleep and is being questioned by the police."

"How is she?"

"There are signs of strangulation and other injures. They think she'll heal physically. Emotionally she's bound to be very fragile."

The effort to contain her reaction to Mai's injuries flushed her features with color and her eyes narrowed with rage. "The girl was Mai, my model. Because of her experience, selling nude drawings of her would be in extremely poor taste. And if they catch the man who raped and tortured her, and this goes to trial...the monster's defense will bring this up and make a big deal out of it. I'm not about to do anything that will make this more difficult for her than it already is or will be."

Monster? Monster! He controlled his own anger by concentrating on the financial repercussions of the whole thing. This shit was going to cost him a fortune.

When she swiveled to face him, he nodded. "I understand."

"That goes for the sculpture I did of her as well. I'll keep it, or give it to Mai if she wants it."

Why hadn't he thought about how she would respond to this? Because he'd never intended for the girl to be found. "No one will ever know it was her, Genevieve."

"She'll know, and I will, too." Her eyes glazed with tears. "It will never be viewed publicly. Not unless she decides she wants it to be."

Shit! That sculpture could have brought in ten thousand dollars, maybe more. "You said you changed her features, Genevieve. No one but you and she will know it's her."

She eyed him with a look on her face he couldn't fathom. "That's the point, Simon. She'll know it's her, and I will, too. She's been raped and tortured. To know people are seeing her naked would be..." She shook her head. "I can't do it to her. If it was me, I'd want it destroyed."

"You can't, Genevieve. It's one of the most beautiful things I've ever seen. Please, just put it away until you can talk to her about it."

That bitch Mai needed to die. But then Genevieve would probably find reason to bury it with her, or place it on her grave as a marker or something. Fuck!

"Can you take that kind of financial hit?" he asked.

"I have another sculpture almost finished. And I'm doing the drawings for the second of this series. I can hold out until I get it done and sell it."

He'd have to push her to finish it quickly. And he'd have to concentrate on selling some of his other artists' work online to make it. Damnit!

"I have to go. I'll be happy to speak to the Richards myself if you feel I need to."

"No, I'll take care of it. What would you like me to do with the drawings?"

"I have others. See if the Richards will allow us to switch them out with the same mats and frames. Just explain to them what's happened. I'm sure Mrs. Richards will understand."

He breathed a sigh of relief. If she had other drawings she was willing to part with, it would make the whole thing less disastrous. If he could sell the Richards on them. He'd have to. "When would you like me to come out and get them?"

"Give me a couple of hours, and you can meet me at the studio. I'll need to clean them up a little."

"I'll be there." He glanced at his watch. "At four. Will that be okay?"

"Yes. That will be fine." She was already far away, worrying about a girl who was a danger to his freedom, and should mean nothing to her. Why did she care about any of this? Mai was just a model. She'd been paid for her work.

"I hope they catch this bastard and put him in jail for the

rest of his life." She stormed out of the gallery. He watched while she got into her car and backed out into the street.

A monster and a bastard. That's what she thought of him. Of what he'd done.

What would she think when he tied her up the first time? The only thing that had kept him from breaking in and doing so was the money. And once he had her... She'd either do as he wanted, or he'd kill her. She was *his*. Everything she did as an artist was his. He'd let her run the show too long. It was time he took the reins and settled things between them.

But now he needed to deal with Mai. He had never left any of his women alive, and wouldn't make an exception with her. He'd have to go to the hospital and see if he could find out where she was being kept. But he had to take care of the Richards first. He went into his office and placed the call.

CHAPTER 25

G ENEVIEVE CAUGHT THE elevator to the fourth floor of the hospital and walked down the hallway to room four-eleven. A policeman sat outside the door, and she paused beside him. "Mai asked me to come by."

He picked up a notebook next to his chair. His utility belt rattled as he rose to his full six feet four inches. "Your name, please, miss, and some identification."

"Genevieve Warren." She dug in her purse for her wallet and pulled out her license.

He studied it and looked up. "You're the artist, aren't you?"

"Yes."

"My fiancée is into art, and we went to the gallery last year on Secret Avenue to see an exhibit and saw *Reclining Woman*. It was like seeing a live woman. I kept expecting her to open her eyes."

"Thank you."

He got back to what she was here for. "Besides her room-mate, you're the only person she's asked for."

Genevieve nodded. "I promise not to upset her. I'm just going to sit with her for a little while and offer her a shoulder to lean on."

"That's probably what she needs."

Genevieve braced herself. When Juliet had said she was empathic, she hadn't known the half of it. There were times when body language and facial expression had nothing to do with her knowing how someone felt. The pain Mai was experiencing was going to be very, very difficult for her to witness and feel.

She knocked on the wooden surface and waited for Mai to invite her in before pushing the door open.

Mai lay curled upon the bed, her eyes dry of tears. Bandages circled both wrists. Dark reddish-purple bruises marred the skin around her neck. An IV trailed into the bend of her arm, also darkened by an ugly black bruise.

Genevieve padded slowly toward her and paused beside the bed. The silent suffering she read in the depths of the other woman's eyes, felt radiating from her, gripped her heart and gave it a squeeze.

Wordlessly she set her purse aside and climbed up on the bed to enfold Mai in a hug. When Mai began to cry, pouring out her grief and confusion in disjointed words and sobs, it was almost a relief.

✧ ✧ ✧

TWO HOURS LATER, with Mai asleep, Genevieve slid off the bed. She tore out a page from a small pad in her purse and wrote a note telling Mai she'd call later and return tomorrow. She left it propped on the bedside table and crept out of the room. A different policeman sat outside the door, this one was shorter and wiry.

"You won't leave her, will you?"

Resentment flashed across his face, but when she contin-ued to stare at him, his expression leveled out. "My job is to stay right here and keep everyone but the nurses or doctors out. That's what I'm going to do."

"The man who did this came close to suffocating her. She almost died. If he comes back to finish what he started…"

"He's not getting past me, lady."

"Good." She tried to project a little more confidence than she felt. "I've left a note for her by the bed, and I'll call later and come back by tomorrow. I've asked her to call if she needs me."

"I'll check in on her in a little while and tell her in case she doesn't see the note."

"Thank you." Her nerves seemed hyperaware of every-thing, and her skin raw with emotion. She didn't feel right about leaving Mai, but Simon was due at her house at any moment.

She'd promised Mai the drawings wouldn't be sold, or the sculpture. It was time she kept a piece of her own work anyway.

Her head was pounding by the time she pulled into her driveway. When she let herself into the house, Butterbean rushed to meet her at the door. She tossed her purse onto the table by the door and picked him up, cuddled him, then set him back on his feet. Crossing to the cabinet next to the sink, she found the aspirin, filled a juice glass with water and washed two down.

She sat at the kitchen table to wait for them to take affect and covered her face with her hands. She felt drained, but Mai had been better when she left. For now.

Why Mai? Why had he wanted to hurt Mai over and over again? She almost died, and he'd brought her back, only to hurt her again.

Finn called himself a monster, but he wasn't. The man who'd done this was a monster.

The doorbell rang, and she raised her head and released a breath. She didn't want to deal with Simon and his demands. But the Richards needed to be appeased.

"You look exhausted, Genevieve." Simon's tone sounded edgy, almost like an accusation.

She bit back a sharp retort. "I'm all right. How did it go with the Richards?

"They understand why you want to withdraw the drawings. They were disappointed, but willing to look at the others to see if there are any they like as well."

"Good." That at least took some of the pressure off her. "I can imagine how much persuasion it must have taken to get them to agree to that. I appreciate all you've done, Simon."

"Mrs. Richards was very shocked at what had happened. She kept looking at the drawings and crying and saying, 'that poor girl.' I thought they'd back out of the deal completely, but she rallied and decided she really wants to see what else you have. I think she was impressed by your sensitivity to the model's situation."

"Women have an instinctive, visceral reaction to another woman's pain when it comes to this, Simon. It's one of the worst things that can happen to any of us. Our bodies are our own, and to be forced to share such an intimacy with a stranger against her will, and coupled with the strangling... It makes me ill to think about it."

It made her ill to hear Mai talk about it. Mai had never known what being with a man was like, and now it would be a long, long time before she'd want a man to touch her again—if ever.

Simon eyed her with an expression of sympathy, but his eyes seemed detached, analytical. She reached out and laid a hand on his arm. She felt nothing when she touched him. Just a void. Maybe this was why she didn't find him sexually attractive, even though he was physically handsome.

"Come into the studio, and I'll get out the drawings so we can go through them together."

"Sounds like a good idea."

In a cabinet in her office she slid open a wide, flat drawer containing the drawings she'd used for sculptures. Some she'd completed, others were just ideas.

"Who is this?" Simon asked.

She turned to see him holding her drawing of Finn. "Just a man I saw one day. I thought he had a compelling face, so I drew him."

"You can draw people from memory with this much detail?"

"Sometimes. I've drawn numerous pictures of my Gran and of Andy."

He turned the drawing to face her. "This much detail after just meeting him in passing."

"Actually, not. His face was disfigured. Sometimes I see the bone structure beneath and can imagine what was before, from what is."

"Disfigured?"

"Yes."

"I don't believe you." Simon's flat tone held a note of suppressed fury.

Silence stretched. Alarm sent prickles up Genevieve's spine, and made the hairs on her arms stand on end. Her heart hammered hard, and her breathing came in shallow gulps. Something had risen between them. Every instinct urged her to get out of the room, to get away from him. Only the weakness of her limbs kept her standing her ground.

She bent and opened the bottom drawer and removed a photograph and the drawing she'd done of the burned man, restructuring his features as they had been before the fire that had killed him. She laid it on the table before Simon. "I once thought I'd become a forensic artist, but decided I couldn't stomach looking at skulls all day and reconstructing faces of people who had died horrible deaths, or suffered as this man suffered."

He picked up the drawing and looked at the photo. His throat worked as he swallowed. "You never mentioned this before."

"There has been no reason to. My art took a different turn when I was accepted in the foreign exchange program and went to Florence."

He lapsed into silence for a long moment. "You're much too sensitive to work in a field surrounding you with death. You were meant to do what you do."

Her muscles shook like Jell-O as she lifted a stack of drawings. She had to get out of this enclosed space and away from him. "You'll be able to sort through these better on my work table in the studio."

He set Finn's drawing down atop the other one and preceded her into the studio. She placed the sketches in front of him and froze when Simon laid a hand on her shoulder. "I hope you'll forgive me for what I said, Genevieve. I just saw the drawing and I thought…I was jealous. I know it isn't an attractive trait. But I've waited a long time for you to get over your grief. You can't blame me for not wanting someone else to come between us before I've even had a chance to win you over."

She deftly dipped out from under the light pressure of his hand. "I still have a few more drawings to get out. I'll be right back."

Her mouth was dry with anxiety as she stacked the rest of the sketches. She carried them to the table. "I'll get us some tea while you look through them."

In the kitchen, she took her time fixing two glasses of iced tea. While she stood at the counter she took deep, calming breaths. She leaned against the cabinet and dropped her face into her hands.

What had been in that room with her? The man she thought she knew, and the man she'd sensed were two different beings. She'd actually been frightened. Was still frightened.

Even if Finn hadn't come into her life, she'd never trust Simon enough for her feelings to grow. She'd never be able to tolerate being controlled. Although to an extent she'd allowed him to control her already. But that would stop now.

He'd been a wonderful agent, but unless he was willing to step back and keep their relationship on a professional level, she'd have to search for someone else.

She carried the glasses of iced tea the studio and, using a

felt coaster, she placed the tea close by his elbow and turned her attention to the drawings he was sorting.

She studied several with a critical eye. She hated judging her work, because she always noticed things she wanted to tinker with and change. She often made adjustments to the sculptures she created from the drawings, making scale models from clay before doing the finished piece. She thought in terms of three dimensions. And though the drawings were sketched in perspective, they still were too flat to suit her.

She pulled out a drawing she did of Juliet from the back. The line of shoulders spine and hips were so perfectly symmetrical, the tilt of her head so beautiful, yet not enough of her features showed to compromise her identity. She extended it to Simon. "This one, I think."

He studied it in silence for a moment. "Yes. This would be a comparable image. Just beautiful. Is there another?"

"I did several." She fished through until she found some of the others. She stacked them carefully so she wouldn't smudge them. Then turned her attention to some of her earlier work. She compared the quality of five years before until now and had to admit she'd advanced.

She sipped her tea and waited. When the phone rang, she went into her office to answer it. Mai's voice sounded almost normal. Her normal sing-song quality, though stifled some, came through. "They're discharging me from the hospital in the morning, and I'm leaving town for a little while."

"Good. It will do you good to distance yourself from the area until they find him. What about school?"

"My professors have agreed to allow me to do work online with them for the rest of the semester. There's only a couple of weeks left."

"I'm so glad. Is there anything more I can do to help?"

"You already did, Gen. Having you here this afternoon to just listen…"

Genevieve could hear the tears in her voice and felt the sting of them in her own. "You can call me any time. And when you feel up to it, I'll come visit."

"Thanks. I'd like that."

"Is Sylvia with you?"

"Yes. She's staying the night with me here."

"Good. Take good care of yourself, Mai."

"I will. And thank you for pulling the drawings and the sculpture. I know how much that cost you monetarily…and otherwise."

"That doesn't matter. You matter more."

"I know you mean that, and it means so much to me because you do, Gen. I'll call in a few days."

"I'll be glad to hear from you."

She hung up the phone and turned to find Simon standing in the doorway behind her.

"I think I've found three equally beautiful pairs of drawings to show the Richards."

"Good." She followed him back into the studio, looked over the sketches, and agreed they were probably comparable to the ones of Mai. Two were some she'd done of Juliet, two were of a child at the park downtown, and the last two were of the sculpture she was finishing now. She used a kneaded eraser to clean up a place or two on each drawing, then retrieved a portfolio for him to carry them to his office.

"Are you going to forgive me for what I said, Genevieve?"

Simon asked, his expression solemn.

"It's already forgiven, Simon. But…"

She dragged in a deep breath, braced herself, and realized she was shaking and her heart was about to fly out of her chest. "I'm used to doing as I like, making my own decisions, seeing whom I want. I think you'd be more satisfied with someone who is more submissive. And there's nothing wrong with that. Some women want a man to take charge of their lives and make all the decisions. But I'm never going to be that woman, Simon. I've been on my own for too long. Been responsible for my own property, my business."

She touched his arm again, briefly. "I think it's best that we keep our relationship on a professional level. It's been profitable for us both so far. We make a good team there, but I think we're both too strong-willed to make it work in a romantic sense. It would be a constant power struggle between us, and that would negatively impact our business relationship."

He stood completely still, his eyes tracing her features, his expression blank.

Her heart raced and her stomach ached with tension. Her mouth was so dry her throat closed entirely when she swallowed.

"You're probably right." His casual tone threw her for a moment.

Relief stormed through her, and the tension tightening her stomach and shoulders released a degree, but there was still something in his demeanor that triggered an anxious wariness.

"I'll get back to you regarding what the Richards say about these other drawings. I'd like to have all six framed, though, and hang them in the gallery."

"That sounds good. Thanks, Simon. I appreciate all you do for me."

"As you say, it's profitable for us both. What would you like me to do with the drawings of Mai?"

"I'd like them back." His distant, controlled tone was giving her the creeps.

"I'll see to it. And we'll talk later."

"Okay."

She followed him through the house and let him out.

She waited for him to reach his car before turning the lock on her front door...and, with a rush of goose bumps, realized she'd been afraid the click of the lock would set him off.

Every moment they were together this time, she'd been braced for an explosion. Her shoulder muscles felt painfully tight.

When Simon pulled out of the driveway, she went to the breezeway door and unlocked it, walking down the steps to Finn's block.

"I'm here." His deep gravelly voice came from the porch. She turned to find him sitting on the front steps, his elbows on his knees. She moved to sit beside him.

"How is the lass?" he asked.

"She's going to leave town for a while until they catch the man."

"Good."

Tears welled up, and she pressed the heels of her palms against her eyes, her elbows on her knees. Finn rubbed a comforting hand against her back. The tears fell faster. When she turned against him, his arm surrounded her, and the lingering feelings of fear and distress eased.

The gradual awareness of his firm, muscular, bare chest distracted her. She breathed in the scent of soap on his skin and his own natural scent. It was like sunshine on clean sheets, with a hint of mint. Her body responded, though she willed it not to.

She drew back to look up at him. He leaned his forehead against hers, and the pain in his expression had fresh tears rolling down her cheeks.

His voice roughened. "I canna kiss ye with this mouth, Genevieve, but I long to."

Her heart tumbled at his words and the look in his eyes.

"If the spell works, 'twill be the first thin' I will wish t'do."

"After six hundred and sixty years, I imagine there will be numerous women you'll want to kiss."

He shook his head. "I have learned my lesson well, lass. I will never make light of a kiss or a caress ever again."

But if the spell didn't break the curse…what then? They fell silent and held each other.

Finn asked, "What does the man Simon do for ye?"

"He's my agent. He finds buyers for my artwork."

"He wants more."

"How do you know that?"

"He was swearing when he got into his car."

He had been so controlled in the house. Spooky controlled. "I don't have those kinds of feelings for him."

"'Twould do ye well to have a man to protect ye."

She started to say *I have you*, but cut off the thoughts and the words. He didn't need that kind of pressure when he was facing…whatever he was facing…tomorrow night.

"He called ye a bitch when he left."

It didn't surprise her, but it still gave her stomach a wrench. "He was upset."

"I dinna trust him, Genevieve, and I dinna think ye should, either."

"We're just business associates, Finn. Nothing more."

"If a man canna be trusted with yer person, he shouldna be trusted with yer money."

The wisdom of his words was undeniable. She was stuck between loyalty to Simon for all he had done to help build her career, and the breathless fear that had overwhelmed her while she was in the office with him this afternoon.

What would he do if she ended their business relationship?

He wouldn't be nearly as controlled as he was tonight. Of that, she was certain.

And why hadn't she noticed his romantic interest in her? When she looked back on the past two years of their relationship, all she saw was his helpfulness in finding a crew to remodel her kitchen and bathrooms, and his concern when she was too devastated to work.

He'd been waiting for her grief to abate after Andy was out of the picture. She shivered at the thought. The paint on Andy's car was from a dark blue ford truck, not the Corvette Simon had before he bought the Jaguar. Simon couldn't have anything to do with Andy's accident.

"I'll fix us some food."

"No need, lass. I caught some fish and cleaned them. I'd like to try my hand at grilling them, if ye'll allow me to."

"Sure." He was slowly becoming a twenty-first-century guy. "Tell me what you'd like to have with them, and I'll fix it."

"Baked potato, loaded…and something green, because ye like it."

Yeah, he was turning into a twenty-first century man. "I have some asparagus, and I don't think you've ever had it before." She'd been trying to introduce him to a variety of vegetables. He'd eat anything, but thus far his favorites were loaded baked potatoes and little else. "I'll show you how to grill it with the fish."

✧　✧　✧

WHILE THEY ATE, they talked about the book he was reading, which was about breakthroughs in medicine.

"I am amazed that anyone survived in my time. Some of the wounds I sustained during my training should have killed me."

"Your body was strong from exercise, lots of sunshine, and plenty of food."

"Better food than had by the villagers who grew it. And I do enjoy my daily baths, where before few of us bathed in the winter. 'Twas too cold, and hot water was hard to come by unless ye lived in the castle." Finn grinned. "I dinna have head lice or body lice or fleas, either, and I've noticed none of the wolves get them, either."

"Something I am very grateful for. Just the idea makes me want to scratch my head." She gave a delicate shiver.

Finn laughed. "The women would comb their hair with fine combs to rid themselves of them, and put fresh rushes with herbs on the floor to keep away the fleas."

He changed the subject to the latest movie he'd watched

on the television she installed just beneath the eaves of the house. He was a little surprised by the language and the love scenes. Though in his time it wasn't unheard of to come upon a couple swiving in a field now and then, the blatant imagery had been embarrassing, but also fascinating to watch.

And it left him with a strong longing for Genevieve. Would making love be as intense as the scenes in the movie? More so, probably, because they had a bond. They were constantly walking the fine line between what they wanted and what they could have.

"Oh, you actually got it to work?"

"Aye." His magic played hell with electronic things. "As long as I put some distance between me and it, 'twill work."

"I'm glad you figured it out. Movies are just pretend, Finn."

It hadn't looked like they were pretending, with them both naked and panting. "Does the woman's reputation not suffer because she's been seen unclothed?"

"No. Though I'm sure some men probably say rather sexist things about her that could be hurtful and inappropriate if she was aware of it. And I'm sure a lot of the women say similar things about the man. We call men who are muscular and well-built eye candy or hunks, but we recognize they're just playing a role, and that they're regular human beings with lives and families off the screen."

"There are hundreds of years of knowledge I have missed. To live in yer world, I will have to study for years."

"What were you best at before all this happened?"

"Swinging a sword and training and caring for the horses."

"You're very good at landscaping too. You did a fine job

setting in the plants and laying the mulch I bought. Being a landscaper or horse trainer are both honorable professions. You'll find your place, Finn."

He hoped so. To survive for so long and then lose his way once he was once again human would be disheartening. He'd find useful work to do so she would continue to have respect for him.

Several cars turned into the driveway and, seeing no way to flee without being seen, Finn crouched on his block until he realized it was Braxton Myers and Henry Sutton with a few members of the pack. But behind them were others.

"There are several groups from town who have heard about you, Finn. They want an introduction."

"For what purpose?" he asked.

"They just want to make certain you aren't a danger to their packs. I explained to them we have welcomed you into our pack, but they seem to think that gives us an edge, though none of our packs are at war with each other."

Finn shook his head. "I had hoped the need to fight over land had ended by now."

"Not land, Finn. Hunting territory."

"What territory do they claim?"

"All of the east forest past the lake."

"I have not been there, other than to look for the lass who was taken. I havena trespassed."

More cars and trucks zipped down the drive and pulled into the yard. Men and a few women poured out of the vehicles and converged on the patio. Genevieve gripped his arm, her fingers digging in with tension. Though he saw no weapons, he recognized the group as a hunting party.

"Go in the house, Genevieve," he murmured close to her ear.

Her features were frozen in fear and concern. "No. This is my property, and they're trespassing."

"I canna protect myself if I'm worried about protecting ye."

"You won't have to protect me. If they harm me, there'll be too many questions asked."

"Not if you disappear," Braxton murmured from behind her.

Finn's concern spiked, and he gripped Genevieve's chin to bring her gaze to his. "Go in the house."

She pulled away from him, her mouth flattened in anger. "No."

He had no choice but to concentrate on the group descending on him. He kept his hands at his sides while the twenty or so people crowded around. An older man, at least six-foot-four, with a wide chest and shoulders, marched up to him. His grizzled gray hair flowed back from a wide forehead, and his beard bushed around his face. "I'm Tate Johnston. Head of the bear clan."

Finn inclined his head in acknowledgement of the introduction. "Finn MacLeod."

"We have some questions for you."

"Ask them."

"How did you know the woman had been taken?"

So this wasn't about hunting territory at all, but suspicion he might have had something to do with the lass's disappearance. "Genevieve knew the lass," he said, gesturing to her. "'Twas she who told me she was missing. She said the lass would never wander off without calling her friend. She thought the wolves would be able to track Mai from The Dish."

"How did you know to look at the lake?"

"Henry searched the scents and said the lass was taken south. The lake had empty cottages and empty boats upon the water. To hold her, and do what he did, he'd have to have an empty place, and away from others. While the wolves searched the cottages, I searched the houseboats. I searched ten before I smelled blood, human blood. That was how I found her. I raised the anchor and broke the line holding the boat in place and towed it to the dock."

"It's a funny thing you found her so quickly. And nothing like this has happened here in Superstition until you showed up."

"You're wrong, Tate," Henry spoke. "You're pairing this with Finn's arrival, when in truth it's happened four or five times in the past six or seven years. Campus assaults, just like everywhere else."

Tate turned his attention back to Finn. "Why didn't you just free her and take her to shore?"

"She was injured, bleeding, and seeing me wouldna have helped her state. I dinna have the luxury of shifting to a human form as ye do."

Henry spoke again. "Finn was with us, hunting in our territory, when the woman was taken after she left The Dish. Also, she didn't have Finn's scent on her. Nor did the bed. The scent was wholly human."

"Would you be so quick to *defend him*," his tone implied he was lying on Finn's behalf, "if you hadn't taken him into your pack?"

Henry had put himself out there as far as he needed. "I hunt with Henry's pack, but I am'na a part of it. How can I be? I am not wolf. But there are no others like me. Is that what frightens ye?"

"We're not frightened of you, gargoyle."

"Then why are ye here?"

"You have no mate, nor a possibility of one." The implication was clear. If he didn't have a woman, he was attacking women to serve his needs, or if he wasn't already, he would be.

"But he does," Genevieve said, she pressed in close against him. Finn automatically put an arm around her, but sent a doubtful look down at her face and released her name on a sigh.

Tate's gaze swung between her and Finn. "You're lying."

Genevieve shook her head. "Your bigotry is showing, Tate Johnston. Does being able to change into a bear make you any more or any less a man?"

The crowd, thus far silent, shifted, and a murmur traveled through them.

"Prove it," Tate challenged.

"Prove what?" Finn asked.

"That you're lovers."

Genevieve's cheeks pinkened. "Don't tell me that in addition to being a bigot, you're also a voyeur."

Henry snorted in an attempt to stifle his laughter.

Tate narrowed his eyes and a deep growl emanated from him. "Kiss her. If she wants you, we'll all be able to tell."

After all the man's questions, that suggestion sent blood rushing to Finn's face. He wouldn't shame Genevieve in such a way. "Are ye afraid, then, that I might move into yer territory and challenge ye?"

"No, you wouldn't survive a challenge."

"I have survived for six hundred and sixty-three years. What makes ye think ye can kill me?"

Another murmur went through the crowd.

"Finn—" Genevieve murmured. "Please." Her worry for his safety was written in her pale face and the taut line of her mouth.

If she was saying that when they were alone, he'd be hard pressed to deny her. But being surrounded by witnesses. The sweet scent of her arousal when she wanted him was meant for him, not an audience. That was what encouraged him to go on, though he tried not to put too much hope in the promise of more. "I winna have ye shamed before the likes of them. What is between us is ours, not theirs. Ye know why I can't allow this."

Henry stepped forward and folded his arms across his chest. "Your own women could benefit from such a strong desire to protect and defend, not only their bodies, but their privacy, and their honor, if you want to use that word," Henry said, his tone droll. His gaze traveled over the crowd. "Couldn't you, ladies?"

There were only six women in the crowd, but none of them would meet his gaze. A woman stepped forward. A smattering of gray was scattered through her chin-length hair, but her skin looked soft and supple. Her eyes rested on Tate as she spoke. "You're the sexual predator here, Tate. You and your men. You don't even try to spare our pride. You parade your infidelities before us like they're badges of honor."

She scanned the rest of the men. "How do you think it makes us feel, knowing we are just one of many, and don't really count for anything special. We're the ones raising the children, cooking your meals, working jobs to help support your households, and you treat us like we're no more to you than the other women you fuck. And you're not even ashamed enough to at least try to hide it. You act like it's your due. A mating like this isn't what I want for my daughters. And it isn't what I want my sons to offer the women they chose to spend their life with."

"Shut up, Allison," Tate growled.

"Show them how you make me, Tate." There was pain in her voice. "You've paraded the cracks in our marriage before the whole pack. Why not that, too?"

Tate stormed toward her. Finn pulled away from Genevieve and leapt forward to grab his arm. Tate tried to shake him off, and Finn looped an arm around his massive chest and held him. Tate twisted and struggled. Finn gritted his teeth with the effort, for the shifter was muscular and powerful. A man broke away from the group, as though to come to Tate's aid. Braxton leapt in front of him, and the two fought.

Tate pushed back with his feet to throw Finn off balance. With a snap of his wings, Finn flew high, suspending the larger man above the pack. He flew toward the bank of trees along the edge of Genevieve's property. "Ye have lost the respect of yer woman through yer own selfish actions, bear shifter. Ye have led the other lads in yer pack to do the same with theirs."

"Who are you to sit in judgment on me? Put me down."

He drove the back of his large head into Finn's face. Pain exploded across the cusp of his eye and cheekbone, and he released Tate, letting him fall the thirty feet to the ground.

The dull thump as he landed was followed by a yell and a curse. In the distance a high-pitched cheer went up. Finn swooped down and landed close beside the fallen shifter.

"You've broken my damn leg." Tate groaned as he twisted to rise. "I think my back is broken too."

The men of the pack ran across the field toward them. Finn blinked to clear his vision, but the eye watered from the pain, and his vision was blurry.

"I lost everythin' I held dear because I didna treat the people who mattered with respect. The mother of my child died birthing him, and I never got to tell her how sorry I was for so selfishly taking the gift she gave me.

"Ye already lost the respect of your women. They hold ye responsible for their men's behavior. 'Tis the men who lead, but 'tis the women who hold the clan together. They are the givers of life and of love. And it is fearsome hard for a woman to stand by a man she canna respect. If ye continue to follow this course, ye'll lose everythin', as I did. And ye'll be as alone as I was."

The sound of the men wading through the tall grass came closer.

Finn could stay and fight them all, or he could retreat, and hope it ended here. He couldn't take on the whole pack alone, and he couldn't ask the wolves to help. This was not their fight.

Finn flew toward the house, pain radiating from his cheekbone to his temple. His eye was already swelling shut.

Genevieve gasped when he landed. "Dear God, Finn. I'll get you some ice." She ran into the house.

"That damn bear has a thick skull. I shoulda warned you," Henry said, leaning closer to examine the damage.

"Aye. 'Twould have been helpful."

"The ladies enjoyed seeing you drop Tate. Allison would have appreciated it more if you'd dropped him on his head."

"'Twould not have done any good. He'll learn a hard lesson when his pack leaves him." With the back of his hand, Finn wiped away the tears determined to run down his face. "They will eventually."

"I need to touch the bones around your eye, Finn. That asshole may have broken a few, and you don't want to lose an eye."

Henry ran a thumb around the eye socket and his cheek-bone. Finn gritted his teeth and bit back a moan.

"I don't think he's broken anything, but it's going to take some time to heal."

Genevieve was back with a plastic bag of ice wrapped in a towel. "The women actually cheered when you dropped him. Who put it into his head you'd want to take over his pack?"

Finn glanced up out of his one good eye into Henry's face, but he shook his head. "You're a new player in the area. And he's losing his grip on his people. Some of the older folks are drifting away from him."

"I'm not a bear." Finn accepted the bag of ice and held it against his eye. The cold seemed to sooth it some.

"Sometimes strength means more, especially when you have a leader who's managed to beat every challenger. Those who want to split from him and his followers are looking for a leader, and you'd be a good candidate."

"I canna lead them. I dinna know how much time I have

left."

Henry's expression shifted to one of concern, and he glanced in Genevieve's direction.

Finn attempted to make a joke to ease the two's their worries. "And I dinna need to take on a harem of discontented women. One determined to protect me is enough."

Genevieve shot him a warning glance. "They were accusing you of something you didn't do. I wasn't going to stand by while they lynched you."

He wasn't familiar with the term, but he had an inkling of what it meant.

They all tracked the men's progress as they carried their injured leader to one of the trucks.

Braxton ran up from the field with the other four men who'd come with them. The first truck pulled out. "You've done some damage, but he'll heal as soon as he shifts." Braxton didn't sound pleased. "He comes on to our wives and girlfriends. But they've all been warned."

Why the desperation to prove his manhood? "I doubt anythin' I said to him will penetrate his thick skull." If the shifter continued on his course, there would be worse trouble, and Genevieve would be dragged into it.

Unless the curse were broken and he became human once again. As a human, he would not be a threat to the bear shifter. "Should his mate leave him, it might make him wake up to what he's wasting."

"I think Allison's already out the door," Genevieve said. "Going after her here in front of witnesses was the last straw. I heard her say she's taking the children and going to stay with her family."

"Maybe that will be enough," Braxton said.

Finn shook his head. "I hoped people would learn from their mistakes, but it seems they just keep repeatin' them."

Henry gave him a slap on the back that jarred his head, and he bit back an oath as pain arrowed through him. "Friend, you have no idea."

CHAPTER 26

SIMON JAMMED THE gas pedal to the floor and shot down the country road. He'd been driving for hours since Genevieve rejected him. *Him.* After everything he'd done for her. And she was offering their business relationship as a peace offering. Like that would be enough to appease him.

There had to be someone else. The way she had reacted when he saw the drawing...furtive, secretive. He'd find out who the man was, and, disfigured or not, he'd regret coming between them. He'd die as easily as Andy.

But he had another problem to deal with first. Mai. He had to find a way to get to her. First he'd go by the hospital to see what kind of security they put in place. If he couldn't get to her while she was in the hospital, he'd deal with her once she was released.

He turned east and drove to the lake. The houseboat he used had been long abandoned, the elderly owner too ill to visit or keep it up, leaving it free to use as he chose. It was still docked, with police tape wrapped around the railing and barring the door.

His cabin was farther uphill from the lake. He pulled the jaguar around the back of the house and let himself in the back door. It took him only a few minutes to change into worn jeans, a faded T-shirt, and tennis shoes. He tucked one leg from a pair of pantyhose into his pocket, along with seven-inch switchblade, tugged a baseball cap down over his hair and, leaving the keys to the Jag on the ring by the door, sauntered out to the old blue truck and fired up the engine.

Twenty minutes later he parked behind a local mini-mart down the street from the hospital parking lot. Before exiting the truck, he pulled on rubber gloves. He cut through nearby yards until he reached the perimeter of the hospital's property, following the fence to the sidewalk and wandering in through the emergency room entrance, where patient traffic was at its heaviest. Conscious of the cameras along the way, he kept his head down and adopted a long, loping stride unlike his own natural gait.

Mai wouldn't be in the surgical wing, pediatrics, maternity, or oncology, but possibly on general medicine on the fourth floor. There would be an officer posted at her door if the country hicks running the police department knew anything about what they were doing.

He bypassed the elevator and took the stairs, careful to keep an eye out for cameras. He eased the door open on the fourth floor and looked through the crack. Midway up the hall a young police officer sat in a chair, sipping a cup of coffee while he read a book.

A heavyset nurse dressed in colorful scrubs came out of a room across the hall. She pushed a computer stand before her as she walked down to the nurse's station, parked the computer next to it, and moved around the desk, disappearing when she sat down.

Simon eased the door shut and took a moment to think

things through. He'd be too exposed if he opened the door and walked down the hall, so he needed some distraction to draw the officer away. Or draw the man to him. Excitement sent a charge of adrenaline through his system, and his heart raced. It had been too long since he'd faced a challenge like this.

Keeping his head down, he went back down the stairs to the third floor, wandered down the hall to the elevators, and pushed the button, sending it up one floor. Next he stuffed the cap in his pocket, took out the pantyhose and, leaning forward, pulled the hose over his head and replaced his ball cap, checking his reflection in the shiny metal elevator door to make sure his features were sufficiently flattened and distorted.

The door opened, and he rushed toward the nurse's station. Two nurses were sitting at the computer terminals keying in information. One glanced up, and he registered her age, about fifty, and weight as way more than she should be carrying, as she said, "May I—" She got no further, because he sprinted around the counter and punched her in the side of the head, knocking her off her chair to the floor.

The other nurse jumped to her feet and darted toward a room behind the station. He grabbed her by the hair, his fingers digging in tight. He drove her head against the edge of the counter, then dropped her to the floor.

The moment the cop grabbed him from behind, he jerked out his switchblade, pushed the button, and slashed the cop's arm. He jerked back and fumbled for his gun. Simon turned and buried the knife hilt-deep in the man's neck, and he went down, choking on the blade and the blood running into this throat.

Simon reached for the cop's pistol—not the standard

thirty-eight he expected, but a nice Beretta. Leaving his three victims helpless and bleeding on the floor, Simon walked down the hall to the door where the cop had been sitting.

He checked the gun's chamber and, seeing a round was already in place, flipped the safety off. He pushed against the door, only to find it locked. He fired three shots into the lock and kicked the door open. Two elderly women cowered in the corner, their bony arms up in the air in a posture of surrender.

"Where's Mai?"

One of the women sobbed and hunched her shoulders. She pointed across the hall.

Moving fast, the rubber soles of his tennis shoes squeaking, he dashed across the hall, hitting the door hard and shoving it open. The bed was rumpled, but empty. He ran to the bathroom, but the door was open, the light off. He flipped it on, illuminating the dull, sparse space. He checked the two storage cabinets, on either side of the room. She'd slipped out past him while he was taking care of the cop.

He rushed out of the room. Spying another nurse coming down the hall, he raised the gun, and she darted into the closest room. He hit the stairwell at a run and caught the snick of a door closing somewhere down below. He followed the sound, then paused on the platform to the second floor to listen. He'd never find them.

Every instinct screamed for him to get out.

He'd been so close. Rage made him sweat profusely. A rash of pinpricks flared up the back of his neck. Swearing, he tucked the Beretta into the waistband of his pants and pulled his T-shirt down over it. It wouldn't hide it well, but it might get him out of the hospital unnoticed.

He hurried down the stairs. At the last minute, he jerked his hat off, peeled off the stocking, and stuffed it into his pocket. Hat back in place, he yanked the door open and loped his way down the hall and out the emergency room door.

Sirens wailed in the distance. He sauntered down the sidewalk, pausing long enough to throw the Beretta down a storm drain. When he reached the perimeter of the hospital property, he took the same route through the yards and back alleys to the small market and jumped into his truck, peeling the rubber gloves off and tossing them on the seat.

Five minutes later he was halfway across town and on his way back to the cabin.

Police cars raced past him toward the hospital.

CHAPTER 27

GENEVIEVE LOWERED HERSELF to the porch step and folded her hands between her knees.

The freshly dug bed of wildflowers was a riot of color. A large clump of fuchsia-hued bee balm was swarmed by several butterflies and bees. Black-eyed Susans bobbed in the breeze, their golden petals dappled light against the dark pink of tall, leggy cone flowers. The taller plants stood at the back while daisies and pink and blue verbena added more pastel shades before them. Tiny clumps of violets and white and blue anemones bowed close to the ground, their understated beauty nestled against the multi-hued greenery of the larger plants.

How long had it taken Finn to find the flowers and transplant them to this bed? His reasons for doing so were plain. He had no money, no material things to give her. If anything went wrong during the spell tonight...

If only they could spend the day together talking, holding each other.

How had she come to care about him so much in such a short time? Because, even though he was a creature, even without money or possessions, he had a dignity and quiet resolve about him she found incredibly attractive. And she was touched by his determination to protect her from ridicule for caring for him.

Because he was a beast in other people's eyes, a more intimate relationship would never be acceptable. He understood and accepted that.

How was it possible that the second man she'd fallen in love with was just as out of reach as Andy was now. The worry that something terrible might happen to Finn ate at her. But her fears hadn't kept her from wanting him, from caring about him.

She went over and sat beside the statue. "I love my flowers. They're beautiful. I love that you found them and planted them with your own hands. You have a future in horticulture or landscaping design."

She leaned against the statue. *I'm afraid, Finn. I don't want to lose you.* "I hope you're not worried. I believe everything will work out, because I know Juliet and Miranda will do their very best. And their best is astonishing." Was there anything else she could do? More than love him?

At the sound of a car turning into her drive, she looked up. She gripped the statue's arm to help her rise and watched while two white and blue police car stopped in her driveway.

What had happened? Adrenaline set her heart racing, and a tremor shook her. Surely no one in the shifter community had reported what happened last night.

The passenger door of the car opened, and a young woman climbed out.

"Mai." She darted forward, Mai met her halfway, and they hugged.

Just touching Mai, Genevieve sensed a change, and she leaned back to look into her face. "I heard about what happened at the hospital. I tried to call, but they wouldn't tell me anything." The bruises on Mai's face where she'd been beaten stood out against her smooth skin, almost like the fingers that had caused them were still in place. "You're sure you're okay?"

"Yes, they are taking me to a safe house." She glanced at the policewoman standing at the car door.

Two male officers walked up from the other car, their hands on their guns.

"Come inside." Genevieve invited. "All of you."

"We'll stand guard out here, ma'am," the broader and older of the two male officers said. He nodded at the younger officer, jerking his thumb over his shoulder, indicating he should go around back.

Genevieve led the way into the house and into her studio.

Mai went immediately to the statue and stood before it. "Do you think I'll get it back?"

The hope in the figure's stance, the bravery with which she faced life was what Genevieve saw in Mai the first time they met. It was the quality that motivated her to encourage Mai to pose for her.

"I know you will. You came here alone, you worked and studied. You're not going to let one asshole undermine what you've accomplished. Sylvia and I and all your other friends are going to be here to support you."

Mai straightened her shoulders. Her throat worked as she swallowed. She turned away and moved to sit on the couch beside her. "Those poor nurses. One has a broken jaw, and the other a skull fracture. And the police officer, the young one, Mark, he's alive, but they don't know if he'll survive. He nearly choked to death on his own blood. The only reason he is alive now is because one of the injured nurses came to and turned him on his side.

"There were two other nurses in the unit. They went from room to room checking the patients and getting them into the bathrooms to lock themselves in until help came." Mai shuddered and wiped a hand over her face.

"If Sylvia hadn't been with me, I don't think I could have dealt with it. She was like, 'Come on, Mai, we're getting the hell out of here.' She's the one who pulled me out of the room and down the stairs. We hid on the second floor while the nurses there called the police and security."

"You were both unbelievably brave." Genevieve placed a hand on her arm.

"Not me. I was petrified, but Sylvia saved me." Her voice shook. "He wanted to kill me, Genevieve. Why would he want to do that? I don't know what he looks like. I can't tell the police anything, because he kept me drugged or blindfolded."

She hesitated to push Mai too much. "You may be able to give them more help than you think."

"How?"

"I know you're still traumatized by what happened, but...though you couldn't see him, you could smell him, feel his presence. You heard his voice. During the initial attack, you felt his strength. You're more powerful than you know, Mai."

The girl's brows crimped in a frown. "I don't feel very strong, Gen. But I don't want him to do this to anyone else."

Dear God. "Don't put that kind of pressure on yourself, Mai." It would only make it harder for her to heal if she carried around guilt that wasn't hers to bear. "You aren't responsible for anything he did. He's the guilty one, and he will be held accountable when they catch him." She infused as much confidence into her tone as she could.

Mai lapsed into silence for a beat, her quiet voice almost a whisper when she did speak. "They think he may have done this before. He was too good at it. Too practiced."

Mai covered her eyes again. "He was wearing a dark jacket. He was white, and the hair on his wrists was dark." Her speech was halting, jerky. "His watch was silver, with a gold stripe on the band, and a blue face with a gold frame around it. It glinted in the streetlight. Why would a rapist have an expensive gold watch?"

The policewoman stepped forward, her body language tense.

Genevieve lifted a hand, encouraging her to remain silent. "Have you given this information to the detective in charge of the case?"

Mai dropped her hands. "I just remembered. I was so frightened I couldn't think. There was an old blue truck parked on the street. A yellow beetle. And my car. He had to be hiding in the truck." She looked up at the policewoman. "Where's my car?"

"It's parked at your apartment, Ms. Chen."

"I want Sylvia to come with me. What if he goes to my apartment and hurts her like he did me? What if he takes her to get to me?"

"We'll talk to Detective Robinson about it once we get to the station," the policewoman said.

Mai's eyes were liquid with worry. "Will you come to the

station with me, Gen?"

Genevieve ached for her. "Yes, of course. If that's what you want."

"I want you there, and I want Sylvia with me. I can't be alone. Not yet. She can't be at the apartment alone. He has my backpack, my books. He knows where I live."

With the waves of panic coming off Mai bombarding her, Genevieve couldn't sit still. "I'll get my purse." She stood. "I'll go by your apartment and get Sylvia. You'll need clothes, so you can use my phone to call her and tell her to pack your bag and hers."

Mai grasped her hand. "Thank you, Gen."

✧   ✧   ✧

FINN RECOGNIZED THE lass, Mai, when she got out of the car. The police officers paced restlessly around the house, keeping watch. Finn fought against the magic's hold to no avail.

The female police officer and Mai hurried out of the house and drove away. The other two officers followed in the second vehicle. After they left, the garage door rose, and Genevieve backed the car out, but pulled forward again so she could shout out the car window, "Finn, I'm going to Mai's apartment to pick up Sylvia and take her to the police station. I'll be back in a couple of hours."

His first instinct was to forbid her. What if the rapist was watching the apartment? What if he followed her back here? He couldn't protect her during daylight. As she drove away, a growl he couldn't voice roiled in his chest.

Fear for her rampaged through him like a brush fire. He struggled to rise from his crouched position, shoving with all his might against the stone his limbs had become. He fought until his head ached and every muscle was on fire, but he couldn't budge his stone prison. If anything happened to her...

He wouldn't be able to bear it.

SIMON DROVE HIS truck into the parking lot and parked. The only place he could think to watch for Mai was her apartment.

Even if they moved her out of Superstition, she'd have to return home for clothing and personal belongings. If she showed up, he'd follow her, and if there was an opportunity to get to her, he'd take it.

If not, he already had his money and identification ready to leave the state. He'd be taking Genevieve with him.

He slumped in his seat and watched the front entrance. When a familiar car pulled into the parking lot, he slumped lower. Genevieve pulled up to the front door and jumped out to open her trunk. A girl he'd never seen before emerged and put two bags in the trunk, then walked around and got into the car. Genevieve got back in the driver's seat and pulled away.

Simon started his truck and pulled out, waiting for them to roll out into traffic before following, keeping a couple of cars between Genevieve's vehicle and his. Once they pulled out onto Main Street, he knew where they were going.

He parked diagonally across from the police station, cut the engine, and kept an eye on the building using his rearview and side mirrors.

GENEVIEVE TOOK A seat across from Sylvia and Mai in the small interview room. The girls' suitcases were stacked in the corner. Detective Chase Robinson's light brown, blond-streaked curls looked like he'd raked his fingers through it most of the day, and the hint of dark brown scruff made his pale skin appear a shade whiter than it actually was. He pulled his tinted glasses down the bridge of his nose, looked over them at Genevieve, and crooked his finger at her.

She followed him out in the hall.

He yanked his glasses off, revealing his eerily whitish-blue eyes. "What the hell have you gotten my girlfriend into?"

For a moment she went blank. There was no way Juliet would tell Chase about the ritual for Finn until it was over. He'd be reading her the riot act about putting herself in jeopardy. "I don't know what you mean."

"She's been studying her ass off. And I happen to like her ass just the way it is."

Genevieve smiled. "I happen to prefer it just as it is too."

His grin revealed lines that crinkled attractively at the corners of his eyes. "If I wasn't sure you mean that in an entirely artistic way, I'd be tempted to talk her out of sitting for you again."

Genevieve laughed. "I'd pay good money to see you try."

That earned her a grimace from Chase. Juliet was as hard-headed as he was.

"She's been giving me a few stock tips and a few suggestions about investments. So far, she's been right on the money. Forgive the pun."

"I see. In that case, I feel a little better. She's going to talk to the owner of the bar about making her night manager."

"Good, she deserves to be. She's savvy enough to be running the place already, even though she hasn't finished her degree yet."

"Yeah, she is. The good thing is, if she's night manager, we'd actually get to see each other more."

"Which I know she wants, too."

"Thanks for encouraging her. And thanks for pulling that memory out of my witness."

"I didn't pull anything. I just told her how strong she is—which she actually is—and reminded her she had more tools to identify him than she thought, like smell and sound and touch. Broad suggestions. She remembered the details."

"The thing is, the man who left The Dish ahead of her was Simon Martin."

Shock traveled from the top of Genevieve's head to the bottom of her feet. It couldn't be Simon. He didn't even know Mai.

"He was wearing a dark jacket, and had on a gold watch. He left a ten-dollar tip for the waitress, and she noticed the expensive watch. What do you think about that?"

"He always dresses well. Was he anywhere close to Mai so that she would notice how he was dressed and transfer the memory onto the man who attacked her?"

"He sat in a booth toward the front of the restaurant. She was in a booth midway back, studying. She didn't seem to notice him. And he never approached her or spoke to anyone but the woman who waited on him."

She needed to be objective when she thought about this, but those moments in her office kept coming back. He'd scared the hell out of her.

"Chase…" She swallowed. "Are you running a background check on him?"

"It's already started."

She bit her lip. "He's been my business manager for three years."

"Yeah." He waited for her to continue. "Just say it, Gen."

She swallowed, and clasped and unclasped her hands. "He's been pushing me for a romantic relationship. The other night at the house, he got a little strange."

"What do you mean strange?"

"He saw a picture I'd drawn of a man and got very angry and possessive. He actually called me a liar. He apologized later, but when I let him know I wasn't interested in pursuing a romantic relationship with him… He just became very…empty, almost robotic, but there was a tension about him, and between us. For several minutes it…it was like…. There was something in the room, and I wanted to run, but was too afraid to move. I kept expecting him to explode."

"But he didn't."

"No, but the way he acted was creepy. Like he'd flipped a switch on his emotions. Just turned them off. Nobody is that controlled, Chase."

His gaze stayed on her, but she could tell his thoughts were elsewhere. "I'll be going around to interview him again as soon as Carter and Brian leave with Mai and Sylvia."

He lowered his voice. "The guy meant to kill Mai, and damn near took three people out to do it. Including one of our own. The guys will be at their sharpest."

"How's the officer?"

"He's in critical condition. The doctors say he must have

had an angel perched on his shoulder to have survived a knife to the throat."

Dear God.

"If you'd sit with them a few more minutes, I'd appreciate it."

"Sure."

"The guys should be here shortly. They're getting their last-minute instructions from the chief."

"Okay." She reached for the doorknob, but turned to look over her shoulder. "I appreciate you letting Sylvia stay with her."

"I think it's a good idea. Sylvia got her out of the hospital room and saved her life. She kept her head, acted quickly. She'll be one more line of defense."

Genevieve nodded. "And moral support. Mai needs that right now."

She pushed the door open and walked back to her seat. The two women's expressions were identical—anxious and expectant. "There will be two police officers accompanying you, and staying to guard you. They'll be here in a few minutes."

The three of them were too tense to talk, Genevieve, because she had just acknowledged there might be something seriously wrong with her business manager, and Sylvia and Mai because they were extremely anxious about what came next.

A soft tap sounded on the door before it opened. Two large men came, in taking up most of the remaining space in the room.

Chase's partner, Carter Pfister, had a reassuring bulk to his build. Wide-shouldered and muscular, he looked like he could take on an army alone and come out on top. "Ms. Chen, Ms. Thorne. My name is Detective Pfister." His tone had an easy, matter-of-fact calm that seemed to immediately sooth Mai and Sylvia. "Detective Underwood and I will be accompanying you to the house. If you're ready to go."

The two women stood. Brian Underwood grabbed their bags and handed them off to a policeman outside the door.

"Thank you for staying with us, Gen." Mai said.

Her features started to crumple and Genevieve rushed to hug her. "You're going to be fine. This will be over soon."

Mai nodded.

Genevieve hugged Sylvia. "I know you'll look after her." Sylvia offered her fist for a bump, and Genevieve laughed and returned the bump.

She left the room to watch them go down the hall toward the back of the office while she wrestled with her own emotions.

Could Simon really be the man who attacked Mai? How would he have found her? How could he know who she was? Had she ever used her name when speaking to him? She didn't think so.

The fascinated look on his face while he gazed at the sculpture flashed back to haunt her. The noise of telephones ringing, the murmur of voices, and the constant movement behind her fell away as her fear intensified. Was she to blame for Mai's attack?

CHAPTER 28

T HE SUN SET with an almost violent display of color. Finn burst free of the base, fueled with rage at being trapped by the magic. It was years since he had railed against the restraint of it, but the need to be free of it, finally and completely, burned inside him now.

Time seemed to pass with agonizing slowness while he waited for Genevieve to return. He dressed, then got water from the refrigerator and gulped it down. He took to the sky, though it wasn't completely dark, circling the area, searching for her car. He spotted it moving toward the house followed by two other vehicles, a red pickup truck and a silver van.

When her car pulled into the driveway, he tossed the empty bottle into the rubbish bin and waited for her to park the car in the garage.

She appeared a few minutes later through the front door, and walked directly to him to press close, her arms around his waist.

"What is it? What's happened?"

"The police have taken Mai to the safe house. It was emotional for us. I'm very worried about her. He's come after her once, I'm concerned he might do so again."

"The men with her will protect her, lass. And because he's

tried before, they'll be on alert."

"Yes. Of course." She pressed closer, and he gave her a reassuring squeeze.

"Ye said ye wouldna go off alone, lass."

"Mai was worried about Sylvia being at the apartment. And since Sylvia got them out of that hospital room alive, Mai naturally wants Sylvia with her."

Finn shook his head. Genevieve's independence would be the death of him. "Yer eagerness to help those ye care about is admirable, but ye must have a care for yourself, too."

She looked up. "I'm being careful. I was surrounded by police the whole time we were at the station." She leaned back. "The ladies will be here in an hour or so to start. How are you feeling?"

"Eager to get this behind me."

She did her best to project confidence, but tension worked beneath her expression. "Do you want to eat?"

"Nay, lass. I'm not hungry."

"Neither am I." She raised a hand to tuck his long hair behind his ear. "Your ears are almost human, Finn. The curse is weakening. You could wait and see how far it retreats on its own. You have time."

He cupped her face in his hands. "I spend most of my waking hours in a stone prison, lass." *Waiting to be with ye.* "I dinna intend to wait any longer."

She nodded, though her fear for him was apparent in the way she held him. "I love the flower bed you created. It's beautiful, and fragrant, and I love seeing the bees and butterflies."

"I can bring you meat for your table, fish from the stream

nearby, berries from the forest, even mushrooms should ye want them, but I canna work to provide anythin' for ye. I canna be a man, Genevieve. I canna walk with ye in daylight. Be a true part of yer life. I canna have a life beyond what I already have. I want to live as a man. Work as a man."

Be a lover to ye. How he longed to say those words.

She turned her face against his chest, and her tears dampened his skin. She pulled away and turned her back to him.

"If I thought you were risking your life because of me, I'd call Juliet and Miranda and tell them not to come. But I know it's more than that." She brushed at the tears and wiped her hands on her jeans. "I want you to be free. I really want that for you."

"I know ye do, lass." He laid a hand on her shoulder to comfort her. "I want that kiss. Once all this is done."

She glanced over her shoulder, her eyes still wet, but offered him a tremulous smile. "There's a saying that you have to kiss a lot of frogs before you find your handsome prince. Maybe kissing a gargoyle will count as two frogs—maybe more."

Finn laughed. "I must finish gathering firewood for the bonfire."

"I'll fix some iced tea and food for when this is behind us. We may both be hungry by then."

"Aye, lass."

After she went into the house, Finn stalked around the studio and entered the forest behind the house to scavenge for firewood.

What if this spell didn't work?

He would continue to be just as he was...or it could make

things worse.

He could be trapped inside the gargoyle forever. He already made arrangements to solve the issue if that was the case. Henry and several of his wolves promised to destroy the statue.

He stacked several fair-sized limbs in his arms and carried them back to the edge of the woods, dumping them in the garden wagon Genevieve used for the heavy bags of mulch he just laid for her. His thoughts continued as he foraged and loaded more wood.

He could be trapped as the live gargoyle. In that case, he would contact the bear shifter Tate and ask him to kill him. It would be better for someone who had no attachment to him to do it.

It wasn't impossible he could be left just as he was now, which was equally unacceptable. He couldn't face eternity living as the monster. At least when he was fighting the German planes, he felt he had a reason for being. But what purpose could he serve as he was, here or any other place?

He was shot at because he was a part of the unknown and unusual, flying overhead. If his presence became common knowledge, they would put him in a cage. Or decide he was a danger and hunt him down. How many times would they try to kill him if the magic wouldn't allow him to die? That would be a hell unto itself.

He could drown himself. Once in the water, the weight of his wings would drag him beneath the surface. All he'd have to do would be breathe in and let himself go. If he could do it. The instinct to live was strong. And it hadn't worked the last time. He found himself back on his block the next evening.

He hauled the wagon around the side of the house and

pulled it out into the middle of the field, where he had already cleared a circle for the fire, dumping the wood and jogging back with the wagon behind him.

His thoughts returned to his internal debate.

Was he a coward for wanting to end this?

He had been so long without a human touch. Until Genevieve. He'd need to have a stone-cold heart to resist her. The way she smiled at him. The way she tucked his hair behind his ears. The way she looked at him. He didn't want to leave her in pain because of his passing, but she couldn't cling to a monster if there was no hope. If he lived, it would be more difficult for her.

Unless he kept looking for a way to break the curse. Because her computer didn't like his magic, he'd asked Genevieve to research magic shops and witches. New Orleans had many, as did some areas of California and New York. Some were probably charlatans, but there had to be others who were truly powerful. If he could find one who understood black magic and would be willing to free him from this...

He couldn't expect Genevieve to wait for him. It might take years. Time meant little to him, but she was human, and deserved a family, and a man to love her. A son or daughter to pass her skills on to, as her grandfather passed them on to her. Though it would kill him seeing her with another man. Just as it had seeing her with Simon.

If Juliet and Miranda could free him from his base, he would be able to travel about the country alone and search for someone to help him.

Having worked up a sweat, he wiped a grimy hand over his face and dried it on his sweatpants. If the witch's spell worked, he wouldn't have to worry about any of this. He just needed to hang on and see what happened.

After he took the last load of wood out to the field and put the wagon back in storage, it was time to clean up and dress for the evening.

He'd just put on a clean pair of sweatpants when the first cars pulled up, and Genevieve went out to greet the witches. The women were quieter, solemn and focused, but for all their deportment, an air of excitement simmered beneath the surface. With every one of them dressed in colorful ceremonial robes, they reminded him of a royal gathering.

The fabric of Juliet and Miranda's robes shimmered with color. Like two iridescent dragonflies, they swooped down on him with another woman in tow who was less flamboyantly dressed in a simple black robe.

Juliet said, "Finn, this is Aubrey McClellan, one of our oldest and dearest friends. She's been a practicing witch since she was twelve, and she's agreed to lend her support tonight."

He could feel the witch's power from a foot away. It was warm and soothing. "I am grateful for your help, Aubrey McClellan."

She studied him for a long moment. Her green eyes kind. "May I touch you?"

Finn extended his hand and she took it, her grip stronger than he expected.

After a short, thoughtful moment she released him. "I'm sorry for your trials, Finn. When is it you hurt your foot and your eye?"

"My foot some days ago, my eye last night."

"Juliet said you normally heal once you return to stone.

What has changed?"

Genevieve stepped forward. "It's my fault, Aubrey." She explained about having worked on his toenail and the repercussions.

"I'd like to try to heal you before we start the spell," Juliet said.

Finn nodded and she placed her hand over his eye.

Finn watched her face while she murmured a spell beneath her breath. The shadow of a bruise showed on her face for a second, and she flinched, but then it disappeared. The pain and soreness he continued to experience from Tate's head butt eased, then dissipated.

He remembered Juliet saying that for every use of her magic there was a price. She had paid the price to heal him. She knelt at his feet and started to do the same to his foot.

He raised his hand. "Wait. I dinna wish to cause ye any pain, and the foot wound is worse. Mayhap ye should save yer power for bigger issues."

Genevieve's scent came from close by. He turned to find her behind him. She slipped a hand in the crook of his arm, her features pale but composed. "I'll take the price for his healing, Juliet."

"No, lass."

"It was my actions that caused it. I should pay for it. You need to be at your strongest for this to work, Finn."

"She has a point, Finn," Aubrey said. "We'll try to do as little harm as possible, but the magic that surrounds you is thick and black as tar. It's going to cause you some discomfort when it comes off."

It had come close to killing him going on. His heart began

to race, and dread lay like a brick in his belly. "I had a wee mind it might smart some when it's banished. But I appreciate the warning."

"Please forgive us for any pain we cause you."

Her apology didn't make him feel any better about the upcoming experience.

"It winna be ye or the others here I hold responsible, but the man who cursed me to begin with. I give ye m'word."

The three witches nodded.

Juliet gripped Genevieve's hand while she murmured the spell. Genevieve bit her bottom lip as the pain from his foot was transferred to her. When his nail was once again whole and the foot had no pain, he turned to check on Genevieve.

"I'm okay," she said, with a weak smile.

The three witches returned to the fold. Another car arrived, and five more witches joined them. The required thirteen had expanded to fourteen. Finn wondered if it would make a difference.

"Ladies, let us begin," Miranda called, and started across the field to the clearing Finn had created with its large stack of wood. The other witches followed.

The closer they got to the clearing, the deeper Genevieve's fingers dug into Finn's arm.

"Ye winna consider staying at the house while we do this?"

She raised a brow at him. "No."

He nodded. He wished she would. His breathing sped up, and he felt a little nauseous. "'Twill be fine, Gen."

"I know." For the first time, she didn't sound like she believed it.

The steady call of crickets and other insects had stopped

while the group trekked through the field.

By the light of the women's flashlights, Miranda and the others stood like spokes on a wheel along the perimeter of the circle. Within the circle, Juliet and Aubrey stood on either side of a small potting table. Bowls, candles, water, and several other items were arranged on it.

Juliet stepped forward, her stance regal as she spoke. "Our intent here tonight is to free Finlay MacLeod from the black magic that has transformed him from man to gargoyle. If it be the will of the Goddess and God, we will succeed. We will call the corners to protect us all from any backlash. Each witch here has provided an object for the ritual, as have Finn and Genevieve. Finn, if you will light the bonfire."

He eased away from Genevieve and went to light the wood. A little of the wondrous lighter fluid she kept in the shed made setting the dry wood alight much easier. The heat from the blaze radiated out to him, and he stepped back.

The women extinguished their flashlights and stood in the firelight. Juliet lit sage, and, walking clockwise, moved around the circle, cleansing it while Aubrey followed her with a broom, literally sweeping out any negative energy.

Finn had researched part of the ritual they were going to perform so he would understand a little of what would happen.

Juliet beckoned to him. "Finn, I invite you into the circle."

He entered the circle, and Juliet waved the sage smoke around him, and from head to toe.

"Genevieve, because Finn is a creature of the air, and you have guardianship over him, I would like to invite you to stand in the east quadrant of the circle." She gestured to her right.

Genevieve entered the circle and stood between two of the witches, while Juliet cleansed her by walking around her with the sage stick.

Then Julia walked to the center of the circle and placed the smudge in a brass bowl.

Next Juliet chose a wand from the objects on the table and once again moved clockwise around the circle, coming to a stop beside Genevieve. She pointed the wand toward the sky. "Oh, ye Guardians of the Watchtowers of the East, I call upon you to witness this rite, to guard this circle and keep us safe. May the element of air rise and ripple, blow the dark magic away from Finn and this place. Let it return across the ocean to the place from whence it came."

Aubrey handed her a stick of incense, and Juliet lit it with a wave of her hand and inserted it in a holder at the eastern corner.

She returned to the table, traded the wand for a dagger, and walked the circle again. At the south corner, she pointed the dagger. "Oh, ye Guardians of the Watchtowers of the South, I call upon you to witness this rite, to guard this circle, and keep us safe. Help us light that which is dark, let it shine bright with love and peace, and banish the anger and hate that bound this magic." Aubrey handed her a red candle, and Juliet lit it with a wave of her hand and placed it at the south corner.

The third time she walked the circle, she raised a small, carved statue, "Oh, ye Guardians of the Watchtowers of the West, I call upon you to witness this rite. To guard this circle and keep us safe. The dark magic drinks from Finn MacLeod's spirit. We ask for the powers of water to wash away the darkness that clings and transforms him. Fill and refresh him instead." She knelt and placed the cup at the western corner.

She took up a stone and walked the circle one more time, this time stopping at the northern corner. "Oh, ye Guardians of the Watchtowers of the North, I call upon you to witness this rite. To guard this circle and keep us safe. From the earth this stone came, but no earth has kissed the stone Finn transforms into each day. Oh, mighty Earth, swallow the magic that encases him, and return it to the realm from which it was summoned." She placed the statue on the ground at the northern corner.

When she rose, she looked to the rest of the group. "Bind yourselves together, sisters."

The witches stretched their arms out and grasped hands.

She called Finn forth and rolled a long pallet out on the ground for him to lie on. He had been so caught up in the ritual, the sense of dread lying like a block of stone in his stomach had dissolved, but now it returned tenfold. Because of his wings, he had to lie on his side. She placed a small pillow under his head, and knelt beside him, holding the dagger she used earlier and a foot-long clay doll. "I need a lock of your hair and a drop or two of your blood, Finn. May I take it?"

"Aye." She cut a lock of his hair with the dagger and affixed it to the doll's head, then pierced the small form's chest with the tip of the knife. When he offered his hand, she pricked his finger and let the blood drip into the hole she made in the clay, sealing it inside the figure.

She set the doll on a cloth the size of a hand towel next to him.

"Powers from the east, south, west, and north,

"We have come to call you forth.

"Drag this darkness from Finlay Macleod and into the
   light,

"Bolster us in our fight.

"Move this curse from him to lay

"Within this figure, this doll of clay.

"Let this evil power reside

"Where it may forever abide.

"Tear it loose and bind it firm,

"Where it will never again cause harm.

"By the power of these fourteen and thee,

"As we wish it, so mote it be."

The witches chanted, over and over, "*Movere ac tenebras.*"
Finn knew what the words meant. *Move the darkness.*

The wind began to whip around the circle, bending the
tall grass flat. The fire, fed by it, rose like a tower, writhing and
dancing over the raw wood. The power built inside the circle,
the pressure of it first pushing down upon him, then burrowing beneath his skin like a thousand ants. Finn gritted his teeth
against the pain. He attempted to breathe through the worst of
it, until a stabbing agony struck his back. His wings seemed to
be folding into his body. The bones crushed as they stabbed
into him, and a scream exploded from his belly.

✧   ✧   ✧

GENEVIEVE CLAPPED HER hands over her ears, unable to listen
to Finn's screams. Tears flowed down her cheeks in streams.
The urge to scream along with him built and built, until she
stumbled forward and fell to her knees beside him. His body
twisted and contorted as his wings started to disappear into his

back. The length of his jaw receded, and he clutched his face, tears bathing it as he twisted and writhed upon the pallet.

She moved to touch him, but a bluish glow emanated around him, pulsing with heat and power, and stinging her when she got too close. The gargoyle's pain-filled grimace was now a man's. Finn's features had reverted to human, and the points on his ears were gone, but something continued to bubble beneath the surface of his skin like hot liquid.

How could he live through this? How could he not pass out from the torture? She prayed they'd stop their chanting. When they didn't, she gripped her hair at the scalp with both hands and squealed in pain along with him. For she felt a part of his pain, sharp and piercing, and she rubbed her arms hard. When his eyes rolled up and he went limp, it was a relief.

Her attention turned to the clay form beside him. It had taken on the gargoyle form, wings and all. For the first time, she believed this might work.

The chanting stopped. Silence as profound as a prayer stretched. A hollow emptiness surrounded them like a vacuum. Her ears felt full. She swallowed to try and make them pop.

The doll-sized clay form started to change. The wings shrank by an inch, then two.

"Noooooo." Genevieve grabbed the doll and held onto the wings to keep them from retreating back into the clay. "Noooooo." She tugged at the clay and shaped it expertly. The tiny face began to shift, and she worked quickly to stop it as well, but though she tried, her hands couldn't work fast enough.

As Finn's wings erupted again, he awoke with a hair-raising scream. She threw the figure down with a sob broke and crawled to him, holding as he writhed in agony. It seemed to go on forever, and when it finally ended, his wings stretched back as they had before. He lay spent, breathing in harsh gasps while she wiped his tears away with the hem of her T-shirt, though her face bore the same evidence of his suffering.

"I love you, Finn. It doesn't matter what you are. I love you."

His shoulders heaved, and he wiped his face with the back of his hand before pulling away and staggering to his feet. "Ye must stop, Genevieve. There is no hope. I am an abomination." He staggered out of the circle and continued toward the trees.

Miranda dropped to her knees beside Genevieve to gather her close, and she buried her face against Miranda's shoulder while sobs racked her, because he was right. For one glorious moment they had hope, and now it was gone.

CHAPTER 29

FINN STAGGERED WHEN a tree root cropped up to trip him. For the first time since become a gargoyle, he felt weak and dizzy. He extended his wings and tried to take off. After a couple of false starts, he got them to work, and he took to the sky.

He rose above the house and circled it, unable to control the need to check on Genevieve. Her tearstained face and broken voice had nearly undone him as much as her words.

He loved her with everything in him, but they could not be together. And now he knew they never would. He could not bear to experience such pain again. He would lose his mind and become the beast again.

The fire had died down to embers, and the witches were shadows as they crossed the field to the house. Several of them doused the flames, while others stood on the patio for a few moments, then broke away to go to their cars. When he was certain Miranda and Juliet remained with Genevieve to offer her comfort and support, he changed direction to fly south.

He came upon the clearing where he brought Genevieve the night they flew together. He glided down and stumbled when he landed, having to brace a hand on the ground to catch himself. He needed to eat to renew himself, but the idea of food set his stomach to churning.

He moved to the stream and cupped his hand in the water to bring some to his mouth. The sight of his rough, malformed hand and claws revolted him. How could he dare touch Genevieve with hands like this?

A groan built in his throat beside his rage, and he roared out his pain. He leapt to his feet, tore a small sapling out of the ground, and heaved it as far as he could. Once he'd embarked on a frenzy of destruction, he couldn't seem to stop. He broke and destroyed, tore up the earth with his claws until they were broken, and the ground looked like a plow had harrowed it.

Afterward he lay on the ground, gasping and exhausted. The silence surrounding him was calming, though the pain of his crushed hopes lodged like a fist in his chest.

His eyes burned with his need to release his grief, but centuries of manly discipline made it impossible.

After a while, he sat up. Seeing the destruction he wrought only compounded his grief. He had destroyed a lovely, peaceful place. Even the fireflies were gone. Finn dragged himself to his feet, and, with deliberate care, began to clean up the mess and replant the trees and other plants he'd ripped out of the ground.

Hours later, when he was exhausted, sweaty, and covered with mud, the call of the sun struck more painfully than usual. He flew toward home.

He landed on the lawn and rushed to bathe away the sweat and mud. The first rays of the new day were glowing far in the distance when he moved to take his place on the stone block, and, at the same moment Genevieve walked out onto the patio and approached him. Her pale skin looked powder-soft in the early morning light. He watched the silky flow of her pajamas as she moved, and noticed the quick flash of her poppy-tinted toenails.

Dark rings stood out beneath her eyes like thumbprints. Realizing she had not slept, he felt guilty for causing her such distress.

"Are you okay?" she asked.

"Aye."

"I meant what I said, Finn."

He swallowed with difficulty. "If I say the words, 'twill only make it harder for us both, *leannan*." When he framed her face with his hands, the delicacy of her bones, the softness of her skin, triggered a deeper ache of loss. "I want ye to have a husband, children, all the things I canna give ye."

She gripped his wrists when he started to withdraw from her. "Don't you ever get tired of be so damned noble, Finn?"

"Not noble, lass. Practical. We Scots are known for it. How do ye know our children wouldna be born with this curse? How would ye explain to them their *arthair* was a creature of the night instead of a flesh and blood man? How do ye know it wouldna somehow infect ye, should we make love?"

"How do you know that my loving you won't eventually break the curse? Your eyes are still blue. Your ears are close to human now. Your brow is not so prominent anymore." Her green eyes had turned grayish with passion. "You *are* becoming human again. We just have to be patient."

He wanted her with an unquenchable hunger. But being with her...should he lose control... "Do ye ken how hard it is for me to see ye every day, touch ye, and not be able to kiss ye, caress ye, take ye to me?"

"Yes, I do. Because it's just as hard for me."

Women had never spoken so openly in his time. Blood rushed south and he hardened. "Genevieve..." The sun rose over the hills.

Genevieve rose on tiptoe and pressed her lips to his. A floral scent clung to her, and her breath bore the faint taste of mint. For half a second, he was just a man responding to his lady's kiss, until the magic rose and yanked him away. As the stone absorbed him, exhaustion overwhelmed him, but the taste of her lips lingered to torment him with a promise that could never be fulfilled.

Simon studied Detective Chase Robinson. The man had questioned him right after Mai's abduction, and now he was back. But there couldn't be any evidence leading this detective back to him, otherwise he'd be slapping handcuffs on him and hustling him out to his car.

"Did you see anyone on the street when you left?"

"No, I'm sorry, I didn't. The street was deserted."

"Where was your car parked? Liz, the owner of The Dish, said you took the same route Mai did that night."

The streets were empty at night, and there were no traffic cameras. "I didn't have my car parked on the street. It was parked behind the Gallery. I walked back there to get it."

"That's quite a walk, Mr. Martin. About eight blocks."

Simon shrugged. "I don't get as much exercise as I need during the day, so I take long walks at night. And Superstition is a relatively safe town. I've never had any trouble here.

Unlike Lexington. I was held up at knifepoint on my way to my car one night there."

Chase's light brown brows rose. "When was this?"

The man's gaze did give him a brief pause. His irises were so light they looked almost white. Had there not been a darker ring of color along the edge, Simon might have wondered if he could see. "It was three years ago, August seventeenth. I remember, because I had a very big sale that day, and my staff and I celebrated with some champagne before I left for home. The man had been in the gallery earlier that day and overheard us talking about it, and thought I'd have some extra cash on me because of it. I was taking the receipts to the bank when he held me up."

"How much did he get away with?" Chase asked.

"Nothing. I fought him off, and he was accidentally stabbed while we fought. As soon he was released from the hospital, he went to jail. It seems he had broken his parole by trying to mug me."

Simon adjusted the crease on his trousers. "Not our normal customer, although to look at him, you'd never have known he had a background in burglary and assault.

"Afterward I decided to pack up and move, since I can sell my artists' work from anywhere. I run a successful website, and have thousands of contacts. Sometimes I ship pieces across the country to California and even Washington state, and share the commission. I always accompany Genevieve's pieces to make certain they arrive safely and are correctly installed."

"I'm sure she appreciates it."

"The collector in New York loved *Reclining Woman*. He sent word Juliet could have a job with his agency any time."

Robinson's jaw tensed.

Simon controlled a smirk. "She really is extraordinarily beautiful. And her sister as well." It was so easy to get a rise out of a man when his girlfriend or wife was involved.

"Yes, they are," Robinson said, his tone neutral. "Did you know Mai Chen modeled for Genevieve?"

"I don't believe she ever told me who the model was for her latest piece. She didn't with Juliet, either. She's very careful to protect her models' identities. And she always changes their facial features in the finished work. The only reason I guessed Juliet had modeled for her is because she and Juliet are friends. I've seen them together, and I noticed a similarity in body type and guessed."

"How long did it take you to walk from The Dish to the parking structure, Mr. Martin?"

"I'd say at least fifteen minutes."

"And what route did you take?"

"South on Kentucky Street, East on Dove Avenue for about five blocks, then I crossed over and went down Trick Street for two blocks, then crossed over again and walked the remaining blocks on Secret Avenue."

"Did you see anyone along the way?" Robinson poised the pencil over his pad, ready to write more notes.

"No. It was very late, but a few cars passed me along the way."

"That's okay, I'll check the business cameras. That should give you an alibi."

"I wasn't aware I needed an alibi."

Robinson eyed him. "At the moment every male in this town is under suspicion. And you were in the vicinity that night."

"Did the young lady identify me?"

"No. But we're checking DNA and fingerprints. Would you be open to giving me a DNA sample and your finger-prints? Both are completely painless."

Sweat rolled down between Simon's shoulder blades. If he didn't cooperate, Robinson would think he had something to hide. He'd been careful, but there was always a chance he'd left evidence behind.

Robinson opened the case he brought with him, put on rubber gloves, then lifted a long-stemmed swab.

How long does it take to get DNA back? Simon opened his mouth, and the detective ran the swab against the inside of his cheek, then closed the plastic tube around it. Wrote his name on it and placed it in the case.

Then he plugged in the electronic scanner and carefully cleaned the glass. "Just place your fingers one at a time against the plate, and it will take a digital reading of each print."

Simon pulled his shirt cuff back and put each finger into the device.

"Nice watch," Robinson commented.

"Thank you. It's a Rolex."

Like any scanner, the light flashed and ran beneath his thumb. Immediately an image with whorls and ridges came up on a small screen. Robinson saved it.

When the last finger was done, Robinson said, "Beats having to clean fingerprint ink off, doesn't it?"

"I wouldn't know, Detective. I've never been printed before."

"Never been a state employee, a teacher, been arrested?"

"No."

"May I look at your watch?"

Simon studied him for a moment. Unlike most small-town cops Simon dealt with, this was no country bumpkin. Simon removed the watch and handed it to Robinson.

Chase took a picture of the watch with his cell phone. "I want a new watch for Christmas, and I really like this one."

"If you show up to work with one, you may find yourself on the wrong end of an investigation yourself. It cost ten thousand dollars."

Robinson whistled. "That's a bit out of my price range." He took another swab and rubbed it around the face of the watch and around the curved edges, Simon's stomach fluttered uneasily.

Robinson sealed the swab, handed the watch back to Simon, then unplugged the scanner and shut it inside the case.

"Just where are you from, Mr. Martin, originally?" he asked, his tone more conversational than before.

"Holcomb, Kansas."

"Isn't that the town…?" Chase's voice drifted off.

"Yes. The town Truman Capote wrote about."

"I read that book in college."

"I've read it, too. He didn't have much to say about the town, only the killers. I left when I was eighteen and never looked back."

"I did the same thing, but I went into the service."

Curious Simon asked, "How did you know I didn't do the same thing?"

"You've never been fingerprinted. The military takes DNA and fingerprints."

"I see." He should have known that.

"You saw the sculpture of Mai in Genevieve's living room."

"Yes. It's one of Genevieve's most beautiful so far."

"You recognized Juliet as *Reclining Woman*, but not Mai as *Water Baby*?"

"Mai isn't really a close friend to Genevieve. She's more of a protégé."

Robinson pounced on the comment. "How do you know that? Did Genevieve tell you?"

Simon shrugged. "I just assumed. She doesn't get involved with her models usually. And besides, she's changed the features on the sculpture. The sculpture doesn't look Chinese. Without that as a hint, how would I know which college student on a campus of students had posed for her?"

Robinson's gaze narrowed. "If you had access to Genevieve's house, I'm sure you'd know where to look for that information."

"I've never been to Genevieve's house without her invitation. I don't have a key."

"I'll be asking her to verify that."

"Go ahead." No one had any idea he had a key.

Robinson flipped his notebook shut and picked up the case.

"Aren't you going to take Keith's fingerprints and DNA?" Simon asked.

"No. Keith has an airtight alibi."

A small twinge of resentment nipped him. "Because he's gay?"

"No. Because there were several witnesses to verify his

location for the time frame of Mai's abduction. Of course, I'll be checking the business cameras along the route you took."

"Okay." Simon would be long gone before Robinson completed that task. And Genevieve would be with him.

Simon accompanied the detective to the front door, and observed the detective while he got into his car.

Keith wandered up. "He's quite yummy, even with those odd-colored eyes. Kind of like a young Bruce Willis, when he still had hair, only taller."

Simon kept his tone neutral. "Too bad he's got a girl-friend."

"How do you know that?" Keith asked.

"She's one of Genevieve's friends."

"He's got his eye on you for that Chinese woman's rape?" Keith asked.

"He's just crossing off suspects. I think he may be investigating half the men in town, and every sex offender in the state. I have nothing to worry about." He turned to see a look of speculation in Keith's eyes. "I didn't do anything."

"It was strange that she was Genevieve's model. And that it happened right after we put the drawings up. You don't think it was someone who came through and saw them?"

"How could they recognize her from the drawings, Keith? Genevieve didn't draw her as Chinese." Sometimes his assistant wasn't very smart. "In fact, I didn't even know she was until Genevieve called and told me she was the one missing."

"That's a relief." Keith smiled. "I mean that the drawings didn't trigger anything. And the drawings you substituted for the originals were just as beautiful. Genevieve needs to do more. They take less time, and they sold much more easily."

There's a thought. "Yes, they did, didn't they?" They'd need a way to bring in money while they were on the road, and that should be as good as any. Which reminded him, he needed to wipe the hard drive before he left, and take his black book of distributors with him. It wouldn't do for the police to know who his contacts were. "I'll be sure to encourage her to do that, and tell her it was your idea."

Keith grinned like he'd won the lottery.

It was good to leave him happy. Since Keith would be out of a job once he and Genevieve left.

✧   ✧   ✧

GENEVIEVE LOWERED THE electric chisel and took up the hammer and manual chisel. After weeks of work, the sculpture was taking shape, and she was doing finishing touches to his back and shoulders. It did her good to have a task to focus on that would take away the disappointment and worry over Finn.

Typical man. No patience.

He was changing. His brow ridge was beginning to recede, and his jaw wasn't as distended. She had photos to prove it.

If she could just convince him to give it some time…

She finished hammering a section away and paused to step back and look at it. A hand touched her shoulder. She yelped and swung around, the chisel gripped like a knife. Recognition brought with it a shaky relief. "Damn it, Chase. You scared the shit out of me." She jerked her protective headphones off and left them hanging around her neck.

"I'm sorry. Take it easy." He gestured with his hand, as

though waving her emotions down. "I just stopped by to ask you some questions."

"You're lucky I didn't stab you with my chisel."

"How does a person contact you if you're hammering away in here?"

"Most people stand at the door and wave their hands around until I notice them." Her heart began to climb its way back down out of her throat. She set the chisel on the worktable and took her headphones and safety goggles off. "Let me take these coveralls off, and we'll go in the house and drink something while we talk. I need a break."

Once they were seated at the kitchen table with glasses of iced tea, she felt a little calmer. "What's going on?"

"I'm looking hard at Simon. I've run a background check on him and haven't found anything criminal, but he's moved about every five years, which in itself is strange, but not suspicious. Though you'd think he'd want to establish his business and stay in one place."

"I took DNA swabs and fingerprints today. He didn't object, though he didn't like it." He shrugged. "Most people don't." He leaned his elbows on the table. "I also took pictures of his watch and swabbed it. It matches the watch that Mai described her attacker wearing. But that doesn't mean he was the one who attacked her. She was traumatized and drugged. And she only glimpsed it for a few seconds before she passed out. I haven't had an opportunity to show it to her, yet. But I've emailed the photo, along with several others, to see if she can identify it out of a sort of watch lineup.

"The thing is... I'd like to have a copy of his travel sched-ule, but a judge won't give me a search warrant since I don't have any evidence to support the request.

"The DNA won't be back for at least a month. It'll automatically be put it in CODIS as soon as it's processed, but the lab is always backed up. I've entered the fingerprints into the IAFIS database. If his prints have come up at any crime scene, I'll know it in a little while. I'm doing a search for similar crimes in all the places he's lived since he left home at age 18, but it's going to be a long process."

"You wouldn't be doing all that if you didn't believe something is off about him," Genevieve said.

Chase remained silent for a moment. "I can't point to any evidence and say yes, there's something wrong, but the guy is wound pretty tight. He was mugged while he lived in Lexington. I have a buddy who's on the force, and he emailed me a copy of the file. The guy who attempted to rob Martin almost died. He had a knife, and Martin turned the knife on him and stabbed him. It was ruled self-defense, but the mugger said he thought Martin was really going to kill him. He didn't just disarm him, he stayed on top of him, threatening to slit his throat until the officers arrived. The officer involved thought the complaint was just a bid to justify less time since the mugger had broken his parole and was going back in. But there's a coldness about Mr. Martin."

There was…and why hadn't she noticed it before? Because he was very good at playing a role. That was what it was. He played a role instead of being himself. "You weren't in the room with him when he confronted me about the drawing. He went from fine to furious in a matter of seconds."

"Does he have a key to your house?"

"I've never given him one."

"If he did have one, how would he have gotten Mai's information?"

Genevieve tilted her head in thought. "I have a contract my models sign saying they accept the lump sum payment for their services so they can't come back and demand more money once the sculpture is finished and sells. And it also gives permission for me to use their image in my work."

"Where do you keep those?"

"In my office in the studio."

"Can I see them?"

"Sure."

She rose and led him to the office. She went to the file cabinet, opened the drawer and pulled the file holding the contracts.

"Lay them on the desk. Would there have been any reason for Martin's fingerprints to be on the file?"

"No."

"When he was in here the other night, what did he touch?"

"Just some drawings and a glass he drank tea from."

She opened the wide drawers in the cabinet. "These."

"Anything else at all?"

"No."

"How often has he been in your office?"

"Two—no, three times in the last year."

"You haven't cleaned in here since he left the other night?"

"No. Though I do clean pretty often. And I keep the door closed because of the dust."

He looked over her desk. "Is the contract the only thing with Mai's name on it?"

"I wrote her a check for her services. And I have her address and contact information in my address book."

"Would anyone but you have reason to have contact with your address book or checkbook?"

"No. I give my accountant copies of everything but not the originals."

"Would you mind if I lifted prints from your address book, checkbook and the contract file?"

"No. But I really don't know how Simon would have gotten into the house."

"But that doesn't mean he doesn't have a key or can't pick or jimmy a lock."

That suggestion gave her stomach a quiver.

"Did you give keys to the workmen when you had your kitchen remodeled?"

"Yes."

"Did he have any contact with them?"

"He was the one who found them for me." She rubbed her forehead. "He checked on their progress when I had to leave and do a workshop in Lexington at the UK for a couple of weeks." She was beginning to understand what made him such a good detective. He was relentless. And she was beginning to admire the way he connected the dots in an investigation.

"I can give you the workmen's numbers, and you can ask if they loaned their keys to the house to him for any reason. They returned them to me once they were done."

"I'd like those numbers. Do you still have the keys?"

"Sure."

She opened her top desk drawer. The two keys were tagged. She held them up.

"I won't be able to get prints off them after this much

time, and more than likely they'd be the workmen's prints. I just wanted to be sure they were still here."

She was grateful he was so thorough.

"I'm going to get my stuff out of the car. Gotta warn you the fingerprint powder is a little messy, but it won't take but a minute to dust your address book and the other things, and I can check them while I'm here."

Genevieve shook her head. "Would you like a sandwich while you're here? It's almost lunch."

He grinned. "Sure."

She left him to do his work.

Thirty minutes later, when he appeared in the kitchen, she set a thick ham sandwich down in front of him with a sprig of grapes and some homemade potato salad. She tried to let him eat in peace, but she could barely taste her sandwich, she was so anxious to learn what he found.

"Martin's fingerprints weren't on your checkbook or your address book," Chase said casually. "He may have wiped the fingerprints off, or he could have worn gloves. There weren't any fingerprints on either of them. Just on the pages. I'm assuming they were yours, since only one person's fingerprints were on them. You said you hadn't cleaned in there in...."

"At least two weeks, because I've been working at my kitchen table instead."

"He may not have gotten the address from your office. Or gotten it at all."

She chewed the bite of sandwich she'd taken and swallowed and set the rest of it aside. "But you think he did."

"I don't know. But gut instinct tells me the guy is strange. Something about the way the police report read from

Lexington. But there's something strange about a lot of people."

Like the void she felt when she touched Simon.

She shoved her chair back from the table and went into the pantry for her purse. She returned to the table with her phone, did a search for locksmiths, called the first number, and arranged for all her locks to be changed that afternoon.

"I keep a calendar, like a business diary, to write down things. Appointments, phone calls made, that kind of thing. I may be able to help you with Simon's travel itinerary. Come back into the office."

They set their dishes into the sink and she led the way back to the office. She slid the calendar out from beneath the desk calendar and flipped it back to the first of the year. "He went to California on January fifth…"

In some instances she even had the names of the hotels where he stayed. She had records of seven trips Simon made in the past nine months, one coinciding with her trip to Scotland three months before. California, Atlanta twice, New York twice, Miami and Orlando, Florida.

"Why is it you know where he was and when?" Chase asked.

"It never dawned on me that he was offering me the opportunity to keep tabs on him the way he does with me. He was very upset when I went to Scotland without letting him know."

"What do you mean he keeps tabs on you?"

"He's always asking what my plans are, when I'll be back, and calling to check in on me. I didn't realize how often he was doing it because I work so much, and the only other people I keep in regular touch with are Miranda and Juliet. And he always asks how the work is going. So I just assumed it was about that, not about me."

"But lately that's shifted?"

"Yes."

"You have a security system, don't you?"

"No. Just electronic locks on the studio and dead bolts on the rest. I've been meaning to get one, but I've been so consumed with my work and other things…"

"I strongly recommend you contact a security company and have them come out and install one right away. As in today or tomorrow. After what happened to Mai, even if Martin isn't involved, you're isolated out here, Gen. You want to be cautious."

"Okay."

Chase pulled a Post-it off a stack and wrote a number on it. "This is Security One, here in town. The alarm systems are routed to the police department. If there's an issue, we come out unless they call us and tell us it's a false alarm. Call them and get the ball rolling."

"I will." Him giving her all this information made her stomach shiver and shake so much she regretted eating the sandwich.

As she walked Chase to his car, he paused beside Finn's statue. "Juliet's been telling me about this guy."

"She has?" Surely not.

"Too bad he's not real. He looks like he could take on a bad guy. If he didn't scare them to death first."

"Finn's not that scary." She leaned against one of his wings. "Once you get used to him."

"Finn?"

"Yeah. That's his name."

Chase shook his head. "You've named the statue?"

"He was already named when I got him."

"Really?" Chase's brows rose.

"Yeah."

"Finn." He studied him a moment longer. "It suits him."

"I think so too."

"Didn't I see a model of him in your studio?"

Model? She'd placed the clay figure on a shelf in the studio but hadn't looked at it since last night. She'd been too disheartened and had thrown herself into her work as soon as her feet hit the floor this morning. Chase was saying goodbye and she forced her attention back to what he was saying.

"Thanks for lunch. How 'bout giving that potato salad recipe to Juliet? It was great."

"I'll send it to you instead, so you can fix it yourself and impress her."

She snickered at his expression.

She waved goodbye as he drove away and dashed back into the studio.

Last night, after Finn flew away, she'd placed it on a shelf in the studio for safekeeping, just as Juliet had urged her to do. She went to it now and took it down from the shelf. The wings were little more than nubs by the time Finn limped away. Now they were full-blown wings, and in proportion to the figure. The facial features that were melted away by the end of the spell had shifted to look more like a facsimile of Finn's gargoyle face.

Hope surged, and her heart pounded in her ears.

CHAPTER 30

SIMON RAGED UNDER his breath, his eyes never leaving the screen as Detective Robinson finished eating and returned to Genevieve's office. What had they talked about? What information was she sharing with him? They had talked as though they were friends. In fact, she'd been more relaxed with this cop than she was with him.

But then Detective Robinson was not a man on the make, just the boyfriend of a friend. There was the barrier of him already being...taken... that had relieved the possibility of any sexual demands between them.

What had she told Robinson? There was precious little she knew about Simon's life, because he was always careful to share only those things that would paint an advantageous picture for her. And she had not become a part of his true life...yet. But she was about to. Very soon.

He resigned himself to the fact that Mai was out of reach, at least for the moment. She was taken to a safe house that first night. He followed them there, but lost her when she'd been moved again, and there was no way to trace her. The officers who accompanied her that first night were back in town, and had obviously passed on their responsibilities to someone else.

Simon knew quite a few influential people in town. He'd

fished for information under the guise of being a concerned citizen, but he didn't really have a true reason for inquiring about Mai.

Had he allowed his need to finish her off put his freedom in jeopardy? When he returned from his abortive attempt to take care of Mai at the hospital, he found a long scratch on his arm. Had one of the nurses scratched him? Or had it happened when he was wrestling with the police officer?

He'd stepped up his timeline, and had just a few more things to take care of before he made his move. He'd emptied his accounts and transferred the money to an offshore account, and made arrangements to have his car driven to their destination—St. Petersburg, Florida—in the next day or so.

Genevieve would enjoy the sun and the beaches there. It was a town that embraced artistic talent, and had an abundant tourist trade. Not that her work was geared to tourists. Her work was meant for a bigger stage. He had helped her gain that recognition. She owed him, and it would soon be time for her to pay up. Whether she wanted to or not.

He closed the software when a tap came on the office door, and he called to Keith to come in.

"I've sold Genevieve's other drawings. I thought you'd like to know."

"All four of them?"

"Yes. The businessman who stopped in, he'd been up at the mines to check out the mushroom farm. He wanted all four as a set for his office."

Eight thousand dollars in one day from four drawings. She was the golden goose. He'd have to treat her with care. "Excellent work, Keith. I'll be sure to tell Genevieve. She'll be very pleased."

The man was grinning from ear to ear as he left.

Simon opened the security software again so he could watch while she answered the phone, and dialed Genevieve's number. She rushed into the house from outside to answer. He frowned when she studied the number on the phone for two more rings before answering on the fifth ring.

"I thought you'd like to know, besides the drawings you sold to the Richards, Keith has just sold the other four."

"That's—" Her expression was blank with surprise. "That's fantastic! Please thank him for me."

"They went for a thousand a piece." He almost felt guilty for skimming the money from her when they would soon be combining their funds once they got to Florida.

"I'm amazed. I would never have imagined my drawings would sell for that much money."

"They were exquisite, although some of it was presentation. The frames and mats set them off to perfection."

She leaned back against the kitchen island. "You and Keith both have a knack for that sort of thing. It's through your efforts that I've done so well."

"Thank you for saying so."

"Well, it's true." She turned her head as a sound came from the front of the house.

"How is your friend Mai doing? Better, I hope."

Genevieve stood motionless. "I haven't spoken to her since the police took her into protective custody." She looked up as a man came through the front door. "I have some workmen here, Simon. I think I need to go."

"Okay. I'll convey your gratitude to Keith."

"Yes, please do that."

He hung up and waited to see where she might be going. She disappeared outside once again, and he closed out the software.

"What are you up to, Genevieve?" he murmured. She was wasting her time and money working on that old house. But it would bring a good profit when they sold it.

They'd be living in a much more spacious place once they arrived in Florida, and she would have her studio downtown, in one of the empty warehouses. He'd already picked it out online. He had only to pay the deposit. Once she'd been conditioned to what he needed from her.

Clare hadn't taken to his special needs, and continually tried to escape. But he had some new ideas about how to handle Genevieve. The warehouse would be the perfect place for it.

✧　✧　✧

FINN SHOOK HIS head as he woke, the grogginess of sleep lingering in a way that was strange to him. He realized he was lying on his side on the slab. Used to waking at dusk and the softer light of the setting sun, the glare seemed harsh as he gazed into the distance and threw up a hand to block the blaze of the low-hanging sun.

For the first time in six and a half centuries he looked upon more than its distant glow and the colors that painted the sky after its passing. He sat up on the stone block and recognized the discomfort of the rock beneath his bare buttocks.

"Finn?" Genevieve's voice came from behind him, wispy

and soft. He twisted to glance over his shoulder and missed the hulking weight of his wings.

"You have a cleft in your chin. I didn't realize that."

Finn touched his chin and felt the faint indention. He raised a hand to his face and stroked his cheek. Beard stubble prickled his fingertips. He hadn't had a beard in centuries. He touched his brow and felt the difference. Why had he not felt any pain during this latest transition? He had slept his way through it.

"I'll get a mirror." Genevieve rushed inside the house and returned a few minutes later with a looking glass. She offered it to him.

Finn's stomach tightened. Seeing his image as the gargoyle had destroyed all hope that night. Knowing he was a monster was hard, but facing the ugliness of it had sickened him. How could Genevieve not scream every time he came near?

He lifted the mirror and looked into it. Blinked, then looked again.

His jaw was shadowed by his beard, and his hair hung down the back of his neck and lay shaggy against his cheeks, but his face was exactly as he had so often dreamed it. And his teeth were no longer the monster's, but human.

He set the mirror aside and pressed the heels of his hands against his eyes to contain his tears.

Genevieve remained silent but rested her hand on his shoulder in comfort. When he finally dropped his hands, she held out a glass of water. He drank deeply, then paused to look at the glass container as he gripped it. No, claws…just square, human fingernails.

He froze for several seconds. It wasn't possible. He swallowed as he turned his hand first one way then the other. "How did this happen, Genevieve?"

"Your voice... It's less gruff, but still deep."

"'Tis the same as it was before the curse."

"The clay figure started changing today, taking on more and more of your gargoyle features. I didn't notice it, but Chase, Juliet's boyfriend did." Her voice trailed away, and her eyes shimmered with tears, though a smile spread across her face.

He attempted to stand, but his limbs felt rubbery. He didn't want to admit it, but he needed to stay seated until he was able to get to his feet. "The magic has left me, Genevieve. I find myself very weak."

She sat down beside him. "It has been a part of you for so long, it has to have been traumatic for it to be torn away, and probably disorienting now it's gone."

"Aye." He searched her face. Would she feel differently now that he was no longer the monster? Could she feel the same for the man as she did the gargoyle?

"You need something to eat."

"Did you call Juliet and Miranda? Do they think this will last?"

"They don't know. They're hopeful, since the clay figure now looks like a gargoyle."

He reached for her hand and brought it to his lips. "If all I have is an hour with ye, 'tis more than I thought I would ever have, lass."

She raised a hand to cup his face and leaned closer to press her lips to his. It had been so long, but his lips parted, and he drank in the taste and feel of her mouth against his.

Her cheeks glowed with color and heat when they broke the kiss. He was pleased to see she was as out of breath as he. His body quickened with need, and his heart beat so he could barely catch his breath. They clung together for several long, intimate minutes.

"Do you want to come inside?" She asked, her tone husky. "I'll cook a meal."

As the monster he had felt smothered inside the auction house. Even standing inside Genevieve's studio made him wary. Would that feeling plague him now he was human?

"Aye."

She rose and gripped his arm while he struggled to his feet, waiting to make certain he was steady. Then she went to the cabinet and brought out a new pair of sweatpants and a T-shirt.

"It seems there are parts of me that are stronger than others," Finn teased as he sat on the concrete bench and put on the pants.

"I noticed," Genevieve laughed. "I thought that part might be enhanced by magic as well, but it seems to have remained the same.

Finn laughed and shoved to his feet. He was feeling stronger now. But human. She was right, it was a trauma to have lost what had given him great strength and allowed him to fly.

She caught his hand and drew him toward the house. Finn tugged her to a halt. "The magic is weak, but it could still harm ye." He tucked a stray strand of dark brown hair behind her ear, simply because he couldn't keep his hands off her.

"I don't think so, Finn. I've been around you for weeks

now, and if it was going to infect me, I think it would already have done so."

"I want to believe that, Genevieve. But I dinna wish to cause you the kind of torment I have known all these years."

She smoothed his hair, and kneaded the back of his neck in a way that tested the limits of his resistance. "What if this is the only time we have, Finn? What if tomorrow you become the gargoyle again?"

He molded her close, and her green eyes darkened. God's blood, but he wanted her to the point of pain. But the need to protect her outweighed everything else. He rested his forehead against hers.

Surely God, the devil, whatever force drove the magic, would not be so cruel. But he'd seen how cruel it was to live without the tenderness of a human touch, the whisper of a kiss, the warmth of an embrace. He could not return to that. But... He leaned back. "What if making love with me causes ye to become like me?"

Her expression of unwavering focus was the same when she was drawing. "Then neither of us will be alone. You can show me if making love was any different in the fourteenth century."

"Lass, after centuries of celibacy, it may be a challenge for me to remember, but I'll do m' best." If he got inside her, he would not last half a heartbeat, but perhaps the second time... Even thinking about it nearly brought him to the brink.

He forced his attention on the wide hall leading into the entrance to the front door, a solar of sorts (they called it a living room now), then the kitchen.

"Would you like to eat, Finn?"

"Later, lass. 'Tis not food I'm hungry for right now." Now he was committed, he was impatient to get wherever she was taking him and spend hours touching her, kissing her, being inside her.

Her eyes were smoky green with passion as she led him down another hall, narrower this time, to a room with a large bed and heavy tables on either side.

"I've wanted to open my home to you before, Finn. But I didn't think you'd feel comfortable inside."

"Aye. I wouldna have. As the monster, I am wary of close spaces. Walls make me feel trapped."

"But you feel comfortable, here with me now?"

"Aye. Very comfortable."

She pulled her T-shirt up over her head and dropped it to the floor.

Finn studied the sheer, lacy bra supporting her breasts. Her pale skin peeked out from beneath the fabric, the lacy image of a rosebud lying against the slope of her breast. He ran a finger beneath the strap, then traced the rose pattern down over the center of the cup and felt her nipple bead beneath his touch. She unhooked the back of the bra and let it slide down her arms.

She was long-limbed, and long-bodied, and as lithe as he had imagined her, yet her breasts were surprisingly generous. He had not dared to touch them with the hands of the monster, but he proceeded to make up for the lost opportunities and cupped her breasts while his mouth covered Genevieve's in a kiss as furiously passionate as the fire consuming him.

Her flesh was softer and smoother than anything he'd ever

felt. He sat down on the bed and pulled her between his legs, resting his head against her breasts and nestling his face against them. "I have dreamt of yer scent. Dreamt of what yer skin would feel like. What ye would taste like." He pressed a kiss to one peak, then drew it into his mouth and sucked.

Genevieve ran her fingers through his hair and pressed closer. Finn gripped her hips and kneaded her buttocks while he turned his attention to the other nipple.

He reached for the button on her jeans and unfastened it. She unzipped them helped him peel them down and off. He fell back against the covers and dragged himself up into the center of the bed. Genevieve followed him and straddled his hips.

"We'll go as slow as you want next time, but I've wanted you as much as you have wanted me, Finn." Her kiss was frantic, clumsy, and endearing, and tasted of iced tea and her.

Finn dragged the stretchy fabric of his sweatpants down, freeing himself. Painfully engorged, his control nearly slipped when her fingers closed around him and guided him inside her. The pleasure of being buried deep within her, of her body gripping his cock, was almost more than he could bear. He pushed deeper, intensifying the contact.

When she began to ride him, he closed his eyes against the sight of Genevieve's breasts rising and falling, the added encouragement too much for his sex-starved body. She rocked, sliding him all the way home again and again. She was so tight, wet, and warm. He found her small, sensitive nub with his fingers, and when he stroked it, she lost her rhythm and her breathing became as loud and ragged as his.

A sensation of pleasure more intense than anything he had

known in centuries tightened his balls, swelled his cock, and made him groan aloud while he spilled his seed.

When he opened his eyes, it was to the sight of her smiling down at him. He urged her down to share a long, slow, thorough kiss. "I've wanted to be inside you since you scrubbed m'willy with a brush, the second day after I arrived in America."

Genevieve laughed aloud and hid her face against his chest. "It was covered with pigeon droppings and algae."

"Aye. But the man inside the statue rather liked the way you held on now and then."

She laughed again, but still didn't show her face. She slid away to lie beside him.

They had not laughed enough together. He would see that they did from now on.

Remembering what he could about indoor plumbing, he slipped out of the bed, hiked the sweatpants back up and went into the bathroom. The place seemed all glass and mirrors. He relieved himself in the toilet. The silver handle would only go one way, so he pushed it down. It was a wonder to see the water swirl until it disappeared.

He studied his image in the mirror while he washed his hands. He looked as he had before the turn. Cleaner, but the same.

There were uncountable things he would have to learn to survive in this world…if he remained human.

He stood in the doorway of the bedroom and gazed at Genevieve, her long, slender body stretched upon the bed, completely nude and open to his perusal. The stirrings of desire ignited all over again.

Her hair tumbled about her face and across her pillow. Turned on her side, the curve of her hip was a thing of beauty, as was the rest of her. If he became the gargoyle again come daybreak, he would not forget a single moment of this night. With that thought, he shucked the sweatpants and climbed back into bed with her.

CHAPTER 31

F ROM HIS OFFICE at home, the snowy security camera reception made it impossible for him to see into Genevieve's bedroom. Simon swore and smacked the computer. There seemed to be some kind of electrical interference in her room. All the others were clear as a bell.

Perhaps there was a problem with the camera or the wiring.

Or maybe she'd found the camera and disconnected it. The idea gave his adrenaline level a quick kick, and for a moment the spike had his heart flying.

No. That couldn't be it. She'd be searching every other room, and thus far he hadn't seen her on any of the other cameras. He wasn't seeing her on this one, either, so perhaps she was outside. She'd been spending more and more time outdoors since finishing Mai's sculpture.

But the piece he saw her working on in the studio was magnificent, and it was almost finished. The model she hired had worked out very well. He was athletic, and his body was very well proportioned. He should have trusted her judgment. It was a shame they'd have to leave the piece behind. On second thought, he'd arrange to have it picked up and delivered to Florida as soon as they were settled.

He'd left her to her own devices way too much in recent weeks. Since their last personal discussion, he thought he needed to take a step back, but now he needed to insert himself into her life again in preparation for the move.

She would fight him at first, of course. He moved to open the lid of a small packing crate. The pot he'd brought home from work was a new creation from an artist in Mexico. The small bag of white pills tucked in the lid was a special gift to Simon. He'd have to send Roberto a bonus next pay period as a thank-you. Since he'd complained to the man of having trouble sleeping so often, Roberto was more than eager to help him. These would do well to calm Genevieve during their trip.

He tucked the pills back into the pot and set it on the top shelf behind his desk. He glanced at the computer one more time. The interference was still on just the one screen. And of course it would be the one he watched most. He'd need to either check the camera or remove them all in preparation for their departure. It wouldn't do for the new owners to find them.

He'd have to figure out a way to get Genevieve out of the house to give him time to do that. Perhaps another workshop at the local college would do it. He'd go over tomorrow and see if he could manipulate her into doing a class for a couple of weeks. He'd call the art department chair and suggest it. It would get her out of the house, and he'd have plenty of time to retrieve the cameras.

He sat down at the computer and closed out the program, then reopened it. Simon caught his breath and leaned closer to the screen. He fumbled for the key to enlarge the one square on the computer to full screen. Genevieve was stretched upon the bed, her pale skin flawless. Her breasts were full, the nipples rosy and puckered. Her body was slender, lean and well-toned. His attention snagged the small triangle of light brown hair at the apex of her legs, then moved on to take in her tumbled tangled hair and the bedclothes kicked to the bottom of the bed.

She rolled onto her side, turned her head and looked toward the bathroom. A shadow projected into the room from the doorway. "No," the word came out a whisper though he was screaming in his head. The man was tall, his shoulders broad and muscular, his sun-streaked blond hair gleaming in the dim light of the bedside lamp. Before he could catch a glimpse of the man's face the picture flashed to static.

With a bellow of rage, Simon leapt to his feet. The desk chair hit the wall, shaking the shelves above and rocking their contents. He lashed out at the computer monitor, and the flatscreen tumbled off the top of the desk. The cord brought it up short and it bungeed back to hit the bottom of the desk with a loud crack. He punched the desk lamp and it sailed off to the right.

"Nooooooo! That bitch lied to me." She told him she didn't get involved with her models, but she had. He had to be the man who posed for the sculpture she was working on now.

He tore at his clothing, and the buttons flew off his expensive silk shirt. He wrestled himself free of the garment. The fabric was hard to tear, but he ripped it to shreds. And with each tear, he screamed, "I'll kill that bitch. I'll kill her. I'll kill them both." Breathing hard, he threw the last piece across the room.

"I'll kill her," he said one last time. But first he'd get his fill of her. Starting tomorrow.

✧   ✧   ✧

GENEVIEVE CAUGHT HER breath as Finn lowered his mouth to her hip, the dip of her waist, and followed the curve of her body to home in on her mouth. His lips and tongue tempted and toyed with hers, reigniting her desire. She wiggled close to align her body with his.

She traced his masculine features with her fingertips, finding them less refined than she had drawn them, but more compelling. The cleft in his chin fascinated her, the full curve of his bottom lip, the scar she'd never noticed beneath one brow. There were other scars visible on his body that had not been there before. The wear and tear upon a warrior's body during a time when men were trained to use swords and axes and spears and knives in both practice and battle. She traced a long scar on his ribs with a fingertip, and when the muscles in that area contracted, he grabbed her hand.

"Ticklish?"

"Aye, a wee bit."

It was such a human thing, a wave of tenderness struck her and she kissed him.

He tucked her lower body in against his so his erection rested against the inside of her thigh, warm and taut. She hiked one leg up over his hip, and they nestled in close together, touching intimately, but not joined.

The temptation heightened their desire. Finn brushed his cheek against hers and his lips were warm against the curve of her cheekbone.

"Is making love to a modern woman very much different

than before?" she asked.

"Aye, making love with a modern woman is ver' different. Ye can get out of yer clothes with more ease." He nuzzled her neck. "And ye smell better, since we didna bathe so oft." He smiled when she laughed. "Yer skin is softer." He slid a hand down over her backside. He looked at her, his expression more intent. "But even more, having ye means more than being with any other woman because of the love between us. I do love ye, lass. It started that first night, when ye were so intent on protectin' yer cat from me, ye stayed close by, even though ye were so scared ye shook with it. The first time ye touched my arm, I thought m' heart might beat out of m' chest from the thrill of it."

Breathless, she continued to stare at him for several moments, overwhelmed by the emotion she read in his face. Her vision blurred with tears. "That was a very good answer. Actually, a fantastic one. Come inside me, Finn."

He turned so she was beneath him, then reached between them to rub the head of his penis against her. Genevieve tilted her hips, eager to take him in. He was long and thick with arousal, and she felt herself stretching to accommodate him. As he seated himself deep, she caught her breath at the sensation, and bit her lip as pleasure spiraled through her. When he started to move inside her, she climaxed almost instantly.

Finn paused to give her time to recover, a wholly masculine grin of satisfaction tilting his irresistible mouth.

Genevieve pulled him down for a kiss. Their lips and tongues tangled, stoking the fires of need again. She skimmed his cheek with her mouth, then nibbled his earlobe and blew in his ear. He shivered and began to thrust in earnest, sensations building again.

She stroked his back, the muscles working beneath her hands as human and desirable as the rest of him. She couldn't touch him enough, couldn't get close enough. She'd opened herself to him long before this moment, and the more she loved him, the more he filled her emptiness. A sweet, powerful wave of fulfillment swept over them both, and she clung to him.

What would they do if he couldn't stay? If he reverted to being the gargoyle?

They'd love each other anyway. For as long as it took. When Finn raised his head to look down at her, she smoothed his hair back. "I love you, Finn MacLeod, for as long as it takes."

CHAPTER 32

FINN WOKE TO the pull of the sun and Butterbean's claws as he kneaded the blanket over his chest and pierced his skin through it. Did the cat feel the magic rising as he did? He stroked the cat and earned a head bump against his cheek. Butterbean leaped off the bed and peered up at him as though waiting for what came next.

Finn turned his attention to the woman curled against his side. He and Genevieve had packed as much togetherness into the hours of night as they could. He at least had memories to cling to if the monster overcame him again. Genevieve eating a meal, making love, laughing with him, holding him, telling him she loved him. They had talked nearly all night, and he had stored every expression, every laugh, every word to memory. When she fell asleep on the couch cuddled against him, he carried her to bed and watched her sleep, his heart tied up with the joy of her body curled against his, the warmth of her breath against his skin.

A dim glow struck the side window and he felt the pull gaining strength.

Genevieve's eyes opened and focused on him with a kind of panicked resistance. "Don't go."

"I am trying not to, *leannan*."

He felt the first ray strike the base and the painful grip and tug of it as it dragged him away from the bed. One second he was holding her, and the next he was crouching on the base, unable to move.

Had he been able to voice his anguish, he'd have roared.

✧　✧　✧

GENEVIEVE RUSHED OUT the door, a robe hastily thrown on over her nudity. She knelt on the rough stone in front of him. "You'll come back to me as human. Remember what Miranda said. You might be the gargoyle during the day and human at night for a while. She thinks the magic's hold will continue to weaken. We just have to believe, Finn. Please try to believe."

She rested her cheek against the stone gargoyle and fought the urge to cry. Would they only have one night, or would he become human again in nine hours? "Try to sleep, Finn. It will help pass the time. I'm going to work, which will help me pass the time."

It would drive her crazy, thinking about the uncertainty of his situation, if she didn't stay busy. She shuffled back into the house to take a shower and dress. After fixing coffee, she stripped the sheets off the bed and put them in to wash, then remade the bed and straightened the rest of the room.

She wandered into the studio and stood in front of the nearly finished sculpture. She studied the figure's jaw, lightly marked the spot where she needed to put the cleft in his chin, then went to work. She took a break at noon to eat a sandwich, and lingered over a glass of iced tea on the patio steps.

She was working over the rough patches with sandpaper when there was a knock on the studio door. She peered out.

Her stomach knotted, her breathing unsteady as her heartbeat escalated, booming rapidly in her ears. Simon peered into the room at her. Genevieve held up a finger, signaling him to wait for one minute. She picked up a hammer from the worktable and carried it at her side as she opened the door.

"I can tell you're hard at work." He eyed the sculpture. "He looks like he could open his mouth and speak at any moment."

She forced a smile. "I think he might be about to lead a charge."

"He does look a little fierce. Is this one going somewhere special?"

"I hope we can contact Dunvegan Castle and see if they'd like to make an offer before he goes on the open market. Since I bought their gargoyle, I thought they might want a replacement." And the castle was where he belonged.

"He'd be right at home there."

And he'd have to take the place of Finn one day when his sculpture disappeared and was never recovered once he became human permanently.

When Simon moved closer to study him, she tensed.

"You've even given him some nicks and scars," he observed.

"He's a Scottish warrior trained in combat with a sword and other forms of sharp weaponry. He'd be a bit beaten up, don't you think?"

"Yes, he probably would. You've given him the face of the man you said was disfigured."

"Yes, I did. He was a soldier. And I thought it was appropriate. No one will recognize him."

"You're always so careful about that." Simon smiled, his stare focused on her in a way that made her stomach tumble. "He's exceptional, as is all your work."

"Thanks. I've also been working on the wire form for the second polymer sculpture, and have it almost finished. I'll be adding the clay as soon as I'm done with my warrior here."

"I'm glad to hear you've been so busy." He frowned and looked serious. "I've ruined things between us, haven't I?"

Her legs shook, so she leaned against the worktable. "What do you mean, Simon?"

"I pushed too hard and got too possessive too soon. I understand why you want to keep our relationship just business. And I agree, it's the way it needs to be, Genevieve. If you can forget the little interlude of bad temper the other night, I'd like us to continue as we were before anything was ever said."

He seemed sincere, but he was so good at playing the part. She nodded because he was waiting for her answer, and she was too scared not to agree.

"That being said…" He got back to business. "I came by to invite you to a celebratory open house at the gallery. Since we sold all six of your drawings, we thought we'd have an open house and invite all the artists we represent to participate. It will be a week from this Saturday."

She thought it might be smart not to turn him down. And after all there'd be other people there. She wouldn't be alone with him. "I'd love to come. What time?"

"We thought we'd run it all day, from nine until closing. It will be in the paper all next week."

"Sounds good."

"I've also transferred money from the sale of the drawings into your account, in case you want to check it."

"Thank you."

"Will your friend here be finished by then?"

"Yes, he probably will. I still have a little work to do on the back of one of his legs, but for the most part he's finished."

"We could transfer him to the studio for the open house, if you're okay with that."

"Sure."

"Good. We'll talk more about the transport later."

He turned to leave, and she breathed an inner sigh of relief. "Thanks for stopping by."

"You're welcome." He closed the studio door behind him. Her hands shook as she set the hammer down. She bent and straightened her fingers, cramped from gripping the hammer so hard they were stiff, and wiped her sweaty palms on her coveralls.

Good agent or not, she couldn't work with a man she was afraid of. She'd have to end their relationship.

But she'd have backup when she did it. Finn or Chase. Someone.

✦　✦　✦

SIMON SWALLOWED HIS anger until he pulled out of the driveway. "Stupid bitch," he growled. She thought having the locks changed and updating her keypad password would keep him out? She'd have to do better than that to keep him from having her. He could pick any lock. Not that he'd need to now.

She'd held onto the hammer the whole time he was there,

too. Something had put her guard up. Probably that detective friend of hers. But it wouldn't do her any good. She'd learn who was in charge. He had a few more preparations to make, then he'd be back. He'd need to collect his truck and do a bit of cleaning up at the cabin.

He turned toward the lake as he pulled out onto the main road.

✧   ✧   ✧

GENEVIEVE MARINATED CHICKEN to grill for supper and prepared a salad. She startled as the refrigerator dumped ice, then swore under her breath.

Simon's visit had put her on edge, and she kept imagining she heard strange sounds. She stretched her arms and rolled her shoulders. Sanding the sculpture had made her muscles cramp. She was a little sore in other places, too. But after a two-and-a-half-year hiatus from sex, it was a good soreness. She smiled as she popped two ibuprofen and swallowed them with water.

She'd decided to find out if Finn would like potatoes fixed some other way besides baked. While she prepared the hash brown casserole and put it in the oven, her thoughts lingered on him.

He was restless because he had nothing to do. His manly pride demanded he provide for her, though she didn't need him to. The responsibility of caring for a mate was perhaps another lesson he'd learned through the curse.

What other qualities did he need to acquire before the curse would release him? How could he learn anything more if it continued to control him?

Butterbean's plaintive cry carried to her. He was probably hungry. She called to him and went into the pantry to get a can of cat food. When she came out of the pantry she was surprised he wasn't waiting for her.

"Butterbean?" she called. "Kitty-kitty-kitty-kitty."

His mewing came from the direction of the breezeway.

She went through the living room, following the sound. She walked through the entrance foyer to the breezeway. She glanced outside at Finn's statue. He wouldn't be awake for another hour at least.

She opened the studio door, and Butterbean shot out of the dark room into the breezeway. How had he gotten into the studio? She hadn't seen him in there while she worked. Her eyes on the cat, she sensed movement to her right. She glimpsed dark hair covered by a baseball cap and tried to shut the door. It exploded outward toward her, knocking her back. She caught herself with a hand on the floor as he jabbed downward with a hypodermic. She rolled away and kicked out at it. It went flying, and skittered across the floor while she scrambled to get her feet under her.

Fingers tangled in her hair, jerked her head sideways, and slammed her into the wall. Pain exploded down the side of her face, and she cried out. Then he jerked her head this way and that until she thought her neck would break. "I'm here to teach you a few things, Genevieve. By the time I'm through, you'll either do as I say, or you'll be dead."

Her head ached, her scalp was on fire, and she could scarcely hear, but she did hear "dead." Sitting at his feet, she thought about Mai, and the realization of what was about to happen crashed over her. She reached up, grabbed his crotch, and squeezed with all her strength.

Simon's scream sounded like he was singing in falsetto. He pounded her with his fist, landing glancing blows on her cheek, her ear. When his fist struck her temple, blackness swarmed her and the floor rushed up to meet her.

✧   ✧   ✧

PAIN TURNED HIS world white while his stomach heaved again and again, and his ears seemed full of cotton. Simon slid to the floor, leaned back against the wall, and curled in on himself. His balls ached so he couldn't breathe. When he could move again, he'd kick her from one end of the house to the other.

Several minutes passed before he felt he could walk. He crawled to Genevieve and slapped her, hard, a couple of times to make certain she was truly unconscious. Her head lolled on her neck.

"You cunt," he screamed, though he hadn't completely gotten his wind back. He limped back to the studio door and reached down on the bottom step to retrieve his bag. He grabbed Genevieve's arm on the way back and dragged her down the entrance foyer and through the kitchen to the hall. Once he had her secured to the bed, she'd learn who was boss.

He stripped the comforter and pillows off the bed. A dull ache in the lower half of his stomach and his balls still plagued him when he lifted her onto the bed. He mourned the loss of his leather cuffs as he looped cotton rope around her wrists and ankles and tied them to the legs of the bed.

When she awoke he'd cut her clothes off. It always drove their fear higher as they became more and more exposed.

She groaned and pulled at the ropes that bound her hands.

Her eyes opened, but seemed unfocused. She had, after all, received two hard blows to the head. If they had caused some internal damage it might cut his fun short. He reached into his bag and withdrew his hunting knife. He'd sharpened it just for her.

He climbed up on the bed and straddled her. "Look at me, Genevieve," he demanded.

She opened her eyes, but they were slitted with pain.

He held the five-inch blade close to her eye, and she froze, barely breathing. "I know you were with another man last night, Genevieve. What's his name?"

She swallowed, and he could see her struggling to remember. "Finlay MacLeod."

"I've never heard of anyone in the area with the name of MacLeod." He ran the tip of the knife beneath the collar of her T-shirt and cut it down the middle. Her bra was red this time, her skin pale against the vibrant color. He wondered if the panties matched.

"He's just a visitor." Her pupils, dilated with fear, emphasized the green of her eyes. Her breathing huffed in and out, her breasts straining at the fabric of the bra and her pulse throbbing visibly in her neck.

He cut across the shirt to the sleeves on each side and pulled the garment away. "How did you meet him?"

"He was hunting in the area, and stopped to get a drink from my water hose."

The straps of her bra gave way to the blade. He tucked the blade under the small piece of material that held the cups in place and gently pulled it up. The bra parted, and her breasts were bared to him. He set aside the knife to cup and caress them. Her skin was smooth and supple, her breasts perfectly shaped and generous.

"It wasn't a nice thing you did to me in the breezeway."

Her expression froze, but she didn't beg him not to hurt her as any other woman would have. His grip on her breasts tightened, and she gritted her teeth. He squeezed them harder, at least as hard as the crushing as she'd given his balls. Genevieve writhed in pain and finally made the keening sound he was hoping for, and tugged at the ropes trying to escape. He released her and she panted for breath while she waited for the pain to ease.

"Where does your lover live?" He admired the bright red finger marks he'd left on her skin.

"Scotland."

"So last night was a farewell fuck?"

"Yes."

✧   ✧   ✧

GENEVIEVE'S HEAD POUNDED, her breasts throbbed, and her stomach roiled. It took all her control not to cry. She wouldn't give son-of-a-bitch Simon the satisfaction. How could she not have seen this part of him? She'd known him for three years, but she never had the tiniest inkling he hid a sadistic monster behind his polite civility.

She had to hold on until Finn woke from the stone. He'd find a way into the house to help her. He had to.

She had to pretend to cooperate with Simon until… *Please God, let Finn come.*

Her composure started to crumble when Simon cut the seams on her cotton pants and peeled them off.

She couldn't allow herself to think about Mai and the pain she experienced. And she couldn't think about Finn.

She had to think about survival. She'd do whatever she was forced to in order to survive.

Chill bumps popped out on her skin when the air conditioning kicked on. Her nipples beaded. Simon's eyes locked on them, and she wanted to twist away and hide her nudity, but the lark's head knot he used to loop the rope around her wrists tightened with every small movement.

Her red panties were scant covering for the most intimate part of her body. When Simon started to cut the side with the knife she tried to scoot her bottom away. The rope tightened around her right ankle to the point of pain.

A slow smile twisted Simon's mouth. "Move again, and I'll cut you instead of your clothes. I *will* have you, Genevieve. You owe me that much for everything I've done for you the last three years."

The price was too high. But if she could keep him talking, it might buy her some time. "You made money off every sale, Simon. Why would I owe you anything?"

"Because you belong to me. And you gave yourself to another man. I ought to kill you."

He was delusional. "I don't belong to you or anyone else, Simon. I belong to myself."

"We'll see about that." He jerked at the red panties. The elastic dug into her skin in the bends of her legs, and the ropes tightened with every movement. The lace gave way, and with it some skin. Her feet and hands pulsed with pain, the blood trapped inside them.

With a sudden brutal violence Simon brought the knife

down. Genevieve yelped and flinched away as it plunged into the mattress close to her head.

When Simon jumped off the bed and started yanking off his clothes, fear and panic overwhelmed her, and tears streamed down her face while her teeth chattered and her legs shook.

✧   ✧   ✧

FINN WOKE BEFORE sunset, again to the same weakness and confusion. He lay on the slab, waiting for it to pass, then fought to his feet. The breeze carried the scent of the freshly mown grass and the lilies blooming in the flowerbeds in front of the porch. It was this time Genevieve always came out of the house and drank a glass of tea while she waited for the grill to heat or for whatever she'd put in the oven to finish cooking.

Finn staggered to his feet and went to the refrigerator for a bottle of water. He drank thirstily, finishing off the rest in a few drinks, then tossed the empty container in the recycle bin. He put on sweatpants and T-shirt and climbed the steps to the breezeway. The door was locked. He went up the front steps, only to find the front door was locked as well. He looked through the beveled glass past the entrance foyer into the kitchen. The room appeared empty.

Perhaps she had driven to the store. He leapt off the front porch and went to the garage. Her car was there.

A small finger of uneasiness wormed its way into the depths of his stomach. He jogged across the yard to the studio door and turned the knob. It was locked, so he shoved against it. The lock held.

He put more shoulder into it, and threw his whole weight

behind it, and it sprang open. He flipped on the lights.

The life-size sculpture in the center of the room was so realistic, it staggered him. It was him, a broadsword in his hand, just as he was six hundred years ago. How had she known?

He sped past it and climbed the three steps to the breezeway. A concave depression in the wall midway down the hall caught his attention. It hadn't been there last night. Something heavy and round had struck there... A hypodermic lay on the floor against the frame of one of the tall windows.

Fear nearly strangled him, and he broke into a run, rushing down the hall to the bedroom until he had to grab the doorjamb to stem his momentum.

The door stood open. Genevieve, pale and naked, lay spread-eagled upon the mattress, a knife embedded in the mattress beside her head, and her hands and feet bound to the bed.

Simon, naked, straddled her, with both hands wrapped around her throat. She choked and gasped, her arms and legs pulling against the ropes, her face red with the effort to breathe.

Rage and fear rampaged through Finn's system, and with a Scottish's war cry he charged through the door. Simon released Genevieve and reached for the knife. Finn dove across the bed, knocking Simon sideways off the bed, and they hit the floor in a tangle.

Simon punched him in the face, rocking his head back, the strike harder than Finn expected.

Finn grabbed the side of the man's head and beat it against the metal bedframe until the skin over Simon's eye burst from the blow and blood streamed down his face. Finn rolled over on top of him and punched him again and again. The man grappled with him, trying to dodge or block his blows, but rage fed Finn's bloodlust.

Finally Simon went limp, and his hands fell away.

Breathing hard, Finn staggered to his feet, where he could now see bright red bruises on Genevieve's breasts and throat. Her hands and feet were purple, and Finn grabbed the knife, jerked it free, and quickly cut the ropes binding her hands and feet on one side. Stepping over Simon's limp form to the other side, he cut the others, and tossed them out of away.

He set the knife on the nightstand and reached for Genevieve. Tears poured down her face, and she clung to him. "I'm sorry, lass. I'm sorry." God's blood, he'd been asleep while she was being attacked. His arms tightened around her, and he rocked her, her pain wounding him like it was his own.

She shook her head. Her voice hoarse, she said, "I tried..." She swallowed. "I tried to keep him talking as long as I could." She buried her face against his chest, while sobs wracked her whole body.

When she calmed a bit, she looked up at Finn. "He couldn't... he...he couldn't get hard, and he was in a rage because of it, and started strangling me.

"You need to get to the phone and call for help, Finn. You need to do it now. The phone's in the kitchen on the counter."

"Aye, I'll do it." His throat felt thick with grief and helplessness. "I love you, Genevieve."

He rushed down the hall to the kitchen, picked up the phone, and stared at the numbers. How could he not know how to work this?

✧ ✧ ✧

GENEVIEVE BIT HER lip as she held back sharp cries of pain. The blood was rushing back into her hands and feet, and they were on fire with pins and needles. She scooted to the edge of the bed, but didn't trust her legs to hold her if she tried to stand up.

When Simon staggered to his feet beside the bed, she yelped, the instinct to run driving her to stand. Her feet were numb, and the painful prickling caused her to stumble. She caught herself with her hands and cried out. She fell hard onto her knees and crawled toward the door.

Simon grabbed for the knife and climbed up on the bed, his naked body spattered with blood, his face a mass of lumpy flesh from the beating Finn gave him. "Kill you," he rasped, and rose to stand on the bed and leapt toward her.

Genevieve braced herself for the weight of his body, the piercing slide of the lethally honed blade.

A large shape burst into the room between her and Simon, and the two fell atop her, driving the breath out of her lungs and nearly crushing her before they rolled away.

All motion ceased for a beat, then two. When she heard a dial tone next to her, she reached for the phone, and then spotted Finn and Simon lying still.

She crawled toward them and cried out when she saw the hilt of Simon's knife jutting out of Finn's ribcage just beneath his left nipple.

His breaths came in labored gasps. "I should have tied him up, lass."

"No, no, no, no. Nonononononono," she repeated over and over, like her mind was stuck in a loop. She grabbed Finn's hand when he moved to pull the knife free. "Don't touch it." Tears streamed down her face. "Don't talk, Finn. Just keep breathing."

When she checked Simon, he seemed truly unconscious.

She dialed 911 and asked for help—an ambulance, EMTs, and the police. Told them she'd been attacked, her boyfriend had a knife buried in his side and she didn't think she should pull it out, and then she set the phone aside despite the dispatcher's instruction to stay on the line.

She clung to Finn's hand.

"I love you, Gen." Each word sounded wrenched from his belly, while his skin leached of color.

Genevieve moved to hold him. If Simon woke again, he'd have to kill them both, because she wasn't leaving Finn. Her tears wet both their faces as she leaned over him. Her breaths came in hiccups. "I love you, and I need you so much. Please hold on."

A warm gush of heat came off Finn's body to circle the room, faster and faster, whipping the curtains back at the window and settling over Simon.

The man's eyes flicked open and his mouth fell open on a scream that raised the hairs on Genevieve's arms and the back of her neck.

He jerked into the air like a puppet with someone pulling his strings. His body twisted one way, then the other, while his feet kicked and he fought against the force. He seemed to shrink, almost like he was disappearing into a tunnel, farther and farther into the distance, until he became a pinpoint of light and disappeared.

It was then Genevieve realized Finn wasn't breathing. "Please no! Please." The words burst from her, high-pitched with pain. She pinched his nose, clamped her mouth over his and breathed for him. Straddling his large body, she started CPR.

The sound of sirens pierced her hoarse breathing, and a crash came from the front of the house. Genevieve's shoulders ached with the effort, and she felt light-headed as she continued the compressions and mouth-to-mouth.

Chase was the first man through the door, his gun drawn. He spoke over his shoulder. "Jesus! Get the EMTs in here stat." He grabbed a sheet off the floor and draped it around her.

Two men came in carrying a medical kit.

When he bundled her in the sheet and pulled her away, she fought against Chase's grip until one of the men said, "He's breathing, and he has a pulse."

She turned her face against Chase's shoulder.

"Who is this guy, Genevieve?"

"He's my boyfriend, Finn."

"Finn?" His eyes widened. "What the hell happened here?"

"It was Simon…." She proceeded to tell Chase everything that happened, her eyes never leaving Finn while they loaded him onto a gurney. "I want to go with him."

"Do you know where Simon went?"

"No, he just disappeared, but he was naked."

"I'll come to the hospital as soon as I've secured the scene, and I'll call Juliet to stay with you until I get there."

It was when they were about to close the door to the ambulance when she glimpsed the base Finn had been tied to for so long. On it crouched a new statue. More a grotesque than a gargoyle, and this one had no wings.

EPILOGUE

Four months later

GENEVIEVE SMILED AS she watched Finn flipping burgers at the grill. He'd become a master at it, no doubt from his experience cooking meat over an open fire. Caleb Falkner, Miranda's live-in boyfriend stood next to him, and they seemed deep in conversation. She heard bits and pieces about a sports team.

Finn closed the lid of the grill and swept up a bottle of beer in his large hand to take a swig. He propped a foot on the concrete bench he used to monopolize so many months before and leaned an elbow on his knee. The late afternoon sun beat down on his sun-bleached hair and tanned features, and her heart swelled inside her with love and gratitude. She had come so close to losing him.

"Do you ever feel left out when you're dealing with this stuff?" Chase asked from the lawn chair beside her.

"No, not anymore. I had enough of it, waiting for Finn to awaken each day. Now he's no longer tied to the magic, I'm relieved." She took a sip of wine. "It's been an adjustment for him." Getting his paperwork sorted out. "Getting his GED. Getting a job. All the things we take for granted that come so easily to us proved a steep learning curve for him. He's brilliant in so many ways. He reads everything and can talk to you about so many subjects. But he had to practice interviewing for a job to get one."

"How's it going?" he asked.

"He loves it. He loves power tools and hammering away at stuff." She laughed. "He's built shelves for my studio and in my storage building out back. He's really good at it. He's found his niche."

Chase tilted his head back. "I know how that feels. I can't imagine being anything but a detective."

"You're very good at it."

"Thanks. And that being said... I thought you might appreciate an update on what I've found. But I'll wait until the girls are here to give it to you."

"Okay."

His face lit up as a car pulled into the driveway. "My date has finally arrived," he said, and he went to greet Juliet and Miranda.

The burgers were cooked to perfection, and since everyone else brought a dish, food was abundant. Laughter, good friends, and love filled their life now.

Genevieve felt blessed.

Finn pushed his plate away and stretched his arm along the back of her seat. His fingers stroked her shoulder, and she placed her hand atop his. Their gazes met, and he leaned in to brush her cheek with a kiss.

Chase stood, and, using a spoon, clinked Juliet's wineglass to gain everyone's attention.

"I want to give everyone an update on what we've learned so far about Simon Martin, so those of us who were involved, can close the book on the whole thing.

"DNA and fingerprints have been submitted as possible solutions for some unsolved cases in cities he traveled to and worked in. So far nine cases cleared because of that, one in Lexington. A young female artist who disappeared three years ago. She was one of Simon Martin's clients in Lexington, and she disappeared a month before he moved here. The police looked at him hard several times, but they couldn't tie him to her in any way other than through their business dealings. Their reason for dropping the inquiry, besides lack of evidence, was he had no motive. She brought business into his gallery, and was growing more and more popular. If he had anything to do with it, forgive the expression, he killed the golden goose. They couldn't see any reason for him to do that.

"Personally, I've seen people do some damn stupid things because they were driven by other passions, and to hell with the money." He shook his head.

"This woman's mother insists Martin was pushing Clare— that was her name—for a personal relationship, but she turned him down. A month later she disappeared. They recently checked his DNA against some blood catalogued at the scene, and it was there.

"I know you've probably heard the report about the remains found at the lake cabin. We identified Clare Bowman's remains yesterday, along with those of the original owners of the property."

"How could he have gotten away with killing the owners and taking over their house?" Miranda asked.

"He told the neighbors he'd purchased the property and their truck from them. They only used the place during the summer, and weren't there often, so no one thought anything of it."

Chase looked to Genevieve. "Gen, we discovered one more thing. The paint on the blue pickup truck Martin had been driving matched the paint found on Andy's car. We believe he's responsible for Andy going off the road, and ultimately his death."

The shock of it brought quick tears to her eyes. If only she had never met Simon Martin. Finn told her months ago that men killed because they coveted things others possessed, and he had included women. She hadn't wanted to believe it.

Finn grasped her hand, cradling it between his. "I'm sorry, *leannan.*"

"Look, tracing back through this guy's life, he had a distinct pattern he followed. Even if we had known, it would have been difficult to predict his next victim. You were just his latest target, Gen, and he happened to bite off more than he could chew with you and Finn. You brought an end to a twelve-year reign of rape, murder, and mayhem. The hours of digital footage we found at his house and in a storage locker in the basement of his house led us to clear several other cases when DNA couldn't."

She was still dealing with the creep factor of the police finding cameras all over her house. Simon had stolen private, personal moments from her by viewing them as his entertainment.

"What will happen to that digital footage, Chase?" Finn asked. "I dinna wish Genevieve's life to be viewed by everyone."

"All of it will be destroyed eventually. Since Martin has

been, for all intents and purposes, declared dead, it's locked away."

She'd be glad when it was destroyed.

"Now it's your turn to tell all."

She raised her brows. "About what?"

"What did you do with the sculpture on your patio?" His gaze shifted to Finn for a moment, then back to her. "The one that appeared after your attack?"

She and Finn shared a look. Leaning forward she turned a wineglass in her hands. "It was too dangerous to leave sitting on the patio, so I locked it in my storage building and had Juliet and Miranda come over and ward the building so he couldn't awaken and escape.

"When Finn got out of the hospital, and it had been cleared for Mai and Sylvia to return home, I called them to come over. The four of us broke the sculpture up into tiny pieces, including the base. Then we mixed it into concrete and poured a new, larger base for Mai's statue. Then I asked Aubrey to come over and attach the base permanently to the statue so he couldn't possibly escape. Just in case beating him to dust didn't end things."

"Where is the statue now?" Juliet asked.

"The sculpture and base were donated to the rape crisis center in town. Mai renamed it Hope."

After several moments of silence, Miranda said, "Wow." Her voice was hushed. "That's... perfect. Mai will be standing on top of him forever. Perfect."

"Aye. She thought it was, too," Finn added.

"How's Keith working out as your agent now, Genevieve?" Caleb asked.

"He's doing really well. It seems Simon left his list of contacts behind, so he's keeping everything going, business as usual. He even found the record of money Simon embezzled from me and several other clients in an offshore account. We'll probably never see it, but the FBI is trying to recover the funds."

Conversation moved away from Simon and the chaos he left behind to other things. The sculpture Genevieve was working on for the library. How the sculpture of Finn was received in Scotland. Juliet's upcoming graduation at Christmas. When Juliet and Chase left to go to work, Miranda and Caleb soon followed.

"I am getting used to the two witches," Finn said as they waved goodbye from the driveway.

She shot him a look. "They have names, Finn."

"Aye, I know." He urged her close and rested his chin atop her head. "'Tis easier to like them now I am human, and they arena threatening to fry my ass."

Genevieve laughed.

"Listening to Chase tonight, I kenned how lucky we are." His voice grew husky and his brogue thick. "The life I have is because ye were brave enough to love me, *leannan*."

"Only partly. The real reason is because you risked your life to protect me from Simon. You died trying to save me, Finn. It was your willingness to sacrifice everything for someone you loved that broke the curse and set you free."

He raised one brow, his expression wry. "And I waited six hundred and sixty-three years to fall in love and to do the rest of it."

"Well, they say Scotsmen are hard-headed. But I think you

may have set a record."

"Says the lass who kissed a gargoyle, looking for a prince." He lifted her in his arms to carry her into the house.

She loved his sweeping, romantic gestures. "Never a prince, Finn. I'm completely happy with just a man, just you." To prove it, she kissed him with all the love and tenderness she felt for him.

Passion and love reflected back at her when she looked into his eyes.

"I have waited several lifetimes to learn what love is. Ye taught me in a matter of months. 'Tis honesty, patience, generosity, bravery and sacrifice. 'Twill take me the rest of this lifetime to show ye how well I've learned m' lesson."

His words caught at her heart. The rest of this lifetime sounded right to her. "We have all the time we need, Finn."

He climbed the steps to the breezeway and pushed the door open. "We'll spend it well, together, *leannan* and not waste a second of it."

He lowered her to their bed a few minutes later, and with his lips warm and ardent upon hers and his hands stroking, caressing, loving her, he proceeded to show her exactly what he meant.

BOOKS BY TERESA J. REASOR

MILITARY ROMANTIC SUSPENSE
BREAKING FREE (Book 1 of the SEAL Team Heartbreakers)
BREAKING THROUGH (Book 2 of the SEAL Team Heartbreakers)
BREAKING AWAY (Book 3 of the SEAL Team Heartbreakers)
BREAKING TIES (A SEAL Team Heartbreakers Novella)
BUILDING TIES (Book 4 of the SEAL Team Heartbreakers)
BREAKING BOUNDARIES (Book 5 of the SEAL Team Heartbreakers)
BREAKING OUT (BOOK 6 of the SEAL Team Heartbreakers)
BREAKING POINT (A SEAL Team Heartbreakers Novella)
BREAKING HEARTS (Book 7 of the SEAL Team Heartbreakers)
Coming Soon!

PARANORMAL ROMANCE
TIMELESS
DEEP WITHIN THE SHADOWS (Book 1 of the Superstition Series)
DEEP WITHIN THE STONE (Book 2 of the Superstition Series)
WHISPER IN MY EAR
HAVE WAND, WILL TRAVEL
(A Magic and Mayhem Novella)
HAVE WAND, WILL TRAVEL: Once Bitten, Twice Shy
(A Magic and Mayhem Novel)

HISTORICAL ROMANCE
CAPTIVE HEARTS
HIGHLAND MOONLIGHT
TO CAPTURE A HIGHLANDER'S HEART: THE TRILOGY

The Highland Moonlight Spinoff Trilogy in parts
TO CAPTURE A HIGHLANDER'S HEART: THE BEGINNING
TO CAPTURE A HIGHLANDER'S HEART: THE COURTSHIP
TO CAPTURE A HIGHLANDER'S HEART: THE WEDDING NIGHT

SHORT STORIES
AN AUTOMATED DEATH: A STEAMPUNK SHORT STORY
CAUGHT IN THE ACT: A HUMOROUS SHORT STORY

CHILDREN'S BOOK
WILLY C. SPARKS: THE DRAGON WHO LOST HIS FIRE